"So what, now she's trying to blame me? That's just like her. So what are you going to do? Let her file a complaint about me? Because I can file one too. And mine will have more merit." I crossed my arms defensively over my chest. Whatever. Let her file a stupid complaint. She'd be the one who looked unstable.

Haliburton and Denning exchanged a look.

"Did you see her again?" Denning asked. "After this altercation?"

I shook my head.

"You're positive?" Haliburton asked.

"I'm positive, seeing as I was here and she didn't come over."

They both looked like they didn't believe me. But why wouldn't they? What was Carla saying about me now? I felt a rush of anger at this woman. Why didn't she leave me alone?

"And you said you were asleep?" Denning asked.

"Yes."

"I see," he said, although his tone suggested he didn't. "Have you been down to the courtyard today behind the Steelworks building?"

I was confused at the change of direction, but shook my head no. "I was at yoga down there this morning, but I didn't go into the courtyard for anything," I said. "Why?"

After a long moment of silence, Haliburton said, "Ms. Fernandez is dead."

Witch Hunt

CATE CONTE

KENSINGTON BOOKS
www.kensingtonbooks.com

KENSINGTON BOOKS are published by

Kensington Publishing Corp.
119 West 40th Street
New York, NY 10018

All Kensington titles, imprints, and distributed lines are available at special quantity discounts for bulk purchases for sales promotion, premiums, fund-raising, and educational or institutional use.

Special book excerpts or customized printings can also be created to fit specific needs. For details, write or phone the office of the Kensington Sales Manager: Kensington Publishing Corp., 119 West 40th Street, New York, NY 10018. Attn. Sales Department. Phone: 1-800-221-2647.

Kensington and the K logo Reg. U.S. Pat. & TM Off.

First Kensington Books Mass Market Paperback Printing: July 2020

ISBN-13: 978-1-4967-1760-3
ISBN-10: 1-4967-1760-0

ISBN-13: 978-1-4967-1761-0 (ebook)
ISBN-10: 1-4967-1761-9 (ebook)

10 9 8 7 6 5 4 3 2 1

Printed in the United States of America

For Riham,

You are the very definition of a strong woman.

Thank you for always believing in me.

CHAPTER 1

*Witch: One who connects with the earth; wise
person; shape bender*

Something was in the air.

I could feel it as soon as I paused in the open doorway
of my cozy loft apartment, even though everything looked
the same. The same dark-gray hall carpet, the same welcome mat in front of my door with the arch-backed black
cats, the same pair of boots my across-the-hall neighbor and
good friend Sydney Santangelo always casually kicked off,
strewn outside her door. Nothing seemed amiss.

I couldn't quite put my finger on it—it was just a subtle shift in the air, a feeling that something, somewhere in
the Universe, had been knocked out of alignment. And as
an empath and overall sensitive person, the feeling was
pretty overwhelming.

Although it could simply be that I'd gotten crap for
sleep last night. My insomnia was back with a vengeance
lately, wreaking all sorts of havoc on my psyche. It had
been like this a lot since Grandma Abigail's unexpected
death last month. I hadn't been myself since, which wasn't
surprising. Losing her meant losing my last family member, and it had left me feeling completely alone.

Plus, it was Monday, and that itself explained a lot. If that weren't enough, a glance at my moon calendar this morning told me we were still in Pluto retrograde in Capricorn, which could yield all kinds of upsets. Pluto was all about our shadow side, and brought about unpredictability and change. And I was a firm believer that everything in life followed the cycle of the moon, which meant some sort of problem waited on the horizon.

A lot of angst for a Monday morning. I could hear Grandma Abby's voice in my head: "Violet, you get out there and face Pluto head-on. There's nothing you can't handle. You're a Mooney, aren't you?"

Wherever she was, I believed she had her eye on me right now, and I didn't want to disappoint her. So I'd dragged myself out of bed with every intention of being at my crystal shop, The Full Moon, promptly at nine with a smile and some good vibes, ready to help anyone who needed it.

But first, yoga.

I made a conscious effort to shake off the mood as I squared my shoulders and stepped into the hallway. I could hear Presley, Sydney's four-year-old daughter, shrieking with laughter in their apartment. I didn't bother knocking to see if Syd wanted to go to yoga. She'd tried it for a while after she moved to town two years ago, then gave it up. She'd told me that the whole experience left her overwhelmed and feeling not good enough. "I can't handle those super skinny yogi chicks eating their Buddha bowls and twisting themselves into impossible shapes," she'd told me. Although I think her hesitation was more about her crow pose going awry during her first and only class, resulting in her falling on her face. At the front of the room, no less.

I thought she was missing the point, but it was none of my business. Besides, everyone falls over when they're learning crow pose.

I made for the elevator, even though I just wanted to go back inside and snuggle up with Monty. My fat orange cat was planning on an exciting day of sleep, and I thought longingly of joining him. I'd seen the gloom of this early January day from my full-length windows, and it was a perfect day to stay in bed.

"Knock it off," I commanded myself out loud. "This is a bad attitude. Today is going to rock."

Deciding to make that my mantra for the day, I got in the elevator, tucking my red hair under my black beret and wrapping my new pink scarf tighter around my neck. I loved my new scarf. I'd gotten it over the weekend when I'd treated myself to a trip to Nordstrom Rack. It was the softest, fluffiest scarf I'd found in a while, and a deal to boot.

I pushed open the lobby door and stepped out onto Water Street into the winter air, flinching as it hit my face. Instinctively, I tugged my scarf higher, covering my nose. And nearly tripped over a black cat sitting right at the bottom of the steps.

"Oh! I'm sorry." I knelt down to pet the cat, who looked unfazed by my less-than-graceful exit from the building. He—or she?—arched and purred, looking for all the world like a model for a Halloween calendar, with piercing yellow eyes and a long slinky tail that twitched ever so slightly. The quintessential black cat. "Do you live here? Do you need to go inside?"

The cat continued to stare at me until an approaching whistle distracted us. We both turned to see Mr. Quigley come around the corner. He whistled an off-key version of

"Moon River" as he pushed his noisy shopping cart ahead of him. When I turned back, the cat was gone. Blinking, I looked around. No trace, not even a blur of black streaking away.

Well, cats were fast. It was all part of their charm. I hoped the kitty found its way home okay.

"Morning, Miss Violet," Mr. Quigley shouted from halfway up the block, finally noticing me.

"Morning, Mr. Q." I waved and decided to wait for him because it was polite and because I did like Mr. Quigley. Today he wore his usual outfit—a giant flannel shirt, black vest, and a furry hat with earflaps that made me think of Alaska. His beard was getting longer. He liked to grow it in during the winter months, which left him looking a bit like Gandalf from *The Lord of the Rings*. "Where are you off to so early?"

"Collectin' my cans," he said, drawing up next to me. He had his ever-present pipe clamped between his teeth, which gave his words a slight lisp. "You?"

Every morning Mr. Quigley went around the neighborhood and collected any cans people had discarded. When he had a good stash, he cashed the money in and donated it to the local food pantry. It was a lovely gesture from someone who clearly could've kept the money for himself. I wasn't sure where exactly he lived, but I guessed it was in one of the subsidized apartments around the corner. I felt a rush of gratitude for my own cozy apartment, and my business that made it possible. And all the little extras I got to enjoy. Like coffee and sushi. And yoga.

"That's nice," I said. "I'm working today, but I have to go to my yoga class and get my coffee first. Walk with me?"

He fell into step beside me. "Weird morning," he said after a moment.

I glanced up at him. "What do you mean?"

Mr. Q shrugged. "Just feels weird around here. Like the calm before the storm."

I felt a chill that had nothing to do with the temperature. Same feeling I'd had earlier this morning.

Before I could ask him about it, Mr. Q's eyes narrowed as he caught sight of another man heading down one of the side alleys. "That's my dumpster," he muttered. "Shyster. Someone's encroaching on my territory. Bye, Miss Violet." He darted down the alley, almost as quick as the black cat, his cart jangling against the concrete.

I continued on down the block, walking as fast as I could to escape the cold. North Harbor was quiet this morning. It usually was in these earlier hours, and then later in the day it turned into a mini Manhattan as the restaurants and bars filled up and people strolled the streets. The sound of seagulls filled the air ahead as they swooped in and out of the river just up the block. The Long Island Sound was so close I could smell the salty air, an added bonus I hadn't expected when I'd moved here. The ocean was my happy place. It filled me with energy and cleared the muck out of my brain. Which was why I always wanted to be within smelling distance of it. And later, when my shop really takes off and I could afford it, I wanted to live smack on top of it.

Something to aspire to.

Shanti, the yoga studio around the corner from my building, had a steady stream of people pouring in despite the early morning hour. Natalie Mann's early class was one of the studio's most popular. Natalie's approach both calmed and energized people, and she had a knack for infusing messages into her classes that always resonated.

I joined the yogis entering the studio, intent on making it to my favorite spot in the back next to the wall. I wasn't confident enough in my yoga abilities to take a spot up front. I fully expected to fall on my face one day also. Luckily, a lot of the early birds preferred the front of the studio, so the back was still blessedly empty. I unrolled my purple mat with a snap of my wrist and grabbed two blocks and a blanket. Natalie spotted me and smiled, making her way over with her burning stick of palo santo, clearing the room's energy for class.

"Hey girl," she said, giving me a quick hug while managing to not set my hair on fire. "Thanks for coming."

"Of course. I need this today." I sniffed the heady scent of wood appreciatively. Natalie arrived early to make the studio welcoming. I admired her dedication to yoga, which she'd said many times had saved her life. Today, though, she looked tired. I got a glimpse of muddy browns and greens in her aura, which was not like Nat. Reading auras was a skill I'd realized I had back when I was a teenager, and while it greatly helped my work, sometimes it gave me insights that I didn't ask for. "How are you?" I asked.

"I'm fine," Natalie said. Her cheerful smile seemed forced. "Busy week. I might need to come in and do a crystal session soon."

In addition to selling quality crystals, holding classes, and bringing in other energy healers regularly, I offered custom crystal consults and crystal "prescriptions" based on the session. It was what I loved best—one-on-one time with clients, using their auras and energy to create a menu of stones that could truly make a difference in their lives. "Of course! Anytime. Just let me know. I have a bunch of open slots this week."

"I will." She flashed me a dazzling smile, looking almost like herself for a moment, then moved on to resume clearing the room and greeting students. When she'd finished, she waved her stick to put out the flame and sat up front, pulling her dark hair into an effortless bun and closing her eyes. "Welcome," she said, and all the chatter quieted.

I settled back and closed my own eyes, sinking into the mat and the smells and sounds of the room, hoping this practice would chase away this gnawing feeling of unrest.

CHAPTER 2

I felt much better after class. I popped into the studio bathroom to change into my work outfit—long, flowy purple skirt and an oversized black sweater—and dusted some glitter over my hair. I felt very strongly that everyone needed glitter in their life on a daily basis.

I was actually looking forward to getting into my shop. I had a bunch of boxes to unpack—my new shipments from the gem show I'd gone to in Colorado had arrived last week, and I hadn't had a chance to dive in yet. And then tonight my boyfriend, Todd, and I were going to try out the new Thai food restaurant that had recently opened in town. The grand opening celebration promised to be a good time.

If he remembers to leave work, a nagging little voice reminded me. Todd had a one-track mind when it came to his bar, Luck o' the Irish. And since the place was always busy, he usually worked late. But not tonight. He'd promised me a date night, and I had every confidence he'd keep his word. He had been trying to be extra attentive lately, because he knew how hard it had been for me to lose my grandma. And I appreciated it.

Yes, life was definitely good.

I packed up my yoga clothes and mat and left the studio, pausing in the lobby to step into my boots before I headed outside. When I stepped out the front door, I saw Sydney sitting on the steps waiting for me.

"Hey, Vi." Syd sprang up, adjusting her hot-pink velvet cape around her shoulders. Syd owned a vintage clothing store, aptly named Yesterday, that she ran both online and from a tiny house—a literal tiny house—currently parked in Charlie Klein's parking lot the next street over. Charlie, a local barber and lifetime North Harbor resident, thought it was great. He'd taken to boasting that her house regularly got him new clients, and called her his secret weapon.

Syd believed in marketing her merchandise, so she always had the best outfits she put together from her selection. Today, she'd coupled her cape with leather pants and cowboy boots adorned with pink rhinestones. Her rhinestone-covered hat attempted unsuccessfully to tame her wild dark-blond curls. Which needed serious taming most days. When she put effort into it, she either had a beautiful head of shoulder-length ringlets, or blew it out into sleek waves. When she didn't, she looked a bit like she'd narrowly escaped a lobotomy. Today was the latter.

"Did you have a good class?" She snickered a little when she said it. Syd and I couldn't be more different when it came to health and fitness. One of her lifelong goals was to lose that extra twenty pounds, but the reality was she got cranky without cake and french fries. And her main source of exercise was her five-minute walk to her shop.

"I had an awesome class. I really needed that today," I said, zipping my coat and shoving my hands in my pockets while refusing to partake in her yoga negativity. "Were you waiting for me?"

"'Course. I need coffee and you know I hate going alone." She pushed herself to her feet, stepping out of the way of the last of the exiting class goers. "Cold," she muttered. "I hate this weather."

"Yeah. Where's Presley?"

"With Josie. I'm going to go pick her up after coffee. She was amped up this morning, so I was more than happy to let someone else get her dressed."

Josie Cook, my mentor and dear friend who worked part-time in my shop, also nannied for Syd. And worked at the art shop, the candy store, and sometimes the flower shop. She was like Mary Poppins, but with side gigs.

"We heading to Pete's?" Syd asked, looking back at me expectantly.

"Yep. Let's go." As we started off, the studio door banged open again and Natalie rushed out. She stopped short when she saw us. "Hey, Syd!" she exclaimed. "When are you coming back to class? It's been ages since I've seen you!"

Syd studied her from the top of her bun down the length of her fashionable Athleta—or maybe Lululemon—yoga pants, then shrugged. "Probably not for a while," she said.

"Oh, that's a shame." Natalie looked genuinely dismayed. "I hope it wasn't because of that crow. Everyone has a tough time with crow." She patted Syd on the shoulder. "Don't let that stop you from joining us, okay?"

Sydney shot daggers at Natalie with her eyes. Just as she opened her mouth, I grabbed her arm and pointed her toward Pete's. "Thanks, Nat. Class was awesome," I called over my shoulder, waving at her as I pushed Sydney down the street. "Can you please be nice?" I hissed as soon as we were out of earshot. "She means well."

"Oh, please." Syd made a face. "No one can be that

sunshine and namaste all the time. And I know for a fact she's not always Little Miss Açaí Bowls and Veggies."

I burst out laughing. "Açaí bowls? What on earth are you talking about?"

She leaned over with a conspiratorial glance over her shoulder, but Natalie wasn't behind us. She'd gone down the street the other way, probably to the gym for a cycling class or something. "I saw her at Potatoes from Heaven the other day. Getting those specialty french fries," she added, with a touch of glee in her tone. "The ones with the garlic and herbs?"

Crinkle-cut garlic-aioli fries, to be exact. I was well acquainted with them, although admittedly my appetite had been almost nonexistent lately, so I hadn't indulged in a while. But they would tempt even the most dedicated of dieters. Potatoes from Heaven was a food truck that came to town every Monday, Wednesday, and Friday and parked in various spots in our business district. They served all kinds of french fries, baked potatoes, even tater tots, with special sauces and toppings and herbs. The potatoes were all organic, at least. And all were to die for.

I wasn't terribly impressed with Syd's revelation, though. "So?" I asked, pausing in front of the coffee shop.

Syd huffed out a breath. "What do you mean, *so*? She acts all high and mighty about her eating habits and her exercise but she's really not perfect either. It's Monday, so I bet you she'll be there later. I'll report back, because I'm planning on going."

"Oh, would you get inside." I gave her a gentle shove through The Friendly Bean's front door. "She never said she was perfect. So she eats french fries sometimes. Big deal."

Sydney sniffed, but let it go. I followed her inside the Bean. My other happy place. I always looked forward to the warmth and camaraderie inside, not to mention the menu. The scent of good, strong coffee hit my nose as soon as I opened the door, and I sighed happily as the blast of warm air greeted us.

"There they are." Pete Santorini, the tall, dark, and handsome owner and morning barista, grinned at us over the top of his espresso machine. He reminded me a little of Jake Gyllenhaal. "You're late."

Sydney batted her eyelashes, ever the flirt. "Miss me?"

"Always, darlin'," Pete returned. "Were you cheating on me somewhere else?"

"Never. Vi had yoga this morning. You know, with all the crazies. So I had to wait for her. I hope you saved us something good."

I resisted an eye roll. Sydney and Pete flirted like this every time I saw them interact. I wondered when they'd just get it over with and get together. Or at least go on a date. Pete was cute, and there was something to be said for being with someone who could keep you in coffee. Sydney wasn't dating anyone, so it might be good for her.

"The fresh blackberry muffins are out back," he said. "Just say the word."

My mouth was already watering, and this could go on forever. "Perfect," I cut in. "We'll each take one."

We joined the four-person-deep line. I perused the chalkboard menu on the wall showcasing Pete's latte specials. He liked to experiment. Today he was offering a juniper and sage latte, which sounded weird but given Pete's prowess with an espresso machine, I figured I'd give it a try. Plus it would make him happy.

Decision made, I turned to Syd. "So what's going on with you? How's business?"

Sydney sobered a little. "Business is good, but I feel like I'm kind of in a war zone," she said.

"What do you mean? Are they still giving you a hard time about the store?" I waited expectantly as we shuffled forward in the line a couple of steps at a time. Syd's innocuous parking job at Charlie's place had hit a nerve around town. There were some elected officials who didn't think she should be allowed to simply park there and operate without all the traditional hoops a business owner would have to jump through. On the other hand, the lot was private property—Charlie had bought the building and lot a couple of years ago—and he was renting it out to Syd for something like five dollars a month, just to be able to say he was doing things by the book. Charlie was one of the more vocal residents in town, and he never hesitated to speak up when he didn't like the direction things were moving.

And these days, there seemed to be a lot of angst in town. Development was once again on the rise for the first time in over ten years, and the town had seen an influx of new entrepreneurs. Usually it was restaurants that came and went frequently, but right now a lot of new retail and specialty businesses were hoping to anchor here. And some people had very definite opinions on how that should go.

Syd usually didn't care. She figured it would all work itself out and she should focus on the things she could control. But today, something was different. She leaned in and spoke softly. "I got a cease and desist yesterday."

Before she could elaborate, a shrill, displeased voice rang out through the café.

"Violet Mooney!"

CHAPTER 3

Conversation through the entire coffee shop petered out as people turned to see who was shouting. I didn't even need to turn around, though, to know who was behind the voice. There was only one person in this town who sounded like a combination of broken nails screeching down a chalkboard and a petulant five-year-old at the height of a massive temper tantrum—Carla Fernandez, one of our esteemed town officials. I felt my face heating up, already dreading whatever this was.

Next to me, Syd's eyes narrowed to slits and she sucked in a breath. I knew Carla was one of the people giving Syd a hard time about her shop. She didn't like me much either, but for the most part left me alone aside from some snide comments about my "voodoo shop" whenever she could get them in. I usually ignored her and tried to keep a low profile. She wasn't someone I wanted to be on the wrong side of. Carla had a reputation for temper, and for flying off the handle at the flick of a switch. And whatever had flicked her switch this morning must've really rubbed her the wrong way given her purposeful march toward me, eyes blazing fire.

The anxiety I'd woken with returned, a small flutter in my tummy. But why was Carla shouting at me? I hadn't done anything.

I tried to ignore the building feeling of dread and pasted what I hoped didn't look like a fake smile on my face. Grandma Abigail had drilled into my head years ago that when someone was being nasty, taking the high road and being sweet as pie was always better. Plus, it threw them off. "Good morning, Carla," I said, my voice oozing sweetness. "How are you today?"

Carla didn't return my greeting. She marched right up to us, bypassing the people in the line behind us. One of them, a guy I recognized as one of the chefs at the seafood restaurant down by the marina, glared at her.

"Hey," he said indignantly, but she ignored him, coming to a stop in front of me with a menacing frown on her face.

She teetered at the top of a pair of stiletto boots, trying—in my opinion—to overcompensate for her short, somewhat plump form. Really, she looked a little ridiculous, especially given the icy patches still lingering on the sidewalks. One misstep and she'd land on her backside, or worse. I wouldn't mind seeing that, come to think of it. Carla's thick jet-black hair was straightened and pulled back into a severe ponytail. She thrust her hands onto her hips and took a breath, readying herself for whatever tirade she was about to deliver.

I tried not to tune in to her aura, but I couldn't help it. Bright, harsh blue colored the air around her head. This was her color, every time. A rookie aura reader might take it as a creative color, but anyone who knew auras well knew it spoke more to her intolerance of others and her too-strong opinions.

"This," she announced, as if she were on a morning newscast and had urgent breaking news, "is a wholesome town. And all your attempts to sully that wholesomeness are not going to work, young lady."

I blinked, trying to process. I didn't have the first clue what she was talking about. Beside me, Syd crossed her arms over her stomach, as if trying to ward off the attack. I almost expected her to get in Carla's face, but she stayed quiet.

"Don't look at me like you don't know what I mean," she continued, stepping right into my space, close enough that I could smell the terrible perfume she always wore. As someone who only wore essential oils for fragrance, the toxicity of traditional perfumes hit me even harder. Especially when it was so close I could almost taste it. "You don't belong here. What on earth are you thinking, holding a séance on our street? We don't call evil spirits into North Harbor! What exactly are you trying to do? You, young lady, are ruining our reputation and I won't have it!"

A *séance*? Was this woman off her rocker? I almost laughed, but I could tell from her demeanor that it would just make things worse.

"I have no idea what you're talking about, but I can assure you you're wrong," I said coolly. "I don't hold séances. I'm not a medium." I turned my back on her, hoping she'd just go away.

"Don't you turn your back on me!" Carla commanded.

The ever-astute Pete, who had one ear perked toward the altercation, abandoned the latte he was making and came up to the counter.

"Hey," he said. "What's the problem, ladies?" His voice

was pleasant enough, but I could tell he was not pleased. Pete was no slouch, and he prided himself on his café being a safe haven for anyone who came in.

Carla ignored him, pointing a finger with a long red nail in my face. It almost touched my nose, and I had to consciously keep from slapping it away. "I knew from the beginning that shop of yours was a problem. It's bad enough you're bringing all the weirdos to town. This is an *upscale place*. And you are jeopardizing any chance this town has to be noticed on a broader scale!" With each word, her eyes blazed brighter until she looked positively manic.

I was too shocked to react at first. I'd put my heart and soul into that shop, and it had a fabulous reputation in the county. Heck, in the entire state. I was contributing to the economy and being a good citizen. I brought people into town because of my reputation, and they often stayed and spent their tourist dollars in other shops and restaurants. And for someone to suggest I didn't belong . . . well, that was unacceptable. Plus, she'd never even set foot inside The Full Moon.

Pete thought so too. "Excuse me." His voice rose a few notches, dark eyes flashing with something dangerous. "This isn't happening in my café."

I appreciated Pete sticking up for me, but I knew I had to stick up for myself. Grandma Abby would expect nothing less. I instinctively reached up and touched the crescent-moon necklace at my throat, a gift from her back when I was a child. I took a breath, then threw up a hand in front of Carla before she could start another tirade.

Which surprised her. Guess she wasn't used to anyone talking back, least of all any of us lowly business owners. I took full advantage of the situation and drew myself up to my tiptoes, as high as my boots would take me. Since I was already taller than her, it wasn't difficult to tower over her. "You can just stop right there. I have no idea what you're talking about, Carla. What I do in my shop is none of your business. You have no right to start attacking me in a public place when you don't even know what you're talking about." I spun around with a swish of my long skirt that Stevie Nicks would've been proud of and faced the counter.

But Carla was That Person who always had to get the last word in. She simply moved around me so she was once again in front of us.

I closed my eyes, silently deploying a tool my grandma had taught me to use on difficult people. I imagined white light and love bursting from my chest right into Carla's heart. It had taken a lot of practice, but once I really got the hang of it, I'd been able to stop arguments and disputes right in their tracks.

But Carla wasn't so receptive. I could literally feel the good energy bouncing up against a force field of resistance.

"How dare you turn your back on me, young lady! I am part of this town's *government*." She puffed her chest out importantly. "And I will say what I want to say, when I want to say it."

I opened my eyes in time to see Pete rolling his at Carla's back. He made a motion with his thumb as if to say, *Want me to toss her out?*

I shook my head. The last thing I wanted was for Pete to be in Carla's sights too. I took one more deep breath, summoning all the patience I had. "As I said already, Carla—I don't run séances. I've tried to maintain a good relationship with everyone in town, and I've done nothing wrong. But now I'd appreciate it if you left me and my business alone." With that, I pushed past her to the counter, and managed to order my latte in what I hoped was a normal voice.

"You and your voodoo store are a blight on this town," Carla said, raising her voice an extra notch higher just to make sure the whole café could hear. "Just like you"— here she tossed her head at Sydney—"with that foolish house parked on the side of the street. And I intend to do something about all of it." With that, she turned and sailed out of the store. I risked a glance over my shoulder. To my dismay, she didn't even fall on her face.

CHAPTER 4

After a fleeting wish for that ice patch a little farther down the street, I shook it off. That wasn't the way to win this fight. My grandma—not to mention my dad—had always taught me to repay unkindness with kindness. Normally I wouldn't have even interacted with her, but she'd left me no choice.

I glanced at Sydney next to me. She stared after Carla, and her face was a mix of pale and a little green. "Are you okay?" I asked.

She looked at me as if just remembering I was there. "Yeah. Are you?"

"Fine. Just forget it," I said, stepping to the end of the counter to wait for my coffee.

But Syd wasn't letting it go. She paused to order her coffee, then joined me. "She has no right to speak to you like that. Or me. Or anyone, for that matter. That woman has some issues. Someone needs to do something about her. What's she talking about, anyway? What séance?"

I shook my head, holding my head up high. People had

mostly gone back to their business, but I could tell they were whispering about the encounter. I hated that feeling. "I don't know," I said, smiling brightly as if none of that had bothered me. "Let's just get our coffee, okay?"

I tried to not make eye contact with anyone, but I saw Anna Montgomery, the owner of the art shop and paint bar a few doors down, staring at me. When she caught my eye, she turned away with a sheepish look. I liked Anna, but I knew she was friendly with Carla. Mostly she just looked embarrassed.

I turned back to the counter. I didn't realize my hands were shaking until Pete pressed my latte cup into my hands. "You shoulda let me boot her," he said with a wry smile, but I could see the concern in his face. "Are you okay?"

"I'm fine." I brushed it off. "I don't know why she's got a problem with me. I just wish everyone would stop staring."

"I think most people in here know exactly what Carla Fernandez is all about," Pete assured me. "Don't worry about it, kiddo. You go open that shop and connect with as many spirits as you want." He winked to show he was teasing. "Warm muffins on their way out for you girls. On the house. You should eat them here so they don't get cold."

Sydney brightened like he'd just given her a million bucks. "Thank you," she said, blowing him a kiss.

"Thanks, Pete. I'll see you later." I threaded my way through the full tables. The only seats available were at the long counter facing the street, which was fine with me. I didn't want to catch anyone's eye and prompt any conversation about the awkward scene. But I also didn't want to run out the door like I had anything to be embarrassed about.

Sydney slid into the seat next to me and sniffed her coffee appreciatively. Her color had settled, and she looked more like herself. I wondered why the encounter had seemed to bother her so much. Syd was feisty, and I couldn't picture Carla getting under her skin. "Smells amazing," she said, uncapping the cup to take a big swallow.

"Yeah, for sure," I said distractedly, sipping my own drink. It was delicious, and I wondered why I'd questioned the flavor in the first place. Pete's coffee was always top-notch.

Sydney put her cup down and watched me with her big blue eyes. "Don't let that witch get to you," she said after observing me for a moment.

"She got to you," I pointed out. "Tell me about this cease and desist. What's it mean?"

"I have ten days to either find a permanent spot for my business and file for whatever it is a business needs to file for, or I have to move my shop out of town," she said. Contempt dripped from her words. "I don't even know if it's legal for them to do that. But it's fine. Charlie and I are dealing with it," she said, flicking her hand as if a mosquito buzzed around her head. "Just don't let her start the same crap with you. You gotta nip it in the bud before she gets on a roll."

Before I could ask how they were dealing with it, one of the counter guys arrived with our muffins, placing two plates in front of us. I could see the steam still coming off them and inhaled appreciatively. I smiled my thanks.

"Vi?" Syd poked my arm, not willing to let it go. "Promise."

"Promise," I said, ripping off a hunk of my muffin and popping it into my mouth.

Sydney made a noise like she didn't quite believe me, then started on her own food. "Do you know what she's going on about, anyway? Are you really having a séance?" She sounded a bit worried.

I wasn't surprised. Sydney wasn't a woo-woo girl either, another way in which we were complete opposites. She'd only been in my shop once when she needed to drop something off for me. I had no doubt she would defend me and my business to the death, but she had no interest in crystals or energy healing or anything she couldn't completely and unequivocally understand. And a séance would blow her mind.

I swallowed and shook my head. "No, Syd. I'm not having a séance. I'm having a healing circle later this week. It's a joint event at the yoga studio—Natalie and I teamed up to do it. I'm sure she's interpreting that as a séance, since she has no clue about anything and doesn't take the time to ask. She's probably envisioning us digging up the graves over at the cemetery afterward."

Despite herself, Sydney giggled. "Now that's a picture. But really, what's a healing circle? You know I don't get all that mumbo jumbo. And I mean that in the most loving way possible," she assured me, resting a hand on my shoulder.

"I know, I know." I sipped my coffee and stared out the window. More people were out maneuvering along the sidewalks, trying to avoid the icy snow banks. I watched Anna Montgomery exit the café, laden down with four giant bags, trying not to fall. She was doing pretty well so far. "A healing circle is a chance for people to come together, meditate, talk, be with each other, whatever the group wants, really. The whole point is to create collective good energy and blast that out into the Universe."

Syd was looking at me like she was concerned about my mental health. "And people actually go to this? I'm sorry," she amended when I shot her a dirty look. "I'm sure it's . . . awesome. And Carla should leave it alone either way."

"It is kind of baffling to me how Carla is so up on everything going on, though," I said. "I mean, she works full-time and she's on the town council. Where does she find the time?"

In addition to her town council duties, Carla was a Realtor in town. She and Natalie's husband, Andrew, ran North Harbor Realty. According to Natalie, they served only rich clients looking for high-end properties within the county.

"She has no life?" Sydney suggested. She glanced at her watch. "I've gotta go get Presley and get the shop open. I'll talk to you later?"

I nodded. "Todd and I are supposed to go check out the new Thai place tonight, if you want to go."

Sydney stuffed the rest of her muffin in her mouth and took another swig of coffee to wash it down. "I'll call you," she said. "I'm not sure what's going on tonight." She re-capped the cup, leaned over and gave me a hug, then grabbed her coat and gloves and headed out the door.

I watched her hurry down the street, head tucked against the cold. I needed to get moving too. I pulled out my phone, wanting to tell Todd about my Carla encounter. I fired off a text.

You're not going to believe my morning.

I waited for the little dots indicating he was typing back, but the phone remained silent. Strange. I usually heard from him by now. I let my gaze drift back out the window, absently toying with the mason jar with white lights tucked into it. Pete had the decoration in every window. They were always lit, and they felt very comforting. They made me think of fairy lights.

After a few minutes I tucked my silent phone back in my pocket and rose to go. I truly hoped the rest of the day wasn't this exciting.

CHAPTER 5

It felt good to be back out in the cold, after the claustro-phobic encounter with Carla. I walked slowly back up the block, sipping the last of my coffee as I went. I felt like my face was still as red as my hair, which is what happened when I was angry or upset. I breathed in the frigid air, hoping the short walk would make me feel better. Still, I looked forward to the comfort and haven of my store.

I turned the corner back onto Water Street, fumbling for my keys in my giant tote bag. My storefront was a couple doors down from my apartment building, making my commute a dream. My morning routine could usually be summed up in a few hundred steps—down the street and to the left for yoga, up a couple of blocks for coffee, and take a right to get back to my shop. But today, every-thing seemed too close for comfort. I half expected Carla to come around the corner and start yelling at me again.

I glanced around cautiously before I pushed my door open. I didn't see Carla. Part of me knew I was being silly. I mean, what was she going to do, come running around the corner and tackle me? Instead, as I panned my gaze around the block, I swore I saw a blur of black in my peripheral vision. The cat again? I focused, trying to catch another glimpse, but nothing. Maybe I was just imagining things. I shook my head to clear it and looked around again. No cat. And no Carla.

I stepped into my shop and locked the door behind me, leaning against it and closing my eyes for a moment. I needed to let the good vibes and the energy of my crystals settle over me. I didn't even turn the lights on yet. Instead, I concentrated on taking a few deep breaths, focused on grounding myself and shaking off any remnants of the morning.

It wasn't long before I felt a vibe shift. Inevitable, given the amount of stones and the positive environment they created. Crystals, since they are sourced from the earth, have natural healing properties. It was a scientific fact. Some people called them magic. While I appreciated the sentiment, I didn't like to portray crystals that way. Instead, I liked to tell people that if they were open to believing in their natural powers and worked with them consistently, the results could feel magical. And my customers constantly proved me right when they kept returning.

Despite what Carla believed, my shop had an awesome reputation. I stocked only the best crystals, mined sustainably and ethically. The Full Moon was also the only crystal shop in the entire county. There were other small metaphysical shops that sold crystals, but mine was unique. My consults and prescriptions were a big piece of that.

Right now, I needed to get my act together. I had people to serve. I straightened and headed to my back room to drop my coat and purse, automatically reaching up to unwind my scarf from my neck.

And found nothing there. "Are you kidding," I sighed out loud. My beautiful new scarf. I'd been so hot under the collar about Carla I must not have been cold enough to notice I'd left it somewhere. It must still be at Pete's, hanging off the back of my chair. I'd have to run back and look for it later.

But I didn't have time right now. I had to open at nine, and my first consult would be in at ten. There was plenty to do before then, for both me and Josie when she got in. I hoped she'd be along soon, once she'd turned Presley back over to Sydney's care. I could use a dose of Josie right now.

I took a moment to walk around, admiring the larger stones I'd arranged in various displays. My extra large raw amethyst had a place of honor in one of the windows this week, simply because it was so beautiful and calming. I wanted people just walking by the window to feel that energy. I also had a lovely display of raw pyrite in various sizes that I'd just gotten in last week. Pyrite was one of my favorite stones—the sparkly gold rock was able to ward off negative energy and instill confidence. I picked up one of the smaller pieces and let it rest in my hand. I could feel the healing properties of the stone literally permeating my skin.

I kind of wished I could stand here all day and hold it.

But I couldn't, so I placed it back on its shelf. I'd grab one of the smaller stones and tuck it in my pocket. On my way to the case, I passed the counter and noticed the voice mail button blinking on the shop phone. I pressed play and sighed as a bubbly voice filled the room.

"Hi, Violet, it's Lisa Daniels, I was supposed to come in at ten. I need to reschedule—my car died on me this morning! I'm so mad. Maybe you have a crystal for that? Anyway, I'll call you later to reschedule."

It was a new client, so I was kind of disappointed, but

it was fine. I felt like my brain needed to reset before I could properly focus on other people's issues, after the morning I'd had. I turned toward my middle counter, a U-shaped display case where I kept the smaller tumbled stones, to grab a pyrite for my pocket.

And heard a frantic knocking on my door.

I spun around, half expecting to find Carla Fernandez there, ready to continue her rant, but it wasn't her. A young woman peered into the window, her hands cupped around her eyes to see inside. I couldn't see much of her face, but I swore I could feel her energy pulsating through the glass—frenetic. Anticipatory. Negative.

I hesitated. I didn't recognize her, and I wasn't ready for some new drama—I mean, for heaven's sake, it wasn't even nine o'clock yet—but she saw me looking right at her. I debated simply slipping out back until opening time, and then if she was still there, I'd deal with it, but in the end, my desire to help won out. I went to the door and unlocked it, opening it just a smidge.

She was young, maybe midtwenties, and wore skinny jeans, knee-high boots, and a motorcycle jacket that was way too light for this weather. Her choppy, shoulder-length hair had more of a presence than she did—platinum blond, almost white, streaked with a rainbow of purples, greens, and blues. Her eyes were sharp and assessing, and latched on to mine in a way that disturbed me. Her gaze was almost invasive. The air around her felt staticky, as if something about the frequency of the street had changed with her arrival. Given the way this day had gone so far, and the weird vibe I'd awoken with this morning, my hackles were up.

But she was waiting, so I pasted a pleasant, if a tad wary, smile on my face. "Yes?" I said, leaning against the door to casually block her view of the inside of my shop.

"You're Violet Mooney, right?" she asked.

I nodded warily. Did I know her from somewhere? I doubted it. There was nothing familiar about her.

"Cool. I had a referral to come get a crystal prescription." She smirked a little when she said the words, making me bristle. People didn't usually come in here to make fun of me. I wondered if Carla had sent her.

I still didn't open the door all the way. "Did we have an appointment?" I asked, knowing full well we didn't.

She shook her head, but offered no other explanation.

"Who referred you?" I asked.

"I can't give away all my secrets," she said with a cagey smile. "But I was told you were a must-see."

I stifled a sigh. I had no time or desire for this today. "I'm not actually open yet," I said, glancing at my watch. "Can you come back in—"

"No!" she exclaimed, startling me with her vehemence. "I really need to see you now. This is my only chance today and I heard you can really help. Please?"

CHAPTER 6

I studied her. Her eyes reminded me of cat eyes, a combination of greens, browns, and yellows that seemed to change color when the light hit them a certain way. Intense. They made me want to squirm. And I was getting bombarded with her energy. It came at me so fast I was having a hard time deciphering it. I mostly got a feeling of tangled thoughts and confusion, but I couldn't put my finger on an actual emotional need—and usually that was the first thing I got when I started to tune in to someone who came here looking for help.

On the other hand, it was early; I hadn't shifted into my work mind-set yet. Heck, I hadn't even finished my coffee. I opened the door wider. "Come in," I said.

She smiled. It was a feline smile that said *I knew I'd get what I wanted.* "Thank you," she said, and breezed past me into the store.

"No problem." I kept one eye on her as I locked the door behind her again. But she was already deep into the shop, taking everything in. She looked like she was trying to commit everything to memory as fast as possible. And she touched everything she passed, which I didn't love. It reminded me of the way a child would approach a place like this, with all the colors and shapes and, in some cases, sparkles that made up the stones. I wanted to pull her hands away, but managed to resist.

"Have a seat," I said, motioning to the chair I kept in the far left near my largest crystal case for my personal consults. It offered a little more privacy than being out in the middle of the shop. "What's your name?"

"Mazzy," she said.

"Like Mazzy Star?" I asked.

Blank stare, then a shrug. "I have no idea."

I figured she wasn't old enough to know who Mazzy Star was. I wondered what kids like her listened to these day, which then made me giggle a little, given that I couldn't be that much older than her. I tried to swallow the giggle and wound up coughing instead.

She didn't even notice. "This place is crazy," she said, still taking everything in.

I couldn't be sure that was a compliment, so I ignored it. "So what brings you here? Aside from your mysterious referral?" I tried to make light of it, but really I was dying to know why she was really here. I wasn't getting a lot of need or desire for a crystal healing.

Would Carla really send in a mole?

Mazzy shrugged. "I'm trying to wake up my spiritual side," she said. "You know. I think the way I've been feeling means there's something missing in my life."

Wake up my spiritual side? A benign enough phrase, but it sounded completely wrong coming from her. Like she'd practiced it. "How have you been feeling?" I asked.

She shrugged again. She seemed to be casting about for a "right" answer. "Just off. Like there's no purpose in my life, you know?"

I almost pushed more, then decided the best course of action would be to give her something and get her out of here. I cursed Lisa Daniels just a little bit—if her car hadn't died, I could've told Mazzy I had an appointment and turned her away without feeling too guilty about it.

"Well, then let's start with the basics, shall we?" I flashed her what I hoped was a genuine smile and went around the back of the case to where I kept some smaller tumbled stones. On the way, I happened to glance in the mirror on the case across from Mazzy, the one that should've reflected her back to me.

Instead, all I saw was a shimmery outline, not even enough to call it a person.

I felt dizzy, as if my blood sugar had just dropped significantly and my body couldn't catch up. The air had gone staticky again, crackling around me like a radio just missing its nearest frequency. I grabbed the side of the case and closed my eyes for a minute. When I opened them again and glanced in the mirror, I saw Mazzy's colorful hair, then her eyes, watching me watch her, curious. This time, she had an actual body. No shimmery outline.

Jeez, Vi. You need to get more sleep.

I ducked my head down to peer into the case and pulled out a tiger's eye, one of my personal favorite stones. I kept one with me at all times, and I had them scattered strategically around my apartment and my desk out back. Tiger's eye enhances your personal power, courage, strength, and determination. For me, it was a deeply healing stone. And it was common enough that people new to crystals didn't get caught up in a name that they didn't recognize or something else that felt too woo-woo for them right off the bat.

I held the stone in my palm, closing my eyes as I approached Mazzy with it. Usually I got a sense for whether

I had the right one, but I felt nothing. It was weird, almost like she'd put up some sort of barrier. Regardless, I needed to give her a stone and get her out of my shop.

I opened my eyes and held the stone out. She took it, warily, as if expecting it to bite her, and closed it in her own hand.

"So what's it supposed to do?" she asked.

"This is a stone that's all about protection and empowerment." I went through the list of attributes a tiger's eye offered: helps accomplish goals, recognizes inner resources, brings clarity of intention, balances yin and yang energy. As usual, I got caught up in my passion for each stone's individuality and probably gave her way more than she wanted to know.

Mazzy looked unimpressed. She opened her palm and studied it. "What do I do with it?"

I wanted to take it away from her. I felt a little sad about sending it out into the world under her care. But too late for that now. "Get to know it," I replied. "First, you need to cleanse it. My favorite way to do that is in the moonlight under a full moon. There's one next Thursday. But if you don't want to wait, you can cleanse it in the sunlight. Or hold it in the smoke of sage or palo santo. Then you can carry it with you, or sleep with it under your pillow, or whatever feels right." I stopped, aware that she was looking at me with a barely concealed smirk. "Something wrong?"

"Is the moon your schtick?" she asked. "Is that why you named your shop after it?"

"My schtick?" I repeated. "I use it like you would use your calendar. It's very powerful." I returned her stare until she looked away. "Anything else I can help you with?"

Mazzy slid out of her seat, a bit uncertainly. "No, I think this is good. How much do I owe you?"

"That one is eight dollars." I waited while she pulled a ten out of her pocket. I went to the cash register and got her change. "Thanks for coming by," I said as she slid the money and the stone into her pocket.

She nodded and turned to go. A loud rap on the door startled us both. I turned to see Todd at the door, peering inside and looking impatient. I went to unlock it. Mazzy followed me. Good, she was leaving.

I held the door open for Todd. "Hey. I was wondering where you'd been."

He stepped in, his gaze going right to Mazzy. Curiosity, I supposed, but . . . was it my imagination, or did they exchange a look of recognition?

Mazzy glanced back at me and waggled her fingers. "I'm sure I'll see you again," she said with that sly catlike grin, and then she slipped out the door with one last, quick glance at Todd. He avoided her gaze this time.

As the door shut behind her, I noticed the air felt suddenly clearer—less staticky, as if the channel had been changed.

CHAPTER 7

I turned my attention to Todd. "Hey," I said.

"Hey," Todd said with that lopsided grin that I normally loved. Today, though, it seemed forced. He came over and kissed my cheek. "Did you already go for coffee?"

Had I ever. A little while ago I couldn't wait to tell him everything that had gone on so far that morning, but suddenly it seemed like a lot and I didn't have the energy. Also, something felt weird right now. Granted, it could've just been me and my mood, but I wasn't so sure.

"I did," I said. "I texted you, actually. While I was at Pete's. The weirdest thing happened."

"You did?" He pulled his phone out of his pocket and grimaced. "Sorry. It was on silent. I went to the gym." Todd ran a hand through his not-quite-red, not-quite-blond hair, which fell perfectly over one eye. "So what happened?"

"Ugh." I locked the door again and motioned him to come in. "Carla Fernandez accosted me at Pete's," I said over my shoulder as I walked to my desk, then whipped around when I heard a crash. "What on earth?"

Todd stood gingerly next to my charcoal-black statue of Ganesha, the elephant-headed Hindu god, which he'd apparently tripped over. I was dismayed to see one of Ganesha's ears was chipped. "Sorry," he mumbled.

"Jeez, Todd. How did you do that?" With a sigh, I knelt down and felt around for the broken piece. Luckily it was all in one piece. Maybe I could glue it back on. Not ideal, but this statue was one of, like, twenty in the world. My grandma's friend had brought it back from India as a gift when I opened my shop.

"It was in the middle of the floor," he protested.

"It definitely wasn't. You know what, never mind. Do you want to hear what happened or not?" I was annoyed with him and couldn't quite put my finger on why, aside from the ear situation.

"Yes. Of course. Sorry. Want me to fix that?"

"I'll do it." I tucked the piece into my desk drawer so I wouldn't lose it. "So Carla comes into Pete's shouting at me about how I'm holding a séance and she's going to run my voodoo shop out of town. Can you believe it?" I looked at him more closely. "Todd?" He looked like he was about to jump out of his skin, eyes skittering around the room, leg jiggling.

"Yeah. Wow. That's weird. So what'd you do?"

"I told her to leave me alone. That I'm not running a séance, but even if I was it was none of her business." I waited for him to praise me. He was always telling me I needed to be more assertive.

But he didn't. "And what did she say?"

"Some vague threat about getting rid of me. I'm not worried about it. She's nuts. Has she ever given you any trouble?"

A quick shake of his head. "Nope. Never. Don't worry about it, Vi. Your store is awesome." He patted my arm, still looking distracted. "So. Busy day today?"

"Yeah," I said, wondering why he was acting so *weird*. "You?"

He nodded vigorously, and his whole body relaxed. He loved what he did, and he loved his bar. "Crazy day, actually. I'm meeting a new distributor, and I've had two people call in tonight already. I actually need to get over there, but wanted to see you first."

I could feel my romantic evening slipping away, but pushed the thought aside. I didn't want to be That Girlfriend, whining about how work was more important than me.

"Thanks," I said. "Hey, by the way. Do you know that woman?"

He frowned. "Who?"

"The one who just left," I said in my best *don't play dumb* tone.

"Huh." He appeared to think about it for a second, then shook his head. "Don't think so. Should I?"

"I don't know," I said. "But you seemed to recognize each other."

"We did?" He gave me his best wide-eyed schoolboy look. Todd was the quintessential boy next door: easygoing, handsome, friendly, everyone's buddy. It worked on a business level—it was one of the reasons his bar was so popular.

Sometimes I got tired of it. "Yeah. You did."

"Nah. She's probably been in the bar or something and recognized me. I see so many people . . ." He let the sentence trail off and flashed that easy smile again. "So about tonight. Depending on how the day goes and how busy it is, we may need to go to the Thai place tomorrow, okay?"

Of course. I bit back the disappointment. "Sure," I said. "Let me know."

"I will. You're the best." He leaned in for a quick kiss. "I'll call you later." He slipped out the door, nodding at Josie as she came in. The two of them did an awkward dance of trying not to brush up against each other as they both navigated the doorway.

I watched Todd go, trying to shake off the weirdness so I could focus on my day. I had so much going on that I couldn't afford to be wasting my energy dwelling on this crazy morning and who he may or may not know. Whoever Mazzy was, hopefully she'd gotten whatever thrill she'd been looking for and would leave me alone now. Same with Carla. Besides, worrying about any of them wasn't going to change anything. I had to focus on my shop and the thousand tasks I had to do.

But Josie paused inside the door, still holding it open. "What's going on in here?"

I frowned. "What do you mean?"

Josie stepped all the way in, sniffing. "Has anyone been in here besides you?"

"Well, Todd," I said. "And some woman came in looking for some help with crystals. Why? I didn't notice any repulsive perfume." Usually I was the first one to sniff out nasty smells like chemical-laden perfumes.

Josie pulled her trademark beret—she had one in every color, and today's was hot pink—off her pile of brown hair and locked the door behind her. "There's a bad smell in here."

"Like what? Gas or something?" I sniffed too, but didn't smell anything. "I thought you couldn't smell gas. Should I call the fire department?"

She didn't answer, but continued to prowl the edges of the shop, sniffing. I watched, fascinated.

"You said a woman was in here. What woman?" she asked, coming back to stop in front of me. There was a sense of urgency in her voice that put my teeth back on edge.

"Her name was Mazzy," I said. "She said she got my name on referral."

"From who?"

"She didn't say." Could this morning get any more weird? Now Josie was acting strangely. It wasn't like her to be asking so many questions. She epitomized the term *free spirit* and usually wouldn't notice if an alien stopped in for a visit.

"Did you open early?"

I shook my head. "She came to the door."

"Why did you let her in before you were open? Did you tell her you were closed?"

I shrugged. "The sign was on the door and it was locked. She knocked. Said it was the only time she had and she felt desperate." I offered up a half smile. "You know me—always wanting to help people." Usually I was proud of that. Today I felt like perhaps that was being used to my disadvantage, although I couldn't quite put my finger on why.

"And what did her energy tell you?" Josie leaned against one of the crystal counters, her fingers tapping a staccato beat—the one mannerism I knew meant she was worried—as her eyes drilled into mine.

I shrugged, trying to keep it casual, but I could feel my heartbeat accelerate. "She tried to convince me she was concerned about something, but she never articulated it. I felt like she was . . . looking for something. Some negative energy. I also felt like she didn't really take what I do seriously. That's all."

I was trying not to make a big thing of it, but I was getting all kinds of signals from Josie that worried me. So I decided not to mention my feeling that Todd and Mazzy had recognized each other. On top of her current stress levels, Josie wasn't a huge proponent of my relationship with Todd. It wasn't something she'd ever said so bluntly, but I could tell by the way her whole being distanced itself a bit energetically whenever I talked about him. And when she was in his presence, she was polite but not overly engaged.

"What did you do?"

"I gave her a tiger's eye. I hope it helps. Listen, my first appointment canceled, so I'm going to run an errand," I said. I didn't want to talk about this anymore, and Josie wasn't going to let it go—I knew her. Once she got on something, she was like a dog with a bone.

I'd met Josie when I was a teenager. I'd just gotten my license and had borrowed my dad's car to go exploring. I'd stumbled upon one of the other now-defunct crystal shops in the county. Josie had been working there. We struck up a conversation, and she introduced me to some stones I'd never heard of. It was the start of a long-term friendship. I went back a few times a week when I knew she would be there, and over time she taught me everything I know about crystals. She'd been encouraging me to open this shop for years before I got it done. Sometimes I think I did it just to shut her up.

"What kind of errand?"

"I need to go to town hall," I said. "I forgot to pay the tax bill on my car." It was true enough, although I hadn't been in any rush to take care of it. I still had a week before I got a fee, so normally I'd be in there the last possible day. "Do you need me to punch out?" I said it with a smile, but I could hear the edge in my voice. I didn't love being questioned like this.

"No need," she said, returning my smile with her own edge. "I'll look into this smell while you're gone."

I still didn't smell anything, but whatever. "Great. Thanks." I grabbed my bag and my coat. "I'll be back soon."

CHAPTER 8

I walked slowly around the corner to the lot behind my building, where I parked my car. Town hall wasn't far, but in weather like this it was far enough that I didn't want to walk. Although I wondered if some extended fresh air might help shake off the strangeness of this day.

I drove the half mile to the suite of buildings that housed the town offices, my mind still on Todd. He'd reacted so oddly about Carla. I expected him to be more outraged on my behalf. Although when Todd was distracted, he couldn't focus on anything else.

I found a parking spot right out front, which made me feel like maybe my luck had changed. Inside, I made a beeline for the elevator to the second floor and the tax assessor's office. But before the elevator arrived, I felt a tap on my shoulder.

"Excuse me. Have you heard about the proposed Harbor Lights Bridge project?"

I turned. And stared. The guy talking to me wore a railroad track on his head. The elaborate contraption protruded from a plain old Yankees baseball cap—how on earth had he gotten it to stay put?—with a small train on the tracks. On either side were what I assumed were bodies of brown, ugly water and . . . dead fish? I blinked, trying to get a better focus.

"Hello?" He waved an impatient hand in front of me, forcing me to drag my eyes to meet his.

"Sorry. Uh, Harbor Lights. Yes, I have."

He appeared to be around my age, but that could've been the scruffy goatee adding years. His face looked really young. He had small brown eyes flecked with green. They darted around the room like he was expecting to be ambushed at any second. The hair visible from under his odd hat hung almost in his eyes. He wore jogging pants and a shirt that said, *There Is No Planet B*.

He beamed at me. "Excellent. May I be so bold as to presume that you oppose the project, given the likely impact to the environment?"

I frowned, ignoring the ding of the elevator as it arrived. A woman pushed past me to get on, pausing to stare at him—or more precisely, at his hat. He ignored her, waiting for my answer.

The bridge project had been a recent, ongoing controversy in town, and it was ramping up because it was due in front of voters next week. The proposal to redirect the railroad tracks that ran through town due to the age and condition of the current tracks would mean building over the river and through the business district. Which would mean taking an office building by eminent domain, which would displace some local businesses, who might then have to move out of town entirely given the current lack of space. The opposers also felt that by redirecting the railroad tracks, it would upset a lot of the river creatures and fish populations.

I generally felt it was a bad idea, although I was disturbed by the claims from proponents that the old tracks would inevitably fail in the next seven years. I imagined by *fail* they meant a train would plummet into the water, and that didn't sound like a good option either.

I gave a noncommittal grunt.

He pointed to his hat. "I hope that's a yes. This is a depiction of what can happen."

I peered at it, more closely this time. "Really?"

He nodded proudly. "It's a mockup of what we believe will happen if the uninformed, money-hungry town officials agree to move forward with this half-baked bridge replacement project." He whipped the hat off and held it out to me. "See," he said, pointing to the left side. "This is depicting the endangered American eels that will be displaced."

I studied the model. It was clever, I had to admit, but it had to be awfully heavy to wear. And hard to maneuver. What happened if he was in a place with low ceilings?

"And these are trout." He pointed to the other side, where my suspicions were confirmed. Upon a closer look I saw a beached fish, its eyes bulging and tongue hanging out, in case anyone wondered if it was dead.

"I see," I said, not sure what else to say.

He was still waiting for something from me. I wasn't sure what, but I needed to get going. I started to turn back to the elevator, but he stopped me.

"Will I see you at the protest on Wednesday?"

"What protest?"

"A bunch of us are gathering down by the river. In the park. To show our support for killing this project."

"I'll try to get there," I said. "If I can close my shop."

"What's your shop?"

"I own The Full Moon. It's a crystal shop on Water Street."

"I've seen it," he said, snapping his fingers. "It looks amazing. Crystals are an incredible part of our earth. I'll have to check it out. " He stuck his hand out. "I'm Rain."

Rain? Could that possibly be his real name, or had he adopted an environmentally friendly moniker to add to his credibility? "Violet," I said, shaking it gingerly.

"Nice to meet you, Violet. Hey, I don't suppose you would consider helping me spread the word about the protest?" He plopped the hat back on his head and dug into his backpack, pulling out a stack of flyers.

"Sure, I'll take a few," I said.

"Sweet." He handed me a stack.

The elevator dinged, blissfully. "I have to go. Nice meeting you, Rain. Good luck with your protest."

"Thanks! Hope to see you there," he called after me as the doors closed between us.

I kept the smile pasted on until the doors shut, then shook my head. I was definitely setting a record for having the Weirdest. Day. Ever.

CHAPTER 9

When I stepped out of town hall nearly three hundred dollars poorer, my phone chimed, signaling a text message. Josie.

Hey. I need to get someone in here to figure out this smell. You should go home for lunch and I'll text you when I know more.

Was she serious? My thumbs flew over my screen in reply.

Can't. I have WAY too much to do! And an appointment soon.

I figured that would be the end of it, but Josie's stubbornness was in rare form today.

Sorry. Can't have customers in here in case it's something bad. I already let people know we were closed and rescheduled your other appointments.

"Are you freaking kidding me?" I sighed out loud. I had no idea what she was even talking about since I hadn't smelled anything, but suddenly I felt too tired to fight it. Plus I had a banging headache that had appeared somewhere between Carla and Mazzy and had only grown

since then. Going home might be my best option. Maybe
I could grab that nap with Monty like I'd fantasized about
this morning.

Fine. Text me later. I'll try to do some work from home.

I climbed back in my car. While I waited to pull out
into traffic, I saw Rain come out the main doors, talking
on his cell phone, that ridiculous hat bobbing around on
top of his head. People blatantly stopped and stared as
they passed him, but he didn't even notice. I shook my
head and drove home.

This time I had to dodge people as I cut through my little alley and made my way toward my building. The
lunch crowd was out in full force, people dashing for
their favorite spots to grab a bite and get out of the cold
while the parking authority guys prowled the streets
looking for unsuspecting violators thinking they could
get away without filling the meters. Mr. Quigley sat on
one of the benches with his markers and portable desk
sketching something, puffing on his long pipe as he
worked, bundled up in a heavy coat and hat. I wondered
if he'd headed off the guy encroaching on his dumpster
territory earlier. He was too engrossed in his work to notice me.

Which was fine. My head ached, and I just wanted to
be alone. The winter sun seemed blinding, especially
glaring off the remaining snow, and I shaded my eyes
with my hands. I'd left my sunglasses somewhere too,
but I didn't care.

Blessedly, I reached the door to my building without
having to speak to anyone else and fumbled with the key,
letting the door slam behind me. I let my bag drop to the
floor and threw my coat over a chair. I stood for a moment, enjoying the absolute quiet. Then I heard a thud
and a loud purr.

I glanced down. Monty had vacated his window perch when I came in, curious about why I was home. Now he clearly sensed my mood and was rubbing against my leg, purring like a little motor boat. I scooped him up and nuzzled my face into his soft fur. Hugging Monty made everything better.

After I'd snuggled him for a few minutes, I deposited him back on his perch. He sat there most of the day watching the town goings-on. It was his kingdom and he ruled it. I'd hung a bird feeder off the window so he could have some feel of a country life, which kept him entertained.

I dug around in my freezer until I found a frozen Indian food meal and stuck it in the microwave. While I waited for it to heat up, I absently chose a Lindt truffle—my drug of choice next to coffee—from a bowl on my coffee table and popped it in my mouth as I wandered the apartment. I felt restless.

I changed out of my clothes and pulled on my favorite fleecy pajamas, the ones with crystal balls on them. When the microwave buzzer sounded, I took out the food and stirred it around, then gingerly took a bite. Too hot. I set it aside. I'd felt hungry, but now that I had food, I didn't really have an appetite.

I made myself take a few more bites, then abandoned it and went into my bedroom. I closed the blinds and crawled into bed. It had been a long time since I'd gone to bed in the middle of the day, but I desperately needed this right now. Just fifteen minutes, I promised myself, pulling a pillow over my head.

It took me a while to fall asleep. When I woke, bleary-eyed, to the sound of my doorbell ringing repeatedly, I opened the blinds and realized it wasn't just dark in my room, but dark outside.

What the heck time was it? I stumbled out of bed, wondering fleetingly if I should change, but it sounded urgent. I hurried out to the door and peered through the peephole, frowning when I saw two uniformed policemen standing there.

The bad feeling returned in full force like a punch in my gut. What was going on? Had something happened to Todd? Josie? The store? Oh God, had there been a gas leak after all and she'd been taken to the hospital? Swallowing hard, I took a breath and pulled open the door.

"Yes?"

I was surprised at how calm I sounded. The two officers regarded me, unsmiling. The tall one glanced at my pajamas, then glanced back at my face, assessing.

"Violet Mooney?" the other one asked.

CHAPTER 10

I nodded. "What's going on? Is it my store?" I would've heard if there'd been a gas explosion, wouldn't I? It occurred to me that was a terrible thought, even as it ran through my mind.

"Can we come in?" the shorter cop said, already moving past me into the apartment, ignoring my question. The pair was almost comically different in height, although they appeared to be roughly around similar ages. Older than me, maybe forties. Or maybe it was their job that made them look older. The taller one wore a hat and carried a plastic shopping bag. Monty, sensing unwelcome company, jumped off his perch with a thud and skulked into the bedroom, probably to hide under my bed.

"Um, sure," I said, glancing self-consciously at my outfit. It seemed I didn't have a choice.

The taller one motioned for me to move inside and followed me, closing the door behind him.

"I'm Sergeant Haliburton, this is Officer Denning," the short one said.

"Nice to meet you," I said, then immediately felt stupid.

"Can you tell us where you've been this evening?" Haliburton asked. "Specifically between five thirty and six?"

I frowned, trying to sneak a glance at the clock. I had to do a double take though. It was almost seven thirty. How had I slept that long? "Here," I said. "I came home for lunch and to take a nap. I guess I took a longer nap than I'd planned. There was a weird smell at my store and Josie—Josie Cook, I'm sure you know her—was going to take care of it for me. Are you sure she's okay?" I was babbling, but couldn't help myself.

Neither of them looked like they were about to answer my question. "Where were you before your . . . nap?" Haliburton asked, and his inflection on the word *nap* suggested he either didn't think much of people who napped, or he didn't think I had actually been napping. A flutter of nerves invaded my stomach, and I pressed a hand there.

"I was at my shop." I jerked a finger toward the window, then realized I was pointing in the wrong direction and pivoted my thumb. "The Full Moon. Well, actually, I was at the town hall. I left my shop to run an errand and didn't go back."

Haliburton pulled a notebook out of his back pocket and wrote something down. "Where is your shop?"

"A few doors down from here."

"What time did you leave there?"

I shrugged, trying to recall. "Around ten."

"And from there?"

"I went to the town hall. To pay my car tax bill."

"So what time did you come back here?" Haliburton asked, pen poised above his pad like a reporter waiting for a scoop.

"Around eleven, I guess," I said.

Haliburton regarded me with blank eyes. "You guess, or you know?"

I frowned. Why was he being snotty? "I'm pretty sure," I said. "The lunch crowd was out already when I got back."

"So you didn't stop anywhere after you left town hall."

"No."

"You came straight back here and you haven't left since?" Denning this time.

"That's right. I ate some lunch then laid down for a while. What is this about, anyway?" I asked, tired of all the questions. Was it suddenly against the law to take a day off from your own shop and stay in bed?

Denning stepped forward and opened the shopping bag, holding it out to me. "Do you recognize this?"

I peered inside and saw a pile of pink fabric. "Oh! Is that my scarf? I thought I'd lost it." Smiling, I went to reach into the bag, but Denning held it just out of reach.

Using his pen, he lifted it halfway out of the bag. "So this is yours?"

I moved closer to study it, just to make sure. It definitely was, but it looked rough. There was a fairly big orange stain, and when I got closer, I caught a whiff of something smelly. Something familiar but slightly rancid. It hovered in the back of my brain, just out of reach. Feeling a pang at my scarf's current situation, I nodded. "I lost it this morning. But what is that smell?"

They looked at each other. Denning tucked the scarf in the bag and closed it. He didn't answer my question.

I was starting to get a bad feeling. Cops didn't usually deliver lost-and-found items, I was guessing. Especially in pairs. "Can I have it?"

"Do you know Carla Fernandez?" Haliburton asked, ignoring my question.

The flutter of nerves turned into a yawning chasm. "Of course. Doesn't everyone?"

"What do you mean by that?" Denning asked. His face hadn't changed, but his tone signaled his interest.

I turned to him. "I mean, she's part of the town council. Most people know her if they live in town and if they're paying attention to anything."

"Did you see her today?" Haliburton asked.

"I did actually. This morning. At The Friendly Bean."

"And was there an altercation between you two?"

I hesitated, looking from one to the other. How did they hear about that? And why did they care? Had she rushed over to file a report against me or something? And how could she think she'd get away with that when *she* was the one being abusive?

Haliburton's hand was poised over his notebook, eyes on me, ready to write down whatever I said. "You've got to be kidding me. The altercation was more on her side," I said. "She has her nose out of joint about my shop. Thinks I'm having a séance—which I'm not—and she came up to me in the coffee line to rant and rave about it."

"She approached you?" They glanced at each other.

"Yes. Started yelling at me in front of everyone." I sniffed, remembering.

"That must have been upsetting," Haliburton said.

"Of course it was upsetting. She embarrassed me in front of half the town. She has no right to say those things about me and my shop. She doesn't even know what I do. And I'm not having a séance. I'm having a healing circle. There's a big difference!" I realized my voice had gone up a couple notches and cleared my throat. They both watched me, blank faced.

"So what, now she's trying to blame me? That's just like her. So what are you going to do? Let her file a complaint about me? Because I can file one too. And mine will have more merit." I crossed my arms defensively over my chest. Whatever. Let her file a stupid complaint. She'd be the one who looked unstable.

Haliburton and Denning exchanged a look.

"Did you see her again?" Denning asked. "After this altercation?"

I shook my head.

"You're positive?" Haliburton asked.

"I'm positive, seeing as I was here and she didn't come over."

They both looked like they didn't believe me. But why wouldn't they? What was Carla saying about me now? I felt a rush of anger at this woman. Why wouldn't she leave me alone?

"And you said you were asleep?" Denning asked.

"Yes." *For the twentieth time.*

"I see," he said, although his tone suggested he didn't. "Have you been down to the courtyard today behind the Steelworks building?"

I was confused at the change of direction, but shook my head no. "I was at yoga down there this morning, but I didn't go into the courtyard for anything," I said. "Why?"

After a long moment of silence, Haliburton said, "Ms. Fernandez is dead."

CHAPTER 11

I stared at him. All the blood in my body seemed to rush right to my ears, and all I could hear was the roaring sound. It had to be affecting my hearing. He couldn't have said what he just said. Could he? Dead? How could that be? Maybe this was some weird, disturbing dream. That happened sometimes when I felt off. I casually reached under my pajama top and pinched my stomach. Ow. Nope, they still here.

The unease and panic that had haunted me all day finally culminated with a moment of *Oh, now I know why I felt so weird and awful*.

They both watched me, waiting for my response. It probably seemed odd to them that I hadn't said anything yet. I swallowed hard and forced my voice to work. "Dead . . . What are you talking about?"

"So you haven't heard," Haliburton said. Again with that skeptical tone. "Ms. Fernandez was found dead this evening," he repeated, in case it hadn't registered the first time. "Down in the courtyard."

I tried to process this. The courtyard down the street

was a lovely little cobblestone area behind the Steelworks apartment building, an old factory that had been
renovated into a mixed-use building of apartments and
businesses. The yoga studio was one of the businesses on
the ground floor. The courtyard was public, and in the
summer the restaurants on that stretch had outdoor seating and bar areas where people congregated. The water
fountain in the middle on the raised platform was a lovely
addition in warm months, though right now it was in the
bereft limbo of winter in New England. The Christmas
tree that stood in its place had just been taken down, and
now it was empty and waiting for spring.

In the nice weather, people spent a ton of time out
there. In the winter, it was pretty empty. No reason to be
there, since there was no outdoor seating and no pretty
fountain to look at.

"How?" I asked finally, as I tried to process all this.
"Did she . . . have a heart attack or something?" It wasn't
so far-fetched, especially the way she wound herself up
over stupid things. Like séances that weren't really
séances.

"It looks like foul play," Haliburton said, watching me
carefully.

Foul play. The words echoed in my ears. While intellectually I knew what they meant; I was having trouble
connecting all of this.

"And a number of witnesses said the two of you were
engaged in a nasty confrontation today." He continued to
stare at me. "Did Ms. Fernandez threaten to close your
shop down?"

I desperately wanted him to stop, to shut up, while I
covered my ears and went back to bed with the blankets
over my head. But he wasn't stopping, and I couldn't just
go to bed, so I simply stared at him as he finished his terrible thought, feeling my knees go weak. I pulled out one

of the barstools at my counter and sank down into it, trying to process. He couldn't have just said Carla was
dead—*by foul play*—then insinuate I'd had anything to
do with it.

"So you're . . . you're saying she was killed," I said,
needing to spell this out more for my sake than his. "And
you're asking me if I killed her." The horror of this
started to sink in. Of course I hadn't killed her, but they
didn't know that. And I had no eyewitnesses to my
whereabouts all afternoon, aside from Monty.

I could be in some trouble here.

"Actually, I hadn't, but since you brought it up. Did
you?" Haliburton asked bluntly.

"Of course not," I said, feeling tears choke the back of
my throat. How could anyone think I'd ever do such a
thing? Anyone who knew me would know this was complete nonsense. Not that these two knew me from Adam,
but still. "How was she killed?"

"We're waiting on the coroner's report." Denning this
time. The two of them were like a tennis match, playing
off each other.

"So what does my scarf have to do with it?" I asked, as
my eyes landed again on the bag that hung from Denning's hand.

"It was found with the body," Haliburton said.

I straightened. "And that's why you're here. Well,
that's easy. I told you I lost my scarf this morning."

Neither said a word.

"It's true," I said. "Besides, I'm sure there were other
people she yelled at today. Why not go ask them?"

They exchanged another one of their glances. I wondered if cops developed some kind of telepathy they used
when they couldn't speak out loud in front of someone.

"Give us an example," Denning said. "Who else would
Ms. Fernandez have yelled at?"

I opened my mouth, then closed it again. The examples that were on the tip of my tongue were people I cared about, like Sydney. And Charlie Klein, who let her use his parking lot. I couldn't force my mouth open. I saw satisfaction on their faces—*see, she's just trying to shift the blame off herself*—and wanted to crawl under a rock.

Haliburton handed me his notebook, still looking triumphant at my hesitation. "We'll need names."

I glared at him. "Don't look so smug. There are tons of people who don't like her. But I'm not throwing anyone under the bus."

"Throwing them under the bus?" Denning asked incredulously. I thought it was a decent performance. "Someone's dead. It's about doing the right thing, not covering for a pal. If you have any information about Carla Fernandez's death, Ms. Mooney, it would be in your best interests to tell us immediately."

"Well, you've got no worries then," I said. "Because I'm not covering for anyone. I have no idea what happened to Carla Fernandez."

Silence. I almost felt like I'd scored a point, until Haliburton spoke again. His voice was colder and more distant this time.

"Ms. Mooney. We'd like for you to come over to the station with us. We need you to make a statement about your day. And I'd like to hear who these other people are that you know of who had problems with Ms. Fernandez."

I felt the blood drain from my face. That was not what I'd been expecting. "The police station? Am I under arrest?" I looked around my apartment, panicked. A million thoughts were flying through my head, none of them good. And Monty. I couldn't leave Monty. He hadn't even had his dinner yet. How could I be under arrest? How could they think I'd kill anyone?

And how could Carla be *dead*? She'd been so full of life this morning when she'd been hollering irrational things at me. Despite myself, I felt tears welling up in my eyes. She wasn't very nice, but she didn't deserve to be dead.

"You're not under arrest. But it would . . . behoove you to cooperate, and we'd like to have you come with us."

My mind raced. Did I have to go? Should I call a lawyer? I didn't have a lawyer, except for the lawyer I consulted with on business-related things when I needed to. I should've listened to my dad all those years ago and gotten an all-purpose lawyer.

In the end, the only thing I could think of to say was, "I have to get dressed."

They both looked at my jammies. I followed their gaze. At least they were cute. I supposed if one had to be arrested in jammies, it could be worse.

"Go ahead," Denning said.

I fled behind the screen separating my bedroom area from the rest of the apartment and grabbed some clothes from a pile I'd tossed on the chair. "Monty," I whispered. "Where are you? I need a hug. I promise I'll send someone to give you your dinner if I . . ." I swallowed. "If I don't come back." Todd would come. Wouldn't he? I grabbed my phone. Our maybe-date at the Thai food place was a distant dream now. And a quick glance at my alerts told me he hadn't texted or called anyway. Sydney had, though. I wondered if she'd heard about Carla. Had they spoken with her too? She had to be on their list, given the cease and desist. If they hadn't found out about that yet, they surely would soon.

Monty peeped out from under the bed. I suspected the word *dinner* had caught his attention. I scooped him up and gave him a hug and a kiss. Tears were brimming in my eyes, even though I tried to convince myself it was silly. I hadn't killed anyone. This would all get straightened out soon.

Wouldn't it?

"Let's go, Ms. Mooney," Haliburton called from the other room.

"Coming." I yanked my pajama top off, and in my nervous haste I yanked my grandmother's necklace along with it. I watched in horror as it fell, in slow motion, to the ground—the broken chain, the moon with its blue topaz in the center landing squarely at my feet. My whole world again felt like it was tilting. I hadn't taken this necklace off in twenty-seven years. My grandmother had made me promise not to, ever, no matter where I went swimming or what I was doing. She'd promised me it would sustain anything I threw at it. And I'd kept my word.

Until now. Barely a month after her death, and I'd let her down.

With shaking hands I bent to pick it up and placed the broken chain and the moon on my dresser. I felt naked without it already. I couldn't remember a time when I hadn't felt it against my skin, cooling and comforting at the same time. I'd get it fixed tomorrow, as soon as this insanity was sorted out. But in the meantime, I didn't like not having it. I thought about slipping it into my pocket, at least, but worried that they'd take it away from me or I'd lose it somehow. So reluctantly I left it on my dresser, running my fingers over it one more time. It was the last blow in a string of them today, and I wished I could go back to this morning for a do-over.

I finished getting dressed and blew Monty one last kiss. "I'll be back soon," I said, and I thought it might be more for my benefit than his. He watched me with concerned eyes. Blinking back tears, I stuck my phone into the back pocket of my jeans and hurried out to my living room.

Denning handed me my coat from where I'd dropped it on a chair when I'd come in earlier. "Ready?"

I shrugged it on and grabbed my bag. "Sure," I said, trying to keep my voice even and unconcerned. "Let's go."

CHAPTER 12

I'd walked by the North Harbor police department a million times—on my way to the train station or the post office or Desi's, my favorite bakery just outside of the heart of town. I'd been inside once, when I needed a sticker to put on my license with my new address. I'd certainly never been driven there in a police car.

I wanted to die. I wondered how many people had seen me being escorted out of my building by two cops. And put in the back seat, no less, like a common criminal. Granted, they were both in the front, but still.

Intellectually I understood this was bad. Carla was dead. Though I wasn't sure that had actually sunk in yet. Not only dead, but murdered. And I'd had a fight with her, which looked bad for me even though she'd started it. And, my fluffy pink scarf had been at the scene.

Thinking about that, I suddenly felt a little better. Anyone who knew me would know—aside from the fact that I wouldn't kill anyone—that I would be way more careful with a favorite accessory, even if theoretically I was doing something bad. There's no way I'd have abandoned my scarf like that. That bolstered me a bit. It wouldn't be long until all this was sorted out.

Officer Denning opened the back door of the cruiser and reached a hand in to help me out. I ignored him and climbed out myself, standing tall. He shrugged and motioned for me to precede him to the door, which Sergeant Haliburton held open. I swept past him with what I hoped was a defiant air.

"This way," Haliburton said, motioning toward the right. If he'd even noticed my defiance, he didn't comment on it. I followed him down a brightly lit hallway to a room with a table and a couple of chairs. He sent me inside and told me to sit, then walked down the hall and disappeared into an office.

Denning paused.

"Water?" he asked.

I nodded.

He walked away, in the opposite direction from his cohort.

I sat, trying to calm my nerves, wishing I'd had the presence of mind to bring one of my calming stones with me. I usually didn't leave the house without putting a stone in my pocket, but there hadn't been time and I'd been too distracted. While I waited, I tried to piece together what could have happened. Who would've been that upset with Carla that they'd resort to murder?

I tried to stay pretty much clear of town politics, but given my position as a shop owner, I had to deal with certain things. Carla's and my paths had first crossed at a town council meeting not long after I'd opened my shop. I'd been asked by some other shop owners to sign a petition lobbying for more parking and meter forgiveness on weekends in the North Harbor hub. On busy days, some people were deterred from sticking around after lunches or early dinners to check out the shops because they had to worry about their meters running out.

Carla had been one of the council members opposed to the idea. Like most things in North Harbor, the issue had raised passions among the townspeople and shop owners, and it had caused some bad blood. People around here took any issue affecting our town really seriously. It was a bit overwhelming at times, but I appreciated the overall sentiment.

In any event, it was my first taste of Carla and her strong opinions. And it seemed to set the stage for the next round of battles as she appointed herself the queen of North Harbor, giving herself say over who got to be successful here. She also seemed to hold a grudge against anyone who publicly opposed her. She took all of it seriously enough that I had to wonder what else she had going on in her life. Maybe a lot of it had to do with her being a Realtor—if she attracted the right clientele to the business district, those people would probably also want to live here. And they likely had the big bucks.

I figured there were other people in town, maybe others on the council, who thought the same way she did, but they were definitely quieter about it. Carla was a bigmouth, and it was her way or the highway. And that hadn't earned her many—or maybe any—friends. But murder? That was a whole other ballgame.

I fidgeted in my seat. I thought this whole stalling and making people wait forever in interrogation rooms was only a tactic they used on television, but I guessed not. In any event, it wasn't cool. I closed my eyes, trying to focus on my breath and stop the stress from taking over, and found myself fervently wishing I was home. Not just my little apartment with my precious Monty, even though I loved it there. No, I wanted to be *home*, at Grandma

Abby's house in the neighboring town of Southbury, at the kitchen table waiting for my dad to come home from work while Grandma Abby made one of her special teas and fed me cookies. I missed her.

I let the feeling of being there wash over me, the memories of feeling safe and loved, and I started to feel better. I could almost feel the mug in my hand, taste the lavender chamomile tea Grandma Abby used to make me when I was especially upset about something. I settled back into my chair, my eyes still closed. Even the chair felt different, once I'd calmed myself down. Softer, more comfortable. I'd always been a big proponent of creative visualization, but it was really working for me today.

I actually felt good, despite where I was. So I just had to hold on to this feeling, even when Denning and Haliburton returned with their attitudes and their accusations. Let them see how little I was bothered by them.

I opened my eyes again, a self-satisfied smile on my face, to see if they'd returned yet.

And froze, wondering if I'd had a stroke. Or maybe passed out and hit my head and somehow was in a strange dream. Either way, I wasn't in the police station anymore. I was in . . . a living room. Sitting on a chair. And not just any chair. Grandma Abby's favorite chair. In our old living room.

CHAPTER 13

I was in her house.

Sitting in her favorite spot, where I'd go when she wasn't home and I needed to feel comforted. Which, after my dad died five years ago, was often. It had been just the two of us after that, and I'd craved her company. I looked around now, half expecting her to appear with a mug of tea, but the house was quiet. It had that empty feel to it, the feeling a space got when its inhabitants left it for an extended period of time. Trying to hold on to their memory in case they came back, but it still started to fade. I hadn't cleaned any of her things out yet—I couldn't face it—but it still felt wrong. Empty. She had left it to me to do what I wanted with, but right now all I wanted to do was keep it the same as she had.

But I couldn't be in her house, because I was in the police station waiting to give a statement. I had to be asleep. Or hallucinating. This day had been stressful, for sure. I closed my eyes and counted to ten, hoping whatever this . . . *vision* was would clear up when I opened my eyes again.

Not that I wanted to be back at the police station, but . . . of course I couldn't be here.

Could I?

I opened my eyes slowly, bracing myself. I was still in the living room. Still in Grandma Abby's chair, where the scent of her lingered on her favorite soft white throw blanket hung over the back of the chair. The scent hit me so hard tears filled my eyes.

I got up slowly, checking to see if my arms and legs worked. Sometimes in dreams my limbs froze and I couldn't move, so I waited to see if that was the case here. Nope, everything was doing what it was supposed to do.

I walked into the kitchen, with the brilliant yellow walls just as my grandma had painted them years ago. Our cheery light wood table with green legs and matching green chairs, the old-style clock on the wall. And the built-in wooden shelving on the wall next to the pantry, where she used to put her favorite spices. Out the window over the sink, I could see the backyard—my old backyard, where I'd spent hours playing on the tire swing my dad had hung for me off the giant oak tree. Where I'd collected leaves for every fall school project. Where I'd dug up rocks and began studying them in earnest, fascinated by all the different shapes and textures and colors.

This was my old house.

How in the name of the goddess had I gotten here? I had no recollection of walking through a door, or driving here. I'd have had to drive. But I had no memory of doing so, or of leaving the police station in the first place. I wondered if I'd had a blackout or something. Unless they'd let me go—or I'd run out and didn't remember.

The air around me turned colder as I considered that option. If that had happened, did that mean I'd . . . possibly done what the cops said? Killed Carla and *forgot*?

I fled out the back door and around the side of the house to the driveway, searching wildly for my car. It wasn't there, nor was it parked on the street. A blast of cold air hit me, and I realized I wasn't wearing my coat, only the sweatshirt and leggings I'd pulled on hastily before I left my apartment with the police. Why had I left without my coat?

I felt around in my sweatshirt pockets for my phone, figuring I'd call Josie, but it wasn't there. It must be in my bag, which was . . . still at the police station.

I closed my eyes and sagged against the big old oak tree that still stood in the front yard, offering up a silent prayer that I would regain my mental faculties and figure out what was going on. It seemed insane, but I thought longingly of the sparse interrogation room where Haliburton and Denning had stashed me. At least I'd known how I'd gotten there, and that my stuff was there. If I could just remember what happened in that room, I'd be able to figure out what had happened next.

I felt a weird sensation in my stomach, almost like I was on a roller coaster and it had just taken the big dive. I pressed my hand into my solar plexus and took a deep breath. Then I opened my eyes.

And nearly fell off a chair I hadn't been sitting on a second ago. I grabbed the edge of the dirty plastic table to steady myself. "What the . . ." I muttered, looking around the empty interrogation room. It was just as I'd left it before I ended up in my old house. Which clearly had all been in my imagination. The stress of the day had gotten to me. Maybe I'd fallen asleep for a minute and dreamed of it because it had been a safe haven for me. That had to be it. My head still felt a little spacey, but overall I felt better.

I heard footsteps in the hallway and raised voices. I glanced up to find Denning and Haliburton arguing with each other as they appeared in the doorway. Then they stopped and did a double take when they saw me sitting there. Denning closed his eyes and shook his head as if to clear it.

Haliburton narrowed his eyes. "Where were you?"

I frowned. "Excuse me?"

"I said, where were you?"

"Right here where you put me," I said, hoping I didn't sound as uncertain as I felt.

"Yeah, but . . . you went to the bathroom or something?" Denning asked.

"I didn't," I protested. "I've been right here." At least I desperately hoped so. There was no way I could've *really* ended up in my old house. It was a crazy dream or a hallucination.

It had to be.

They both looked at each other, then looked away. "Forget it," Haliburton muttered, stalking into the room and slamming the door. He shoved a notepad and pen at me. "Write down everything that happened today. Every place you've been. Times. All of it."

I took the pad and pen. I wasn't going to add in the trip down memory lane to my grandmother's house. "Aren't you going to ask me more questions?"

"No," he said, his voice sharp. "Just write it down."

I obliged. I wrote slowly and carefully, trying to think of everything just as I'd told it to him earlier. Denning stood in the doorway, watching me the whole time as if I were some weird specimen he had to study. Haliburton barely watched me at all, and checked his watch repeatedly. When he wasn't checking his watch, he was checking his phone. He made me nervous.

I stopped writing when I got to my nap. Of course, after that the police knew everything because they'd shown up at my door and caused all this chaos in the first place. I pushed the notebook back across the table at him.

"What now?" I asked.

CHAPTER 14

Far away from the North Harbor police department and the fountain where Carla Fernandez's body had been found, in a parallel realm to everything Violet Mooney was experiencing at that moment, a Magickal Council meeting was about to get underway. It was a meeting Fiona Ravenstar loathed attending, but she had to because, well, someone needed to be in charge. And that someone needed to be her because, let's face it, if she didn't, the whole witch community that had taken eons to build and morph into what it was today would probably just fall apart. That's how incompetent some of the so-called leaders of this generation were.

And it was no mystery why. Fiona watched them now, most of them on their *smartphones*—and really, if you had to call a phone smart, what did that say about people?—and she wondered what on earth a witch was doing with a smartphone. How did most of them even come by a smartphone? When witches—especially the ones around this table, who had more power in their pinky fingers than they knew what to do with—became dependent on an object like that, it was alarming.

It represented all that was wrong with their world today. This generation of witches—and this included those her age or older—were too enmeshed in the mortal world. It was one thing to share space with mortals, but it was quite another to become so fixated upon their way of life that it got in the way of the important business going on here. Business that had to do with saving their heritage.

Especially with such important matters on the docket. Most urgent was the pending election to fill the seat left by Abigail Moonstone's shocking death a few weeks ago. Much talk about Abigail's successor had ensued, but no one at this table, including Fiona, was in a position to alert that unknowing successor. And if that didn't happen before the election, they were in big trouble, because a definite undesirable was in the lead, according to the latest Broom Poll.

But something else weighed almost more heavily on Fiona's mind. According to the Moonstone tradition and heritage, Abigail had no time limit on her life, unlike some witches. Not a lot of people knew that, but Fiona did. And the fact that she'd died now, leaving an empty chair, was disturbing.

They had one week.

She felt the strong urge to do something childish but terribly funny to get her colleagues' attention. As she pondered what that would be, with one eye on the clock to track the minute hand to when they could start despite the fact that two members of the council hadn't bothered to show up yet, she felt a strange sensation flooding her body. Her arms, legs, even her fingers started to become numb, and she felt a rush of something rising through her, all the way up to her head, sending her off-kilter.

Fiona hadn't felt like that since she was a toddler, trying out her powers for the very first time without realizing what she was actually doing, or how powerful she would one day become—head of the Ravenstar Witches—a family who had fought for, and won, power and privilege for witches everywhere. The Moonstones were the only other family in the stratosphere even remotely close to being as powerful, although in Fiona's mind they weren't even close. It didn't stop her from staying one step ahead, though. She was a confident witch, but not a stupid, egotistical one. She hadn't gotten to where she was by being cocky.

"Are we starting, Fiona?" An impatient voice sounded to her left. She vaguely registered Hattie Blandon, who thought she was infinitely more important than she actually was.

Fiona ignored the voice and tried to focus on the feeling in her body and where it was coming from. She closed her eyes, and the vision hit her like a ton of bricks. A beautiful red-headed woman, silently calling for help. Fiona could feel the despair, fear, and loneliness in her plea as she'd never felt anything before. And it shook her to the core.

Fiona wasn't prone to emotional outbursts. At least not the touchy-feely kind. When she got angry, it was another story. Until then, she ruled logically and consistently, doing what she felt was best for the greater good. She tried to stay out of emotional quagmires and people's personal dramas.

She hardly even engaged in her own any longer.

But today, she felt something she hadn't felt in nearly thirty years. She squeezed her eyes closed even more tightly and forced herself to concentrate harder.

The redhead came more into focus, and Fiona could see her face clearly. It was a face she hadn't seen in that same nearly thirty years, but she'd know it anywhere: Violet. Her daughter. And she was in trouble.

A collage of images passed through her brain, like a slideshow on fast-forward, moving so quickly she could barely grasp them. Cobblestones. A lifeless body. Something pink. A hand ripping a shirt off and a necklace with a crescent moon falling to the ground. An orange cat. An ugly, gray-toned room. Violet leaning against a tree, full of despair.

Violet needed help. And Fiona had somehow gotten the message. The spell Abigail had cast all those years ago was finally, miraculously broken, and she could see her daughter again.

Fiona rose abruptly, knocking over a glass of water on the table when she jostled it. With one crook of her index finger, she caught the cup. The water flowed backward, into its place, and the cup once again stood straight. "This meeting will need to be postponed," she announced, leaving no room for argument. "Please reschedule it," she said to Frances Hazelton, the secretary, then turned without waiting for any kind of response and waved her hand, disappearing into a cloud of purple smoke—her favorite way to travel.

She appeared in the grand parlor of her home in a shower of her trademark glitter and called for Zoe. Her younger daughter floated to the top of the wide, circular staircase, earbuds in her ears, one foot still tapping to a beat only she could hear. "What's up?"

Fiona grimaced. Another one with the technology. She'd never wanted to let Zoe have a taste of the mortal world, but in the end she couldn't control everything.

"We're going on a trip," Fiona announced, sweeping up the stairs. "Get some things."

Zoe perked up, pulling out her earbuds and tucking her long black hair behind her ears. She bent down to tie her red Converse sneakers. She loved trips. She loved adventure, period. It had been a challenge for Fiona to have a daughter even more headstrong than she was, who wasn't afraid to use her powers on a whim. Teaching Zoe best practices with her powers had helped her ground her own. "Where to?"

"I'm not exactly sure what it's called," Fiona admitted. "It looks like one of those rancid little towns in the mortal world where everyone is in each other's business and you can't even make them disappear without getting into hot water. But it doesn't matter where it is." She took a deep breath. "We're going to get your big sister."

CHAPTER 15

Pete Santorini and his date, a woman named Tiffany who'd been coming into The Friendly Bean for the past couple of weeks and unabashedly flirting with him, happened to be walking by the North Harbor police station when two women appeared in a puff of purple smoke.

It hadn't been a particularly fun night for Pete, until now. He'd only gone out with Tiffany because she'd asked. Really, he was interested in Sydney Santangelo, but just hadn't found the nerve to ask her out yet. Which wasn't like him. Pete usually had no problem asking for what he wanted. But this girl was . . . special. And he got the feeling she wouldn't say yes to just anyone. So he kept putting it off, and instead he'd gone to the new martini and piano bar that had recently opened on Water Street, a stone's throw from Violet's store. Tiffany had indulged in one martini—or maybe two—too many. Pete had lost count. But when she'd become louder and more giggly, planting sloppy kisses on his cheek with bright-red lips, he knew it was time to go.

And since he hadn't had too many martinis, he knew exactly what he was looking at when the purple smoke cleared, leaving a shower of glitter on the sidewalk.

Fiona Ravenstar. Witch of all witches. Which meant things were happening.

Tiffany, foggy from her martinis and feeling good, had to stop short so as not to bump into the two women who'd appeared in front of them, seemingly from out of nowhere. The older one had wine-colored hair tipped with blond and cut in an edgy, misshapen bob around her chin. She wore a floor-length green velvet dress with high-heeled boots. The other, younger woman had long black hair and wore something resembling a long tutu with a lacy tank top, despite the cold weather, and fire-engine-red Converse sneakers. She shivered, obviously regretting her poor choice of clothing.

Tiffany blinked and took a step back, looking over her shoulder uneasily at Pete. Probably trying to see if he could see them too.

But he wasn't admitting to anything. "What's up?" he asked.

Clearly unnerved, she glanced from him to the two women, who were arguing—something about *Should we just pull her out of there*—and who didn't even acknowledge that anyone else was around.

"What the heck is that," she said, way too loudly in the way drunk people did without realizing it. "Do these people not know Halloween was months ago?"

He frowned. "What's what?" he asked and kept walking, pulling her along with him as if no one else was on the sidewalk. As he passed the women, the older one glanced at him. He gave her an imperceptible nod as he passed, which she returned.

Tiffany didn't notice. She still looked alarmed, but bent

her head and kept walking, stepping in that too-careful way one did when one was tipsy. "Nothing. Way too much to drink, I guess," she muttered. "Those stupid drinks were strong." Then she slowed, pulling her hand away. "Did you put something in my drink?"

Pete sighed. This was the problem with mortals. They couldn't see what was right in front of them, and if they saw it, they convinced themselves it wasn't really there. Of course, he was perpetuating that tonight, but it would be easier than trying to explain how two witches had suddenly appeared on the sidewalk.

"No," he said. "Come on, I'm taking you home."

She didn't look convinced, but she allowed him to lead her to her building, where he made sure she could get inside safely, then gave her a kiss on the cheek and told her to get some sleep.

Then he walked away, glancing behind him only once to see her brushing glitter off her coat, still looking totally bewildered at what may or may not have transpired.

On his way home, Pete detoured down a small alleyway that led to the back door of Hubert's, the local candy shop. It was way after hours, but there was always a group of them there on Monday nights. Most nights, actually. The fairy lights in the window glowed warm and comforting against the dark, cold night, a signal that they were his kind. He rapped three times on the door to be polite, then, with a quick glance around to make sure no one was watching, snapped the leather bracelet around his wrist, vanishing from the sidewalk.

He reappeared in the basement room where Krista Carmichael, the candy shop owner, sat with a few others, including Josie Cook. They all looked up expectantly when he came in.

Pete looked solemnly around the table at each of them.

Their faces were in turn worried, anxious, excited, and anticipatory. It was a tense time in their community right now, with the pending council election only one week away. Not to mention all the mortal-world drama that they couldn't escape. Well, had chosen not to escape, to be exact. Some witches opted to stay in their own realm, while others ventured out into the mortal world to get a taste. Many of them stayed, an attempt to live in two worlds that didn't always work out as planned.

"Well?" Jonas Friedman, a local fisherman, finally asked.

Pete sat down and put his feet up on the coffee table. "Something's going on. Fiona's here."

"She's here?" Krista asked anxiously. "With Violet?"

"Not yet. I saw her out on the street. She must not have found her yet."

"Yes! She's here!" Krista shot to her feet, fist pumping the air. In doing so, she startled the sleek black cat with the bright-yellow eyes who had been curled under her chair. He stalked over to sit near Pete instead. "That's the important part. Now she'll make it happen. Don't underestimate Fiona."

"I don't know," Pete warned. "Violet wasn't expecting this. I'm sure she'll be reeling. I wonder how she got past Abigail's spell?"

No one knew.

He looked at Josie. "You'll help her, right? You'll explain how much this matters?"

Josie picked through a bowl of jelly beans on the table, methodically plucking out the pink ones. "I'll do everything I can to help Violet, of course. But she has to come to me. I can't just insert myself in this without her understanding who I am. Who *she* is. It will just push her away. And you're right, Pete." She nodded. "Violet will be reeling. She's got a lot of anger toward her mother. She thinks Fiona abandoned her. Fiona will have to tread carefully."

"Doesn't matter," Ginny Reinhardt broke in, shaking her head vehemently. "Violet will totally be open to her. Especially once she knows what's at stake." Ginny was one of the younger members of the group that hung out here, and she still had an optimistic view of their world. Too optimistic, in Pete's eyes, given the state of everything right now.

"Don't be so sure," Jonas warned. "We have to have a contingency plan in place. There's too much at risk to let everything rest on a girl who hasn't even been involved in our community. Who doesn't know her rightful place in it."

"Violet is a smart girl," Frank Mercury, one of the town councilmen, broke in. "It's Fiona I'm worried about. She's got a tendency to come on too strong. She could scare the girl away." With a sigh, he stood. Frank was a big man, and the ceilings were kind of low in here. Pete always expected him to hit his head, but he never did. He was a witch, after all. "I have to go. Have you all heard the news?"

Most of them nodded, murmuring their disbelief. Krista spoke up. "Sure did. Didn't hear the details, though."

"What news?" Jonas asked, looking from Krista to Frank. "What? I had to go see my daughter at school." Jonas's daughter, Ariella, was in training to become a teacher at the top witches' school in his *other* world. Which meant he'd been away from North Harbor and the rest of the mortal universe all day.

"Carla Fernandez. Dead."

Jonas's mouth dropped open. "How?"

"Murdered." Frank shook his head. "I actually have to

go make a statement with the rest of the council. Keep me posted." He clicked his ever-present Montblanc pen and vanished from the room.

Krista sighed. "Meeting adjourned, everyone. We should get some rest. I think things are going to get crazy around here."

CHAPTER 16

In front of the police department, Fiona and Zoe still argued, although Fiona had lost interest after recognizing Pete. She'd seen him before at council meetings when something critical was on the docket and public comments were welcomed. She had been surprised to see him here, of all places, but perhaps she should have known.

Fiona had gotten a feeling as soon as she'd landed on the sidewalk that this was a magickal town, and meeting a kindred literally that same moment was all the proof she needed. It gave her a small sense of satisfaction that no matter how hard Abigail and George had tried to keep Violet from her true heritage, she was drawn to it without knowing why or even how she fit in.

Their argument was silly anyway, with Zoe being dramatic as usual, and Fiona was tiring of it. Fiona often loved that her daughter's personality so closely resembled her own, but at times like this she understood the challenges the people closest to her must have experienced during her younger years.

"You didn't tell me it was going to be freezing," Zoe said accusingly, wrapping her arms around herself.

"Well, how was I supposed to know? I'm not monitoring the weather around the world." Fiona closed her eyes and waved her hands down her body. A black velvet cloak appeared in their wake.

"I need one too!" Zoe said indignantly.

Fiona sighed. "Really? Do I have to do everything for you? Haven't you been practicing more practical things than how to give yourself flatter abs?" Nevertheless, she focused the same hand motion on her daughter. A long red wool coat matching her sneakers appeared.

Zoe grinned. "Sweet. Thanks, Mom." She paused to admire the coat.

"Let's go," Fiona said, motioning to the front entrance. "We came here for a reason and we're wasting time." She marched up the steps to the police station and shoved open the door, surveying her surroundings. What a dreadful sort of building this was. Sparse and gray, even in the lobby that wasn't supposed to be for criminals.

Her first instinct was to simply lift her daughter out of that awful room she'd seen in her vision and send her back home—to Fiona's home, where she'd belonged all this time—but she had learned patience over the past twenty-seven years. She was still no expert at it, by any means, but at least she could function without flying off the handle at everything these days. And she had an inkling that it would be worse for Violet if she reacted that way.

Her daughter probably didn't remember her, after all. She had only been five years old when they were separated. It would be best to keep their reunion as drama-free as possible.

Which was an oxymoron, Fiona realized, but still.

She walked up to the bulletproof glass, behind which two police officers stared openly at them. One was clearly in charge of the desk—he was sitting behind it, fingers poised over a computer keyboard. The other stood behind him, mouth slightly agape. Fiona defiantly tossed her hair, sprinkling glitter all over the counter, and leaned in near the holes meant for speaking. "I need to see my daughter," she announced.

The standing cop didn't bother to hide the tiny smile that played across his lips. "Who's your daughter, ma'am?"

"Violet . . ." She racked her brain for the variation of the name she'd heard George had settled on for his mortal existence ". . . Mooney."

The cop's smile faltered a bit as he tried—unsuccessfully—to hide his disbelief. "Violet?"

"You know her?"

He nodded.

"Well, then why is she still in this rotten building?" Fiona demanded.

"I . . . I didn't realize she was," the cop said. "Let me see if I can find out what's going on." He leaned down and said something to the dispatcher that Fiona couldn't hear, then turned and walked into the bowels of the building.

They both watched him go. Zoe sighed. "Why don't you just let me put a spell on these fools that will make them forget the whole thing? Wouldn't that be the easiest way to fix this?"

Fiona considered this. It would, of course. But Zoe's skills were still young and a bit clunky at times, and she couldn't be trusted with something like that. Fiona could do it herself, but easy wasn't always best. And easy sometimes—fine, often—brought its own mess along with it. Especially when witches imposed their idea of easy on the mortal world. The two often didn't jibe, and left an even bigger problem than the original in its wake.

It had taken her many years to learn that lesson, and it was one she still railed against when actually confronted with a mortal situation. Which in fairness, she hadn't been in a long time. After she and George had split, Fiona had retreated back to the world she knew, the world in which she was most comfortable. A world where witches stayed with their own kind and the rules of society were clearly spelled out for all parties to understand. Not that they were always followed, of course, but at least there wasn't the gray sludge area that you had to deal with when combining a witch and a mortal kind of life.

"Enough of this," Fiona snapped at the other officer. "Go find my daughter now!" She flicked her fingers at the seated cop, who sat in stunned silence as his chair careened backward out of the office and down the hall, narrowly missing running over a cop walking into the office. It was as if a tornado-strength gust of wind had blown through the station, upsetting everything in its path.

CHAPTER 17

Someone banged on the interview-room door. Haliburton's head shot up from reviewing my statement. He looked relieved to be interrupted. Denning reached over and pulled the door open.

The cop who regularly frequented the Bean in the morning and Todd's place on his lunch break—Gabe, aka Sergeant Gabriel Merlino—stuck his head in, his eyes lingering on me for a moment before shifting to his colleagues. I felt my face get red and dropped my eyes back to the table. He'd probably heard that everyone thought I was a criminal—not just a criminal, a *murderer*—and now he'd always look at me differently.

"Hey. Are you done with Violet? She's got some . . . people here to pick her up."

My head snapped up. People? Who? Todd, hopefully. And maybe he'd brought Sydney. I knew he would come once he heard. I hadn't had a chance to text him the details, but news traveled fast in our little five-square-mile town. And he had to be looking for me.

"Yeah, we're done." Haliburton looked at me. "You can go. Thanks for coming in."

Denning stepped aside to let me pass.

"Come on, I'll walk you out," Gabe said, glancing at his colleagues.

I followed him down the hall. He didn't speak until we got to the door leading into the lobby—into freedom. I hoped it lasted.

"I heard about Carla," he said in a low voice once we were out of earshot. "Is that why you're here?"

To my dismay, tears filled my eyes as I nodded. "They actually think I had something to do with it."

Gabe frowned and appeared to be thinking that over. "Don't worry. We'll get to the bottom of it." He squeezed my arm, a friendly touch that was supposed to be comforting.

"Thanks," I said, swiping at the tears. I wondered if he was humoring me, or if he really believed I didn't do it. "Is Todd here?"

He cocked his head at me. "No."

"I thought you said I had people to pick me up?" I said.

"I did." He pulled the door open, shooting me a quick grin. "I've never heard you mention your mom before. She looks like quite a character." He motioned for me to go ahead of him.

I stopped and stared at him, my throat going dry. "My . . . What are you talking about?"

My mother had vanished from my life when I was too young to even remember much about her, and my father and grandmother never wanted to discuss her. All I knew was that she'd left us when I was five, and I'd never seen or heard from her again. When I'd been really young, I'd made up fantasies about why she'd left. She'd been kidnapped. My life had been threatened and to save me, she had to stay away from me. Someone had cast a spell on her. As I got older, I wondered if she was dead. As bad as that would be, it would almost have been better than knowing she just hadn't wanted me.

After all this time, I'd finally come to some sort of peace with it. My family had been my dad and my grandma. Now they were gone, and I didn't have a family. Simple as that. Gabe had to have his information wrong. Or someone was playing a joke.

All these thoughts were ping-ponging around in my head, making it hard to hear anything else.

Gabe was watching me, looking concerned. "Your mother. That's what she said, anyway." He pointed through the little window into the lobby, where I could see two women waiting. Both were clearly impatient, although it was manifesting in different ways. One was older, sleek and stylish and looking like she'd just stepped off the set of a movie. It wasn't just her outfit, velvet on velvet, high-heeled boots, fancy hair. It was the way she carried herself, like she was used to attention and thrived on it. She was also a ball of tightly strung energy—I could see it even from where I stood across the room. She looked like she'd explode if anyone poked her.

The other, younger woman leaned against a wall, playing with a strand of long, so-black-it-was-nearly-purple hair, looking around as if she'd rather be anywhere but there. One foot clad in a red Converse shoe jiggled impatiently while she waited.

Uncertain, I looked at Gabe. "That's—they're here for me?"

"Yes." He frowned. "What's wrong?"

"I don't know them," I said under my breath.

"What do you mean, you don't know them?" he asked slowly. "Is that not your mother?"

I shrugged helplessly. "I don't know. I haven't seen

my mother since I was five. I've never seen—that other woman."

He sucked in a breath. "You're kidding."

I gazed at them. "I wish I was," I murmured. I didn't recognize her at all. Not a smidge. If it wasn't for that weird feeling I was getting, I would think someone was either playing a trick on me, or I was looking at the wrong person in the waiting area. Not that there was anyone else there. I'd imagined this day for a very long time, and in all of those fantasies, I guess I'd never worked out how I would recognize her or know her when or if I did finally meet her. Did she look like me? I couldn't really tell.

I ignored the little voice in my head that was trying to whisper something to me and kept my focus on these two strange-looking people in front of me.

Gabe's face was the picture of concern. I wondered how many other cops were watching this very odd reunion attempt. I refocused on my visitors, my mind racing as I tried to figure out what to do here. How had they found me? And most of all, why were they here?

"Do you want me to get rid of them?" he asked.

I shook my head, not wanting to draw more attention to myself.

Gabe nodded and swung the inner door open, letting me step through. "Okay. Call if you need me. And I'll find out what's going on with the case. Don't worry, Vi. We'll figure it out."

But I'd stopped listening. I knew he was waiting for me to leave, but I was frozen in place. The women had swiveled their heads in unison toward the door when Gabe opened it, and they were both openly staring at me. I locked eyes with the older woman, and felt in spades that weird feeling I'd felt this morning when I'd opened the door to my apartment and knew this day was unlike any other.

That same staticky sound that had pursued me all day crackled in the air around me. I resisted the urge to cover my ears. I had no idea how long our staring contest lasted, but I broke the gaze first and made a beeline for the door. Whatever was about to happen, I didn't want to do it in front of the cops.

"Violet!"

I ignored her and shoved the door open. I didn't look back, but I could sense them behind me, though it was odd that they made no sound.

Once I hit the sidewalk, I took a deep breath, gulping in air like I'd been locked up for years. My pause was enough for them to turn up on either side of me, closing in.

I turned to my alleged mother. "Who *are* you?" I asked. "And why are you here? More importantly, how did you find me *here*?" I waved a hand at the building behind me, nearly whacking a woman trying to skirt around the three of us to move down the sidewalk.

The younger one's eyes got really wide. "Jeez. She doesn't even recognize you," she said to the older one. Then she turned to me and held out a hand covered with rings—not just on every finger, but multiple rings on each finger, ranging from giant stones to plain silver bands. I caught a glimpse of a gorgeous amethyst and wanted to ask her where she'd gotten it, but it wasn't really the time or place. "I'm Zoe. Your—"

"Violet," the other woman interrupted, "I know it's been . . . a long time, but you have to know me. In fact, I know you do." She stepped forward and grasped my arms with long fingers, also covered in rings. Her nails had glitter on the tips, and I could see it sparkling in her hair. When she touched me, I felt dizzy, like I'd come into contact with some illicit substance that affected my nervous system. "I'm Fiona. Your mother."

Hearing the words come out of her mouth was surreal.

I yanked my arms free and crossed them over my chest, shaking my head. If this crazy woman covered in glitter was my mother, maybe it was a good thing she'd ditched me as a kid. My dad had been super stable and loving, as had Grandma Abby. She'd tried to be both mother and grandmother to me, and she'd done a really good job. And I hadn't had to deal with a lot of the issues my girl-friends in high school had, fighting with their mothers about every little thing, getting grounded left and right, arguments about boys. Maybe I hadn't really missed having a mother that much.

"You're out of your mind," I said coolly. "I haven't had a mother since I was five. I highly doubt she's about to turn up now, at a police station, here in this tiny little town." I thought of Mazzy suddenly, and the sense I'd gotten that she'd been there for another reason. Some sort of reconnaissance. "Who sent you? And why? Does this have something to do with Mazzy?"

Something passed over Fiona's face, almost impercep-tible but I caught it. *Aha,* I thought triumphantly. I was on to something.

Zoe watched us, eyes pinging back and forth between us.

"I understand how you must feel—" Fiona began, but I cut her off.

"That's kind of a ridiculous thing to say, considering you don't know me at all," I said. "So don't even try to convince me you *know how I feel.* And even if you are . . . who you say you are, how did you even find me? And why now?"

I was acutely aware of the fact that the middle of the street was not the best place for this conversation. It wasn't as busy as it could have been, but it wasn't deserted, ei-ther—people walking their dogs for one final evening potty, others leaving restaurants or the movie theater. I wanted desperately to go hide in my apartment before anyone noticed me. It was a double whammy of embarrassment—being released from police custody and having these two here arguing with me on the street.

How had my day gone so far down the toilet?

"We should get off this street corner," Zoe said, as if reading my mind. "I mean, if you don't want to draw attention to us," she added dryly.

But Fiona ignored her. "I haven't been able to contact you before now," she said. "I'll explain the whole thing later. But it's because of the necklace. The one you took off today."

Instinctively my hand went for my throat, where my silver moon with the blue topaz had rested for all these years. I felt naked and exposed without it. But how could she have known about this necklace, anyway? My grandmother had given it to me long after my mother had left.

"Abigail gave it to you," Fiona said, those dark, almost black eyes intensely focused on mine. "She gave it to you to keep me away."

CHAPTER 18

My entire world tilted a little bit. This woman, who-ever she really was, knew about my grandmother. That she'd given me this necklace, the special necklace she said had been in the family forever, stressing how very, very important it was to us, and that once I put it on, I needed to treasure it and never remove it.

I needed to know how she knew that. And what she meant about it keeping her away.

I motioned for Fiona and Zoe to follow me, and went around the corner into a little alleyway next to the police station, hoping for some privacy but not wanting to bring them to my apartment. Too late, I heard voices and was dismayed to see two people, a man and a woman in the shadows, engaged in an intense conversation. They weren't near the streetlight but still . . . I took a closer look.

The curly hair and cowboy boots were a dead give-away—it was Syd. The guy looked vaguely familiar, but he was more shadowed than she was. I caught a glimpse of a scruffy goatee. I thought about calling her over to bail me out, but that would prompt more questions than I was ready to answer. I hesitated, not entirely sure what to do next.

But after a quick glance over her shoulder, Syd grabbed the guy's arm and dragged him out the other side of the alley, vanishing around the corner. I wasn't even sure she'd realized it was me, but either way, she didn't seem to want to be seen.

I didn't have time to ponder this. Fiona still waited for me to react to the bomb she'd just dropped. I could feel her shifting from foot to foot in those ridiculous heels, practically breathing down my neck.

I took a deep breath and turned to look at her. "This all sounds like a great premise for a movie," I said, mustering up all the sarcasm I had the energy for. "What does that even mean, she gave me the necklace to keep you away? What, does it have some sort of magical powers?" I snorted to show how stupid I thought that sounded, but she didn't react, just kept looking at me with that slightly concerned face and those unreadable eyes. I didn't care— she could stare at me all she wanted. Besides, a mother doesn't let a piece of jewelry keep her away from her kid. *If* she loved her kid enough.

"You say that," Fiona said in an amused tone, "like it's preposterous."

I rolled my eyes. "If that's all you've got, I'm going home. I'm tired and it's freezing out here and I've had a really crappy day." I could feel tears in the back of my throat as I said the words. It *had* been a crappy day, topped off with an evening right out of a bad movie, and I needed to go home and decompress.

A lingering feeling of guilt nagged at me when I realized how snotty I probably sounded. What if she was my mother? I wasn't exactly being welcoming. But then I shoved it aside. Seriously? She's gone for all these years, then comes back out of the blue—literally—and blames my recently deceased grandmother for a twenty-seven-year absence?

"Thanks for coming," I said, giving them a curt nod, then I turned and walked away.

"We'll come with you," Fiona said from behind me. Her voice was so close to my ear I nearly jumped.

"That's not necessary," I said through gritted teeth, but before we could argue further, a bunch of kids turned into the alley, laughing and talking loudly. The smell of smoke wafted behind them.

From her spot leaning against the wall as if this whole thing bored her, Zoe let out a long sigh. "Seriously," she said. "I'm about to turn all these people into some fun animals if we don't get out of here. Where do you live, Violet?"

I turned and arched my eyebrows at her. "Why?"

"Because you just said you wanted to go home," Zoe said in a tone that suggested I needed to catch up.

"Yeah. Alone," I said.

A look passed between Zoe and Fiona, then Zoe grabbed my hand.

Before I could snatch it away, I felt that same weird sensation I'd felt earlier today when I'd imagined myself back at my grandma's house—that bottom-dropping-out-of-my-stomach thing. I closed my eyes to ward off the sick feeling I was sure was coming.

When I opened them again, I was in my living room.

Now I did feel light-headed, like I was about to faint. Unless I already had. What other explanation was there for me to keep forgetting how I'd ended up in certain places today—places I didn't remember physically going to? This whole thing had to be one long, strange dream. I desperately wished I could wake up.

Monty jumped off the windowsill and came over to sit in front of me, meowing loudly. I reached down tentatively to touch him. Yes, he was real. Yes, it seemed I was really home. I'd be relieved, but . . . I cast a cautious glance over my shoulder. Zoe and Fiona were standing behind me in a pool of glitter, looking around my loft apartment like they were in a museum of foreign objects—the sheer purple curtains I'd hung over my giant living room windows, the lights I'd strung up in various places around the room. My salt lamps. The crystals filling almost every free space. The screen that separated my bedroom from the living area that depicted a full moon over the ocean.

Seriously—how had we gotten here?

Zoe stared at Monty. "I always wanted a familiar like this." She shot Fiona an accusing look and reached out a hand to touch his fur. I backed away so he was out of her reach. A look that may have been hurt passed over Zoe's face, and her hand dropped.

Fiona managed to give Zoe a look without taking her eyes off me. "Too common," she said. "I always wanted you to stand out."

I had no idea what they were talking about, but now she was insulting Monty too. "Hey," I started to say, but Fiona cut me off.

"We need to talk," she said.

"I'm not really in the mood to talk," I said wearily. "Besides, you've been gone for twenty-seven years. Why do you want to talk today, of all days?"

"I know it's hard for you to understand," she said, holding up a hand to halt my protests. "I hope you'll be able to open your mind enough to hear the story. But the bottom line is, I was able to connect with you today. I knew you were in trouble. And I wanted to help."

I didn't know how to respond to that. Monty twisted in my grasp, trying to get free. I let him go, and he jumped out of my arms and headed under the bed.

I thought about joining him.

"How exactly did you know I was in trouble? You have a direct line to the police department?" I dropped onto my sofa and closed my eyes.

"Well, Mom, she's definitely your daughter. She's very dramatic," Zoe said.

I opened my eyes and glared at her.

"What's there to eat around here?" Zoe asked, ignoring my look.

"Eat?" I repeated. "This is one of the worst days of my life and you want to eat?"

"I'm hungry! Mother pulled me out of the house with no warning," Zoe said.

"There's plenty of food around. Just go outside. You'll need my key." I reached for my purse.

Zoe gave me a long look, gave her hair a tug . . . and disappeared. The air where she'd stood crackled as it settled.

Speechless, I looked at Fiona.

She gave me a small smile. "She doesn't need a key."

That dizzy feeling was back. Probably I hadn't drunk enough water today. I definitely hadn't eaten enough. There was no way people were disappearing in front of my eyes and I was teleporting around town.

"Listen. I don't know what's happening, or whose idea for a joke this is, but I wish you'd leave me alone." I felt hysterical tears coming and tried to hold them back, but I couldn't. It had been such a long, crappy day, and I was exhausted, and Carla was dead, and where was Todd, anyway? He was supposed to be the guy who was always here for me, and the day I needed him most he was nowhere to be found. Good thing I hadn't been waiting around for our date.

But Fiona didn't look like she was about to offer any kind of comfort. Her eyes had gone dark, and her lips were pressed so tightly together I worried they might be the next things to disappear. She took two steps toward me so she towered over where I was sitting.

"Look. I know this is a shock, and believe me, I will explain everything. But you need to stop your little pity party, get your act together, and listen to me," she said urgently. "You are Violet Raven Moonstone, and you are three-quarters witch. You belong to the Moonstone and Ravenstar families, which are the two most powerful, respected, and admired families in the witch realm. You have the potential to be a very powerful witch in your own right. And right now, your community—your *extended family*—needs you to step up and own your power and own your lineage." She pointed a long glitter-tipped fingernail at me. "There's a lot at stake. And you have a responsibility."

I stared at her, my mouth literally hanging open, trying to take all that in.

"Besides all that, we need to get busy figuring out who's trying to frame you for killing someone," Fiona went on. She flashed me a small, sharp smile. "So let's get to it, shall we?"

CHAPTER 19

My head spun. I felt dizzy and a little sick as I tried to process all the problems in her statement at once. Someone trying to frame me. My name—Violet Raven Moonstone? I had no middle name on record. And my last name was Mooney. My dad had spent hours when I was a child telling me about the long line of Mooneys, a distinguished group of academics who had devoted their lives to teaching such lofty subjects as literature, astronomy, and political science. It was one of the best things about being a Mooney, he'd said—and it was something I would carry on.

When I was young, I'd balked at this idea, because I'd never thought of myself as a teacher, but I didn't want to disappoint my dad. If I did, he might disappear like my mother had. Because why else would she have gone away unless I'd disappointed her? But when I eventually worked up the courage to voice that to him, he merely chuckled in that soothing, quiet way he had, smoothed down his ever-present argyle sweater, and said, "Don't fret, V. The best teachers usually aren't in classrooms anyway."

I hadn't known what he meant at age seven, or even twelve, but later after I opened my shop and really began to see how I could help people and teach them to take charge of their own well-being, I remembered his words and felt like I finally understood them. Life had started to make sense.

And here I was, upended once again. Not only upended, but in trouble. Possibly on my way to jail unless someone figured out who'd really killed Carla Fernandez.

For a few long moments, nothing in the apartment moved. Our eyes were locked on each other, each waiting to see what the other would do next. Until the air crackled again, and I heard a thud and a muttered curse from behind the screen. Zoe appeared a minute later, looking annoyed.

"That bed isn't in the best position," she announced. "Don't worry, I don't think anything broke," she added for my benefit.

"You have to work on that overshooting," Fiona said to Zoe. "You almost did it earlier with the three of us. I had to course-correct you or we would've ended up on the wrong floor."

Zoe sniffed. "You don't need to help. I'll get it."

"Yes, yes, of course. You'll get it." Fiona waved a hand at her. "Miss Independent. Sit. Violet and I were just getting to the good stuff."

Pouting, Zoe dropped onto the sofa and began rifling through her food bag.

I finally found my voice. "The good stuff?" It came out as more of a squeak, and I cleared my throat to start over. "You just . . . waltz in here and expect me to believe all that nonsense about witches and lineages and whatever else you just said?" I rose, forcing Fiona to take a step back so I could stand. "Plus, I still can't figure out how you know anything about what happened today."

"Of course I expect you to believe me. It's all true." This time, Fiona's voice softened and she reached for my hand. "Violet. I'm your mother. The last time I saw you, you were five"—her voice broke a little there, which surprised me almost as much as her crazy insistences that I was a witch—"and you were wearing your Wonder Woman outfit. Your father and I had agreed to divorce, and we were having a terrible time coming to any sort of resolution over what to do with you. I don't mean literally," she hastened to add, but I hadn't even noticed her choice of words. "That was the day that, well"—she cleared her throat—"we don't need to discuss that now."

I was stuck on the memory of myself in my favorite Wonder Woman outfit. Maybe it wasn't a conscious memory, but Grandma Abby had so many pictures of me in that outfit, it was hard to deny it. I especially loved the fake gold cuff bracelets, big enough on my tiny child arms that they almost reached my elbows. How would she know that if she wasn't who she said she was? *That was the day that . . .* what?

"I would've swooped you away with the snap of my finger, but Abigail . . . had powers that rivaled mine. And George didn't want you to follow in my footsteps." Fiona hesitated. "How is your father?"

"He's dead," I said. "He died five years ago. Cancer."

My mother's jaw dropped. I could tell she wasn't expecting that. My eyes narrowed. "If you're so magical, why didn't you know that?"

"I'm a witch, I'm not omniscient," she snapped. "Your father renounced all his powers a long time ago. Let me guess. He didn't even try to use any to save himself. I'm surprised Abigail didn't do it for him. He always was a momma's boy."

"He didn't . . . what? What do you mean, 'his powers'?" My head felt like it was going to explode.

"Oh. Violet." She looked at me with pity. "I just told you you were three-quarters witch. Which means your father was half-witch. Until he decided he didn't want to be, and that you weren't going to be either. Abigail put the same kind of spell on him as she did you. She was thorough, I'll give her that."

I was having a hard time wrapping my mind around all this talk of powers and spells and magic and especially my father—my college professor, tweed-jacket-wearing father—as a witch, even half of one. I started to giggle. I was probably the only one who heard the note of hysteria in it. "A witch. That's really what you're calling yourself. I can't believe you expect me to sit here and listen to this with a serious face."

Her head snapped up, eyes blazing. "What I'm *calling* myself? It's what I am. It's what *you* are. And if your other family hadn't been so selfish and vindictive, you wouldn't have wasted all these years thinking otherwise." She leaned forward and grasped my shoulders. "Violet. You're a smart, powerful woman. You have to know that, somewhere in your heart."

When her hands grasped my shoulders, I felt like she'd plugged me into an electrical socket. Like there was some kind of current passing between us.

CHAPTER 20

I gasped and took a step back, trying to put distance between us. I didn't know what scared me more—thinking that she was there because someone wanted to mess with me, or thinking she was there because what she was saying was true. But . . . how could it be? If I was a witch, I'd like to think I would've figured it out by now. Then again, I guess I'd always been a bit of an underachiever, content with where I was.

I desperately wished for my father to show up in this room right now and help me. If he'd been a witch like Fiona said, why couldn't he? And why had he died in the first place? Same with Grandma Abby. And what was all this talk about powerful families and me having a responsibility?

I had so many questions my head spun. I shook my head to clear it. "I know I'm smart," I told Fiona. "And because I'm smart, I know this is all a bunch of nonsense. I don't know who put you up to it, or what you have to gain, but it's not fair for you to come in here and expect me to just take everything you say at face value."

"Fair?" Fiona nearly shrieked the word. "You want to talk about fair? What your grandmother did wasn't fair. To you or to me. Or to our community. And that's why we're all in this situation right now. You, and me, and our whole world." She waved her hand, and the air snapped again, leaving glitter raining down on my floor. "A world that you don't even know about, but one that's so important to our heritage. So don't talk to me about fair. Abigail chose wrongly. Selfishly." Her chest was heaving, and I swore I could see silver fire shooting out of her fingertips.

"That's enough." I pointed at her with a shaking finger. "Don't say another word about my grandmother. She was around for me all those years when *you* weren't."

Fiona stepped back like I'd struck her. I could see Zoe out of the corner of my eye, frozen in place, watching us like we were her favorite TV show and she didn't want to miss a word.

But I couldn't slow the words. They needed to come out, and I wasn't holding back. "I'm not sure why you're here now. You have another daughter. She's probably better suited to you anyway. So why *are* you here? Why did you come?"

Zoe sucked in a breath, pausing from unwrapping her sushi. "Hey. What's that supposed to mean?"

The tension lifted, just a smidge, as Fiona and I both turned to stare at her. Zoe started to laugh, apparently unconcerned with the mood in the room. "You think I'm better suited to her? You should've seen yourself just then," she said to me. "Talk about twinsies. Have you noticed you both use the exact same hand gestures when you're mad and trying to make a point? Only you"—she pointed at me—"don't shoot glitter everywhere. Yet."

I sent her a withering look. I didn't need this chick coming in here and making jokes about everything like some kind of bad supporting actress in a drama I didn't even know I was starring in. But she returned my stare with a wink.

I sank into my purple chair and reflexively dug my hand into the candy bowl on the side table. I needed a good Lindt truffle right now.

But before I could unwrap it, my mother pointed at me and . . . it vanished from my hand.

I stared at the place where it had been, blinking slowly. "What the . . . ?"

"You shouldn't eat chocolate," Fiona said. "You'll get fat."

Across the room, I heard Zoe snort. I felt my face get red. I might be a lot of things, but one thing I certainly was not was fat. Still, I glanced down at my waistline to see if any rolls were visible or something. Hardly. I'd barely eaten since Grandma Abby died.

But Fiona had moved on from my disappearing chocolate truffle. "You want to know the truth about your grandmother? Then listen up. Her name was Abigail Moonstone."

I rolled my eyes, a childish habit that I'd made a huge effort to kick. "This again? Her last name was Mooney. Like my dad's, and like mine."

Fiona waved a hand, dismissing my statement. "They changed their name so they could live here among the Lulus." She said the word like it was dirty.

I frowned. "What the heck is a *Lulu*?"

"That's her current slang for non-witches," Zoe filled in helpfully. "You know, because you guys and your Lululemons. She's kind of fascinated with that word. If you think that's bad, you should've heard some of the other less flattering ones," she added.

Was she for real? Lululemons? "I have some in my closet," I said to Zoe. "I guess I'm guilty as charged."

"I know, I saw them when I ended up on the floor in

there," Zoe said. "I actually like the pink ones. With the stripes?"

"Sale," I said immediately. "They are cute, right?"

"Girls," Fiona said through clenched teeth.

Zoe sat back on the sofa and popped a tuna roll into her mouth.

I refocused on Fiona and waved a bored hand, as if I couldn't be bothered with this story but had nowhere else to be. "Go on." But really, my heart was close to pounding right out of my chest. Part of me wanted to block my ears at whatever she was about to tell me. The other part was hungry for the knowledge. And the reason why my mother had left me twenty-seven years ago and thought she could just show up now with a grand story about witches and magical powers.

"The Moonstone family helped create the standard for modern witches," she said. "Along with my own family. Our ancestors were among the most powerful in bringing the practices of witches back into the light, after all the history of pain and torture and oppression. I'm sure you've heard the sayings: *We are the granddaughters of the witches you couldn't burn* is the most popular. And it's very true."

I had heard the sayings. I actually had a sticker with those very words on them in my shop. I didn't tell her that. Instead, I stayed quiet, my eyes fixed on her, waiting for more.

"We can get into the details later. What's important is, after years of turmoil and endless work and strategizing and waiting and planning, the people from our two families gained power in our government and put our world back on track. It's a world where women reign, and men understand the value of that. Most men," she amended. "And now with Abigail gone, there's a chance that the balance of power could shift and fall back into the wrong hands. Not just men, but people who don't have the same values. Who don't understand the benefits of sharing space with Lu—mortals." Those piercing eyes were fixed on me, unblinking. "Unless her only heir steps up."

Her only heir. She couldn't possibly mean me.

"You said something about my necklace," I said suddenly, my hand reaching for my bare neck. "What did you mean?" Without waiting for her to answer, I got up and raced to my dresser, where I'd deposited the broken chain earlier. It was still there. I picked it up, flooded with relief. I wondered if I put it back on if Fiona would vanish? I certainly didn't need this overpowering, insulting, glitter-laden woman in my life.

Then I hesitated.

Did I want her to vanish? The thought crept up on the edges of my consciousness without my even understanding where it had come from.

I let the gold chain drip through my fingers as I pondered this. I had no family now. My dad was gone. He'd never remarried, and I had no other siblings. My grandma was gone. I didn't really know much about her relatives, but none of them had surfaced after her death, so as far as I was concerned, there weren't any. I had my friends, I had Todd, but I had no family.

But what kind of a family were they, really? I mean, she'd just vanished on me. One day she was there, the next day she was gone. And it wasn't like she hadn't wanted children, if she'd gone out and had another one. So there had to be some reason she hadn't wanted *me*.

But something had brought her back.

Fiona watched me curiously as I came out of my room, the necklace dangling from my fingers. "Are you hoping I'll go away if you put it on?" she asked, and though her tone was amused, I caught a hint of something else in it.

I flushed, but didn't bother to answer. "I want to know what you meant. That the necklace kept you from me."

But Fiona didn't answer. Instead, she motioned to the necklace. Unwilling to let it out of my grasp, I held it in the palm of my hand, offering it to her for inspection. "It's beautiful," she said simply. "I'm sure you enjoyed wearing it."

I ran my thumb over the stones. "I did," I said softly. "It made me feel . . . safe." I looked at her defiantly. "I'm going to get it fixed."

Fiona nodded. "Of course you should. It doesn't matter, my love. The spell is broken. I'm here now." She spread her hands wide. "For better or for worse. So we'd better figure it out. And whatever you decide about me, you must realize that you need help here on the mortal plane."

CHAPTER 21

My buzzer sounded, jolting us out of the moment. I rose and hurried to the door, yanking it open to find Todd on the other side. Annoyance and relief warred for the reigning emotion, but I had enough battles to fight that I pushed the annoyance to the back burner. "Where have you been!" I exclaimed, throwing my arms around him.

He hugged me back, but I could feel him tense almost instantly. I pulled back and saw his gaze had moved over my head to lock on Fiona.

I waved my hand in front of his face. "Hello?"

He refocused on me, and I noticed that he looked exhausted. Whereas this morning—a lifetime ago—he'd seemed refreshed and energetic, now his whole body slumped. His eyes were red, and he needed a shave. When he spoke, his voice sounded kind of alien, like he was forcing it. Oddly enough, he didn't ask who my guests were.

"I just heard," he said, dropping his voice and moving his gaze away from Fiona to look at me. "About Carla.

And what they did to you. I was crazy busy at work all day. I'm sorry I didn't get to talk to you sooner. Are you okay?" He stepped back, holding me at arm's length, taking inventory.

I leaned in again to sniff. I could smell onions and french fries. And I was suddenly aware that I was famished. Aside from my coffee and Pete's blackberry muffin before . . . everything, the only other food I'd had was a few bites of my frozen Indian lunch. And it was catching up with me at that moment.

"I'm fine," I said, but I realized he was barely listening to me. He kept sneaking glances over my shoulder at the occupants of my living room, and I swore I saw fear on his face. I rubbed my eyes. It had been a long day, and everything was playing tricks on me, clearly. Still, my stomach was doing crazy flips, some kind of warning. "What's wrong with you?"

"Nothing. Tired." He trailed off as Fiona, who had been watching our exchange, swept over to him, holding out a regal hand.

"Good evening. I'm Fiona. Violet's mother," she added, for full effect.

His surprise didn't strike me as genuine. I watched curiously as he reached for Fiona's hand. He winced when she shook it, as if she'd hurt him somehow. "Violet's . . ." He looked at me, as if waiting for me to verify. I gave a little shrug.

"You'll have to pardon her. She's having a hard time believing I'm really here," Fiona said with a smile, looking him up and down. "And you are?"

Todd said nothing. I'd never known him to become speechless so easily.

"This is Todd. My boyfriend," I said, shooting him a look.

"Boyfriend," Fiona said. "How lovely. And your last name, Todd?"

"Langston," he said.

"Lang . . . ston." She turned that over on her tongue, a look I couldn't quite read in her eyes. "You missed a lot of the excitement tonight."

He cringed, shrinking back from the words. "It was a busy night at work. I didn't hear until just a while ago. Violet didn't mention you were coming for a visit." He gave me a sideways glance, a little chastising. Which immediately got my back up. *He* was giving *me* attitude? When he'd been nowhere to be found all day, especially during all of this? Never mind our abandoned date night, which he hadn't even acknowledged.

"Oh, we surprised her," Fiona said.

"We?" Todd raised his eyebrows and looked around.

"Violet's sister is here as well."

Zoe waved her chopsticks from the couch.

Todd lifted an uncertain hand before shoving it back in his pocket. "It's, uh, nice to meet you," he said.

Fiona said nothing. Todd's gaze roamed around my apartment as if he'd never seen it before, looking everywhere but at the human occupants.

"Hey," I said to Todd. "I need to talk to you." I dragged him into the hall, closing the door behind me. And immediately was engulfed by that same staticky noise I'd been hearing all day. It had to be stress. I pressed my hands over my ears, trying to block it out.

Todd looked concerned. "Are you okay?"

I glared at him. "Not really. You heard I got dragged to the police station?"

"I did. I'm sorry. I can't imagine why . . ." He trailed off, scuffing his toe on the rug. "They'll figure it out," he finished lamely.

I was tired of people telling me that. "Who told you?" I asked.

"About you? Pete. He came by when I was locking up."

How did Pete know? And how was I going to face any of these people again?

Todd looked down at the floor, shoving his hands in his pockets. The forced smile had disappeared, leaving his mouth turned down in a grimace. "I'm sorry I didn't know. I was pretty tied up today."

"Tied up," I repeated, letting the disbelief come through in my tone. "Does this have something to do with that woman?" I may have sounded paranoid, but I figured I deserved it after all this.

His head shot up. "What woman?"

"The one in my shop this morning. You clearly recognized her," I said. "Mazzy." Her name tasted sour on my tongue.

"I have no idea what you're talking about," Todd said, but he'd always been a bad liar.

"Of course you do," I said, with absolute certainty. His vibration screamed dishonesty right now, and it felt like yet another knife in my gut. "Who is she, Todd? Because I felt like she was definitely there for more than a crystal consult."

We stared at each other for a long moment, then he sighed and shook his head.

"I told you I don't know her. And I'm sorry about tonight," he said. "I have no excuse, Vi. I meant to call earlier. But I got sidetracked and I honestly didn't hear anything until someone turned on the news at work. And I didn't hear anything about you until Pete told me, and I came right over."

"Yeah," I said, trying to keep the quiver out of my voice. "And we all know how much your bar means to you."

He ignored that. "What happened at the police station?"

"They wanted to know if I'd killed Carla, because everyone saw us shouting at each other this morning."

"Come on, Vi," he said, as if I had imagined the whole thing. "That's no reason to think you killed anyone."

"You think I don't know that? I'm not the one suspecting me!" I was done talking to him. I reached for my door and jiggled the handle.

Shoot. It had locked behind me, ruining my dramatic moment. I rapped on it.

Fiona opened it a split second later, telling me she'd been listening the whole time. And I'd had enough. Of this day, and of all these people. I wanted to go to bed with Monty and pull the blankets over my head, with my rose quartz crystal under my pillow. Maybe tomorrow things would make more sense, or Carla wouldn't be dead. This whole thing would be a bad joke or some fake reality show that someone was filming.

"Okay," I said. "Everyone out. I need you all to leave. Like, now. I need some peace and quiet and I need to process this craptastic day."

"But I'm still eating," Zoe protested from the other side of the room.

"Well, I'm sure you can conjure up a table and a chair somewhere." I stepped aside, holding the door wide. "You too," I said to Todd, when he continued to stare at me from the hallway.

"Me?"

"Yes! Everyone. What part of 'everyone' don't you understand?"

Todd frowned, but he seemed to know better than to argue with me. "I'll call you tomorrow. Get some sleep." He glanced at Fiona and mumbled, "Nice to meet you," then fled down the hall. I heard the elevator ding a second later, then the sound of the doors sliding shut.

I waited, looking at Fiona expectantly.

Fiona offered me a tight smile. "He's subpar, my dear. I hope it's nothing serious."

I stomped my foot. "Out!"

Fiona looked back at Zoe, gave a nod, then with a twitch of her head, the two of them vanished, leaving only a stream of glitter in their wake.

Silly me. Of course they didn't need me to hold the door. I waited a moment for them to show up again in another colored puff of smoke or something, but the apartment remained quiet. I locked the door, then leaned against it and closed my eyes. I felt bone-tired, as if I'd been awake for days. But the reality was, I'd slept most of the day away. And doing so had hurt me.

Monty peeked out from under my bookcase, carefully checking to see if the coast was clear. When he was certain it was, he leaped into his window perch and settled in, one eye on the street below. The energy in the apartment had already shifted. The electric currents powering the air had subsided, and everything seemed to settle back into something normal, recognizable. I took a deep breath and strode to the bowl of stones I kept on my bookcase. My fingers automatically closed over one. When I opened my hand and looked at it, my stomach flipped. Moonstone. My name, apparently. I rubbed it between my palms, taking comfort in the smoothness of the stone, letting the healing power of the crystal take over.

I thought about Fiona and Zoe vanishing in a puff of glittery smoke. I wondered how they did that. If they were really magical like they said, did that mean they could just conjure up their own signature exit and entry fanfare, kind of like the walk-on music celebs chose for their events? Or did it come ingrained in whatever powers they possessed?

And did all this mean that I had some of these powers too?

It was the question I'd been avoiding all night, ever since that niggle in the back of my brain suggested that my ending up at my old house tonight hadn't been a dream or a hallucination. Maybe I had effectively beamed myself there, for lack of a better term, kind of like the way Zoe beamed her way into my bedroom earlier with her sushi.

It seemed surreal.

But I had bigger problems than my alleged family. Namely, Carla Fernandez and her tragic murder. Someone had killed her today, and my property was at the scene of the crime. And I was a suspect.

Fiona was right about one thing. I had to figure out who killed Carla, if for no other reason than to save myself. But there was no way I was taking help from her, or from any magical source, if that was even a real thing. I needed to do it myself.

So I'd better get to it.

CHAPTER 22

I picked up my phone, then put it down again, not sure who to call. I'd thrown Todd out, and he seemed to have other things on his mind tonight anyway. I could call Josie, but I didn't want to worry her. I also didn't want to explain the Fiona and Zoe piece of the puzzle. Which left Sydney.

I was surprised I hadn't heard from her by now. She had to have heard about Carla, and I figured the first thing she'd do was call me. If she was home, there was no way she hadn't heard me and Todd arguing in the hallway. And if I knew Syd, she'd have come out straightaway to find out what was going on. But nothing.

Then I remembered the alley tonight, and her speedy exit. Maybe she was still with that guy, whoever he was. Which I was also curious about.

I picked up my phone again and texted her.

Where are you? Did you hear about Carla?

I waited, but my phone remained silent. Which was weird. It was kind of late, granted, but Syd was a night owl. I wasn't about to sit around and wait. "I'll be right back, Monty." I went across the hall and knocked on Syd's door, pressing my ear to it. It was quiet inside. I didn't want to wake Presley, but I needed Syd to help me figure this thing out.

I knocked again, then threw caution to the wind and rang the bell. A minute later the door was yanked open and Sydney peered out at me, her unruly curls swept up in a messy clip. She looked like she'd been in bed, which at eleven thirty seemed early for her.

"Sorry to bother you," I said. "But I can't believe I haven't heard from you tonight!"

She kept the door halfway shut. "What's up?"

"What's *up*?" I asked, incredulous. "Are you kidding me? You didn't hear about Carla?"

Her eyes closed, briefly, her hand going to her throat. "I did. It's crazy."

"Well, it's even crazier because the cops were here asking me about it because of what happened this morning. I wanted to see if you've heard anything. Can I come in?"

"No," she said, holding the door when I reached for it.

I stepped back, surprised and a little hurt. "No?"

"I mean, Presley's sick," she said. "I've been dealing with that all night since I got home. And wait. I'm still half-asleep. What do you mean, they were asking you about it?"

I didn't really want to have this conversation in the hall, where nosy Mrs. Owens could easily be eavesdropping right now. "Can you just let me in?" I asked, exasperated.

She glanced behind her, then held up a finger and stepped out of my sight. When she returned, she had her keys in her hand and motioned to my door.

"Sorry. I didn't want to wake her. She finally got to sleep," Syd said when we were in my apartment with the door cracked so she could listen for Presley. "So what have you heard? They have no idea who killed her?"

"That's what I'm trying to tell you. They must not, because they think it's me. Since practically everyone in town saw us fighting today." I collapsed onto one of my barstools. "They came here. To my door. And made me go to the station to make a statement." I left the scarf detail out. It made even *me* feel guilty when I knew full well I didn't do it.

Her mouth dropped open. She forced it closed and sat down on the stool next to me. "Why would they do that? Everyone knows you'd never do anything like that."

I sniffed. "Obviously not."

"That's ridiculous. And plus, she had enemies. She was a nasty person, Vi. *And* she was in politics. The combination is pretty deadly. Any number of people could've done it. It's just a matter of who disliked her more than most. Frankly, I'm surprised it's taken this long."

I was a little taken aback by that response. I'd had a few of the same thoughts but immediately felt guilty and chased them away—and I never would've said them out loud. I remembered the cease and desist order and wondered if Carla and the town had a leg to stand on.

"Syd. You can't mean that," I said quietly. "She was murdered. No one deserves that."

"I didn't say she did. I'm just saying anyone could've done it," Sydney said. "But you're right. I shouldn't have said it. So what's next? They didn't arrest you, did they? Did you post bail? This is so ridiculous, Vi. It's insane." She sprang up off her stool and paced my kitchen. "We have to *do* something! A lawyer. That's it." She spun around and pointed at me. "We need to get you a lawyer. I'm gonna ask Charlie. He knows everyone. Where's my phone?"

"Syd," I interrupted her tirade. "They didn't arrest me. They just needed a statement. I don't want a lawyer. That means I'll look guilty."

"No, it won't. You have to protect yourself, Vi. Let me call him."

"No. God." I got up myself and went to the cabinet for something to do. Tea, I decided. I'd make tea. "Want some?" I asked, holding up a tea bag.

"Sure," she said distractedly, then glanced at the floor. "What the heck happened in here?" she asked, motioning to the trail of glitter throughout my apartment. "Were you scrapbooking or something?"

I'd forgotten about Fiona's trademark leave-behind. I made a mental note to sweep it up after Syd left. "Scrapbooking? When have I ever scrapbooked? No, I, uh, was working on a display for the shop and spilled some glitter," I lied, filling my electric teapot with water and flipping the switch on. "Anyway, I can't believe you missed all this. Then there was the whole thing with Todd too. Didn't you hear that? When did you get home? And hey, who was that guy you were with in the alley, by the way?"

I was alarmed to see that her face had gone from slightly green to stark white. "Jeez," I said. "What's wrong with you? Did you catch whatever Presley has?"

"What? No. I just . . . no. I'm tired. The guy was no one. I bumped into him when I was walking home. He asked me for directions."

Directions? What I'd seen was a more intense discussion than directions, but maybe I was remembering it wrong. I had just been released from the slammer, after all, and met my long-lost mother for the first time since I was five. I could've been applying the drama from that encounter to Sydney's. Suddenly I felt exhausted. What if I couldn't remember anything right?

"Directions?" I asked. "To where?"

"What?"

"Where was he trying to go?" I asked.

"The new Thai place," she said, her eyes going up and over my head.

I knew immediately she wasn't telling me the truth—that over-the-head gaze was her tell—but it seemed an odd thing to lie about. "So what time did you get home?"

"God. I don't remember. Probably nine? I had a crazy afternoon. I did manage to get my fries this afternoon, though. That was definitely important. Good thing I got there when I did too—your skinny friend was buying all the fries." She was trying to make me laugh now. Or forget about my original question.

"My who?"

She waved an impatient hand. "Your vegan yoga friend. I gotta tell you, I don't think the cheesy fries are vegan."

"Natalie?" I felt a surge of impatience. I didn't care about Natalie's french fry habit right now.

"Yep. Anyway, then I had that, uh, painting class thing tonight. I was on my way back from that when I stopped to give that guy directions."

She was all over the place. "What painting class?" I asked.

She nodded, kind of impatiently. "Yeah. At The Muse." Anna Montgomery's store. She did fundraising paint parties every week to support a charity. "It was for the local animal rescue."

"I didn't know you were going to that. I would've gone with you." At least I would've had an alibi.

Syd shrugged. "Last minute thing. The woman who runs the shelter came into my store today and asked if I was going. I figured since she was buying a bunch of stuff I had to say yes. Anyway, back to this mess. They can't seriously suspect you, Vi. And even if they did for a minute, they let you go, so they must be over it, right?"

I somehow doubted they were *over it*. If it was anything like the cop shows on TV, they may have let me go, but they'd be working on building their case. Which meant I had to move fast to prove my own innocence. I took a deep breath. "I need to figure out who killed her."

Sydney stared at me like I'd sprouted a second head. "You need to," she repeated. "Why would you need to? Isn't that what the police are for?"

The water had started to boil, so I pulled the pot off its base and filled our mugs. I searched in the cabinet for my truffles, because chocolate was kind of necessary in times like this, but couldn't find them, and my bowl next to my chair was mysteriously empty. Where on earth had I put that bag? Giving up, I slammed the door and turned back to Sydney. "Because if they want to close the case fast and think they have a good suspect, they might not bother looking for the real killer," I said. "And I could use some help. You in?"

"Vi." Sydney shook her head vehemently. "That is not a good idea. We aren't detectives. You can't pretend to be a detective!"

"I'm not going to pretend to be a detective. I'm just going to casually ask around to see if anyone was extra upset with Carla." I shrugged, putting on the false bravado. "It's my life on the line."

"You know I love you," Sydney said, grasping my hand. "But I'm telling you, Vi, it's not a good idea. Let the cops do their jobs. I mean, we both know you didn't do it, right? Come on, you're a total do-gooder."

I knew she meant that as a compliment, but it still kind of stung. And why wasn't she tripping over herself to help me, like I would do if the rhinestone-studded cowboy boot was on the other foot?

It stung, but I didn't want to show it. "So, what? You think I should just sit back and wait for them to arrest me?"

"Of course not," Sydney said. "But they aren't going to. They're going to figure out who really did kill her, and then it's all good. Right?"

"Syd. Someone was murdered. I don't care how you feel about her," I said, cutting off whatever she was about to say when she opened her mouth. "I don't think it's going to be *all good* no matter what happens here. I'd just like to try and keep myself out of jail."

"I understand," she said after a minute. "But Vi, it could be dangerous. I wish you'd stay out of it."

I focused on adding honey to the tea so I didn't have to answer. But my mind was swirling with possible reasons why my best friend not only didn't want to help me, but didn't seem to want me doing anything to help myself.

CHAPTER 23

I spent most of the night tossing and turning until I fell into a restless, unsettled sleep. When I woke, the sun was streaming in through my blinds, which I'd forgotten to shut. I'd overslept, I realized with dismay when I managed to grab my cell phone and focus on it with bleary eyes. "Ugh," I groaned, dropping it back onto the table. I didn't want to move, but I didn't have a choice.

I rolled over and gasped when I saw two brilliant yellow eyes staring into mine. Monty, I thought, and almost settled in to go back to sleep. Then my eyes flew open. Monty didn't have yellow eyes. He had brown eyes.

I refocused. The black cat. The one I'd seen in the neighborhood yesterday. But how on earth had he gotten in here?

He must live in the building somewhere. And he'd slipped in at some point last night. It was hardly surprising. There had been enough people coming and going in various ways. Although how had I—and Monty—not noticed? "You must be someone's cat," I said.

He (she?) simply stared at me, unblinking.

I began to feel a little uneasy, then chided myself for acting crazy. He was someone's lost cat, period. He'd probably slipped back in last night when Sydney and I were in here with my door ajar. I made a mental note to look for posters around the neighborhood or down in the lobby when I left.

Which would have to be soon. I needed to get to the shop. I still had yesterday's million things to do, today's new list of tasks, and appointments. I hoped. Unless my clients had heard I was suspected of murder and canceled on me. Then I realized I'd never heard back from Josie about the smell she insisted had been in the shop yesterday that she was going to have taken care of. I fired off a quick text.

What happened with the smell? Gas? Dead mouse? Are we all clear?

While I waited for Josie to reply, I pulled up the Channel Seven news website to see if there was any update about Carla Fernandez or her killer. I scanned the headlines. Pretty much the same as last night. Local councilwoman found dead. Foul play suspected, police are questioning suspects. No arrest has been made. No danger to the public.

Meaning it wasn't a random crazy person.

Josie hadn't responded. I threw my covers off and headed to the kitchen to make coffee. I wasn't going to the Bean this morning. I just didn't have it in me. I would make a pot and take a travel mug and that way I wouldn't be buying a sugary latte, so it was a win-win. Besides, I didn't want to see all my neighbors, all the people who would be whispering and pointing at me, or at the very least staring at me, trying to see inside my brain to know if I really had killed Carla as my guilty pink scarf suggested.

Ugh. Not the best thoughts to start the day.

I grabbed my laptop off my nightstand and plugged

Carla's name into a Google search. Sydney had said last night that Carla had a lot of enemies, and it was a matter of finding out who disliked her "more than most."

The phrase rang in my head. For sure, Carla had her opponents—Sydney being one of them—but she had to have proponents too. No one was universally reviled, and the mere fact that she was still on the council was a testament to a strong supporter base. It wasn't as black-and-white to me as it was to Syd—most people had *some* redeeming qualities, and to make a blanket statement about her lack of popularity would put pretty much everyone in town on the suspect list.

No, there was a certain type of person toward whom Carla seemed prejudiced for whatever reason, and that could be the right starting point.

Not surprisingly, there were a lot of results. She was in the paper almost weekly, given her role on the town council, which was quite active, coupled with her outspoken personality and her tendency to be über-conservative in her views on how the town should be run, and what kind of an image we should have. I skimmed a few of the most recent articles, looking for clues or anything suggesting that someone was out to get her after a decision she'd made or a position she'd taken.

There were a few of them. Starting with last Monday's meeting, during the public hearing about a co-op specializing in alternative healing activities moving into one of the town-owned buildings for rent. There was some weird charter in the town, the article explained, that mandated public input before the town rented out any of its space. Mostly likely to avoid the appearance of impropriety or favoritism.

What should have been a very non-controversial topic, though, had exploded into a debate about voodoo-like practices. I frowned. Carla definitely had a fixation on the word *voodoo*. It was what she'd accused me of too. The woman who owned the co-op had actually been driven to tears by Carla's commentary during the meeting, which included things like "witch doctors," "scams," and generally taking advantage of "gullible people who have nothing else to hold on to."

Pretty harsh for a woman who wanted to bring a community resource offering massage therapy, acupuncture, and an essential oils classroom, among other positive things. The rest of Carla's colleagues had disagreed with her, and in the end all her protesting didn't have any sway over the application being approved, but still. Seemed like a lot of unpleasantness for nothing.

I clicked back to the search list, scanning for anything interesting in recent weeks. I paused when I saw Charlie Klein's name, and clicked that story open.

Another Monday-night council meeting, and Charlie had gone during the public comment period to lambast Carla about the noise she was making about his property. The article quoted him as saying she'd "done enough damage in town trying to make things into her fairy tale," and the good people of North Harbor wanted her to stop. The article wasn't very long, and had actually been about another agenda item, but this had warranted a mention.

I sat back against my pillow. Charlie and Sydney had become unlikely friends when Syd moved to town, and Charlie had been looking out for her ever since. I'd heard Charlie had lost a daughter years ago. Maybe he saw Sydney as a surrogate. Whatever the case, Carla seemed to be hitting them pretty hard, and I couldn't understand why. Charlie's parking lot was off the main strip where all the action happened. The tiny house wasn't even visible from this street, and definitely not part of the "downtown" area. Just one street over was into residential territory, and neighborhoods started to take on the persona of a truly diverse town—which this was.

I glanced over at Monty, sulking in the corner while the other cat prowled around my apartment. Monty definitely didn't like this. I wasn't sure what to do about it either. I didn't want to toss him or her out if he or she needed a place to stay, but if another family was searching for their missing cat, I didn't want to be an unknowing party mucking up the works.

I closed my laptop and got out of bed. I sidestepped the piles of glitter in my apartment, choosing to ignore the whole Fiona thing for the time being. After putting the coffee on, I fed both cats, then got in the shower. Nothing from Todd. You would think he'd be groveling for my attention after yesterday. Unless he was too scared to call me. Either way, I was disappointed in him.

Men could be such jerks.

A long, hot shower helped. After, I worked some curl amplifier through my wavy red hair while I studied myself in the mirror. Tired, I thought critically. Stressed out. Faint creases in my forehead, smudges under my eyes. Not as bad as I feared, though. A little concealer and some eye brightener and I would be good to go.

I put on one of my favorite dresses—purple with sparkles—and my purple combats, let my hair air-dry, applied my makeup, and headed out to the kitchen. The coffee had brewed and smelled delicious. Lovely and strong. I poured a quick cup and sipped it while I filled my travel mug, changed Monty's water bowl, and threw some lip gloss, my moonstone, and my phone into my bag.

I should probably let the cat back out so he or she could find their way home. I didn't see it anywhere, though. "Black cat?" I called, knowing I sounded ridiculous.

Monty gazed at me from the top of his tree. His demeanor had changed from sulky to relaxed. I didn't see the black cat anywhere. Which was a little weird, given I lived in a loft and could see the whole apartment. I waited another few minutes, then grabbed my coat and walked out of my apartment. I paused outside my door. The night had ended kind of abruptly last night, with Syd not budging on her stance about letting the police figure out Carla's demise, and me feeling abandoned.

I didn't want Syd and me to have a weird vibe between us. I needed to make it right. I didn't have a lot of close friends. Syd, Josie, and Natalie were the closest people I had, and I didn't want to lose any of those relationships.

I went across the hall and raised my hand to rap on the door. It flew open before I could, but no one was there.

Cautiously, I poked my head in. "Syd?"

"No, darling," a voice said from behind the door.

CHAPTER 24

I froze. "Hello?"

Fiona appeared in front of me. She stretched out her arms as if to hug me, but I stepped back.

Her smile faltered, just a bit, but she covered it quickly. "Good morning."

"What . . . what are you doing here?" I asked, craning my neck to see around her. "Where's Sydney?"

"The young lady who lived here? She's moved. She's got a much nicer apartment down the street. No offense," Fiona added. "But she needed more space. With her daughter and all."

I felt the now-familiar headache starting to pound behind my temples. Pushing past Fiona into the apartment, I opened my mouth to shout for Sydney.

And stopped short, turning in a slow circle. Sydney's apartment, which usually looked like a bomb had exploded in it, looked . . . not like Sydney's. The usual towering pile of mail was not on the counter, and her usual morning coffee cup, laden with milk and sugar, wasn't staining the countertop. Presley's cereal bowl was missing too. And the living room—where was the funky red rug with the spirals on it? And the battered coffee table with her piles of *Glamour* and *Allure* magazines? The half-dead spider plant she kept trying to rejuvenate?

And for the love of God, where was *Sydney*?

Had I accidentally beamed myself somewhere again? But I swore I'd just walked across the hall and knocked on my friend's door, like I'd done so many times before. Including less than nine hours ago. But she wasn't in her apartment, and as was pretty typical over the past twenty-four hours, I felt like I'd fallen down Alice's rabbit hole and had completely lost sight of the daylight to climb back out.

I turned on Fiona, furious. "What have you done with her? She was here last night." It hit me that I didn't know this woman at all, despite her insistence that we were blood relatives. What if she *was* a witch, but a bad one? Or what if she was some nutjob with her sights on me, and she'd done something to my friend?

"Violet."

I refocused. Fiona frowned at me. She shook her head slowly. "My goodness. I can see what you're thinking. Where did you get such an imagination? It certainly wasn't from your father, and I doubt it was from me."

My hands flew to my head, as if my thoughts were appearing in bubbles around it like in the cartoons. "This is impossible." I decided I must have a brain tumor or something. As awful as that would be, it would at least explain all the crazy crap that was happening. "I was here last night. I had a whole conversation with Sydney after you all left. Her kid was sick. There's no way she could have moved since then. People don't just move overnight, not when they have a whole apartment and a kid to pack up."

"Yes, well," Fiona said vaguely. "It wasn't planned. But she's very much alive, all set up in a lovely apartment. Very happy. And so am I, because now I can be your neighbor." Now she did lean forward and kiss me on both cheeks, beaming.

"My . . . *neighbor*?" I took another look around the apartment, this time focusing on the new decor—modern-looking art on the walls in the shapes of constellations. On one wall, there was a giant scroll that read *Ravenstar*, followed by lines of text in a language that didn't look familiar to me. And the ravens, positioned around the room. Creepy. Staring at me.

Fiona followed my gaze, nodding with satisfaction. "Zoe and I live here now." She cast a critical look around. "Needs some work, of course. But our most important things are here. Oh, don't worry," she said with a casual wave of her hand, multiple silver rings flashing in the early-morning sunlight. "I'm not here to cramp your style. I just want to get to know my daughter. Think of this as a long-term slumber party." She winked. "I promise I'll give you your space."

I stared at her, uncomprehending. "But . . . how?" My feet, which previously had felt frozen to the ground, finally moved, and I walked slowly into the living room. If I hadn't known better—if I hadn't been here myself, just a few hours ago—I would've said I'd imagined Sydney, Presley, and their belongings. Although, Sydney *had* been acting strangely last night . . .

No. I shook the thought off. The only strange thing about last night was a murder and the cops thinking I had a part in it.

"Well, it was apparent last night that you might need some support," Fiona said. "With everything going on, and since I wasn't impressed with that boyfriend of yours." She said the word *boyfriend* like one might say *cockroach*. "So Zoe and I decided we would relocate. And it will be a lovely opportunity for us to catch up. Don't worry, dear. Like I said, your friend is not far away. Now. Where does one get breakfast around here?"

"Why don't you just conjure something up," I said, a little bitterly.

But Fiona just chuckled. "I suppose I could, but I really want to get a feel for our new town. Did I hear something about a bean?"

Fiona wanted to go to the Bean. My place. Where my friends were. Where I'd eventually have to explain her. How had she even heard of it?

Maybe I didn't want to know the answer to that.

It also registered that Fiona wore an outfit remarkably like the one I'd chosen for myself this morning, although her dress was orange, which set off her hair—which was a coppery blond today—nicely. She wore a different pair of high-heeled boots, maybe even higher than the ones from yesterday. Which seemed a silly choice given the season and the weather. Then again, I guess she didn't have to walk if she didn't want to.

"It's The Friendly Bean," I said. "But I'm not going today."

"Oh, come on now. I thought you went there every morning?"

How did she *know* that? "No." I held up my mug. "I made coffee."

"Well, save it for later. We'll go get some together."

"I really can't," I said. "I have to get to work. I have an event to get ready for—"

"I love events!" Fiona clapped her hands. "What is it? I'm sure I can help."

"I don't think so," I said.

"Tell me anyway." It came out pleasantly, but I felt like it was more of a command, and before I could register how I felt, I was speaking.

"It's a healing circle. My friend from the yoga studio and I are putting it on."

Fiona frowned. "A what?"

"A healing circle," I repeated. "Where a bunch of us get together and do a group meditation for peace and love. We think the town needs a lot of healing. Even before last night."

She smiled. "My daughter, the do-gooder."

I bristled a little. Sydney had called me the same thing last night. At least I knew she'd been kidding. Well, sort of. I still wasn't sure if Fiona was making fun of me or if this was just her style. "What's wrong with that?"

"Nothing, my darling," Fiona said, and she surprised me by coming over and planting a kiss on my forehead. My skin tingled where her lips touched me, and I wondered if that was our mother-daughter connection, or just my imagination. "It's quite admirable, in fact." She studied me intently, and I felt that odd feeling again—like I was being scrutinized, sized up.

I couldn't get a handle on what her assessment of me might be.

"We'll have plenty of time to plan your circle. Come have coffee with me." She linked arms with me, her tone leaving no room for argument.

I cast about for some other good reason to decline. Finding nothing, I settled on a lame observation instead. "It's not really the weather for those." I nodded toward her shoes.

"Don't be silly." Fiona waved me off. "It's fine. And this way you can introduce me to all your friends. And we can see who might've held a grudge against that woman."

I felt like I was being led to the gallows, but it didn't seem like I had a choice. So I swallowed my protests and resigned myself to the fact that I was going for coffee with my mother.

Who now lived across the hall from me.

How had my world gone so far off the rails?

CHAPTER 25

"I can't stay long," I reminded her once we were in the elevator. "I have to open my shop. I lost out on most of the day yesterday."

"I understand," Fiona said. "I can't wait to see your shop."

She was still holding on to my arm. I tried to give it a tug free, but she held tighter. "This way you can keep me from falling, since you're very worried about that," she said with a wink. "In my unsensible shoes." She inspected my boots. "Those are very interesting. What are they?"

"Docs," I muttered.

"Docs?" she repeated.

"Doc Martens," I explained. "It's a brand. You know, like *Lululemon*." I couldn't keep the sarcasm out of my voice, but she didn't take the bait.

"Fascinating. So. Your shop."

"What about it?" The elevator door opened, and I stepped out into the lobby. My building manager, Kate, stood there with a bunch of boxes. I held my breath, waiting for her to zero in on Fiona and demand to know where her other tenants were, but Kate merely smiled and told us to have a nice day.

"What you do there. What you sell. How it's doing. I want to hear all about it," Fiona said.

"Oh. Sure." I pushed the door open and stepped out onto the street. It was colder than yesterday. I could smell the hint of snow in the air. Fiona sniffed too. "I remember this," she murmured, almost to herself.

"Remember what?" I asked.

"This smell. The feel of the cold air." She glanced at me with a small smile. "I remember taking you sledding in that big park once, when it snowed quite a bit. I didn't really know what to do with the snow, but your father did. What was that park? Do you remember?"

"Central Park," I said. My brain reached for the memory, but I couldn't quite get it. At the same time I felt it—fresh, cold air, my breath puffing around me, wet snow, the exhilarating feeling of flying down one of the hills on my little sled, wondering what would happen once I reached the bottom. Was my mother there waiting? Or had she been at the top seeing me off?

I shoved the pieces away. Trying to add my mother to a memory wasn't helpful at all. I picked up my pace. She still held on to my arm. It wasn't until I glanced down at the sidewalk, where only yesterday piles of icy snow still lingered, that I realized they were all gone. I swore I could see them up ahead, but as we got closer, there suddenly didn't seem to be any.

"Violet!"

The moment was over, and I cringed at the sound of my name. I turned slowly, not sure what to expect—someone else accusing me of murder? Someone wanting to gossip about Carla's death?—but it was only Charlie Klein, waving at me from under the awning of the sushi restaurant.

I brightened. Maybe Charlie had some intel on Sydney's day yesterday, given that he saw her every day. Or Carla and who may have killed her. "Hey, Charlie," I called back. "How are you?" I pulled my mother over so we could talk to him. I could feel the impatience exuding off Fiona next to me.

When we finally reached him, he looked Fiona up and down. "Good mornin'," he said. "I'm Charlie."

She nodded, her gaze also sweeping him from head to toe. "Fiona."

I noticed she didn't mention that she was my mother and wondered why, given her enthusiasm for me to introduce her to my friends. I also noticed at the same time that I was relieved she hadn't. The news was already going to spread like crazy, but with Charlie at the helm, it would've been like putting it on the billboard visible from the highway. His barbershop doubled as a living, breathing gossip column.

"What's going on?" I asked. "We're going to get coffee."

"At that fancy place? I won't go in, but I'll walk with ya."

Charlie and his friends hung out at the old diner in town. He refused to drink anything he deemed "fancy."

He fell into step beside us. "So that's somethin', eh? That news last night about Ms. Fernandez?" His whole face puckered when he said her name, like he'd just sucked on a lemon.

"It is something," I said. "Who do you think would've done that?"

Fiona perked up and leaned in, listening intently for his answer.

He leaned on his cane, appearing to think hard. "Why, I

don't know, Miss Violet. Seems to me there are a plethora of people," he said with a little laugh. "I mean, how do you narrow it down? Coulda been anyone. Her husband—soon to be ex, I heard—or that business partner of hers, maybe. I always wondered how he stood her."

"Charlie!" I exclaimed, horrified. "You shouldn't say that." At the same time, I wondered how I'd forgotten that Carla's business partner was Natalie's husband, Andrew. They'd been working together for a couple of years now at the realty office.

Andrew was a good guy. I pushed away the question of how he'd stood Carla all this time. This must be crazy for him. I wondered what would happen to the business, and if this would have repercussions for Natalie. It had seemed like such an isolated incident, but now I saw just how many people it touched, whether they were Carla fans or not. As for Carla's husband, I didn't know him.

Charlie's eyes were twinkling at my reaction, which was kind of disturbing. "I'm just makin' a point, Miss Violet," he said. "Carla's husband's actually a decent guy. He's outta the country anyway. But heck. Someone seemed to have done it, right?"

"Someone bold, for sure," I said. "It happened in such a public place." Which also gave me the creeps. Someone who could murder another person almost in the middle of the street, well, that said something. Even if it was pretty dark out.

He shrugged. "She was always making mischief in a public place, weren't she? I mean, didn't she hammer you just yesterday in Pete's place?"

I felt my face redden and glanced at the ground. My mother cleared her throat next to me.

"Nobody *hammered* me, Charlie," I muttered.

"Huh." He snorted. "That's not what I heard."

"What did you hear?" I asked.

"That she came atcha like that wrecking ball took down the old warehouse over there." He made a vague gesture down the street. I remembered the warehouse he was talking about. It had been just around the corner, and it was an ugly old building. The town had finally sold the property on which it stood, and the new owner wasted no time in demolishing it and building a new building that had some high-end apartments and a Peruvian restaurant on the ground floor. This had all happened soon after I'd moved to North Harbor. "And that she called you a voodoo lady or something," he continued.

I felt Fiona stiffen next to me at the description, but ignored it. I tried to brush it off. "She was just being unreasonable," I said to Charlie. "She must've woken up on the wrong side of the bed or something."

"Mm-hmm," Charlie said noncommittally, still watching me with those keen, watery eyes. Likely waiting for some gossip. "You mean to tell me you're all broken up about her?"

"Charlie. Someone's died," I said. "You can't tell me you don't feel *something*."

His look of disdain told me all I needed to know.

"But she's got to have family who loved her," I tried again. "Everyone has someone who loves them. At least feels bad for them."

Charlie grunted. Blissfully, we were just about at the crosswalk.

"We've got to run. Nice seeing you, Charlie," I said. Without waiting for an answer, I took my mother's arm and tugged her along, wishing for the light to change, before I realized I hadn't asked about Sydney.

Fiona must've read my mind—which, knowing what I knew, was not just a phrase anymore. Out of the corner of my eye, I saw her lift a finger, ever so slightly, and flick it at the light as if she were flicking a mosquito away. And the light changed immediately from green to red, not stopping at orange, causing a car coming down the street to slam on its brakes. Fiona smiled at the driver as she glided across the street.

"Coming, darling?" she called back at me.

CHAPTER 26

"Did you do that?" I hissed, mortified, as I hurried across the street after her.

"Do what?" she asked innocently.

"That!" I waved at the light. "The traffic light business."

Fiona winked.

"You can't do that! If you're going to hang around here you have to behave," I said, aware that I sounded like an awkward parent who hadn't yet mastered how to deal with her own child.

Fiona stopped right in the street, threw back her head, and laughed. I noticed again that the sound wasn't unpleasant, and that it did tickle the edges of my memory, stronger this time.

"Not funny," I said, pulling her all the way onto the sidewalk.

"Of course it is," she said, strolling along like she had all day and the whole street to herself. "My daughter telling me to behave is quite funny, actually. You're lucky

I've mellowed over the years. A remark like that could've turned you into a toad or something years ago." She winked at me.

I suspected she wasn't joking.

It felt kind of surreal, walking down the street with her. How many times had I imagined a moment like this. Going for coffee with my mother. A moment where my mother was a part of my life. Of course, in my moments we were best buds and partners in crime and told each other everything. I'd romanticized my own mother even though I knew next to nothing about her.

And now here she was, and I had no idea how to feel or what to think. But she certainly wasn't what I expected. *Witch* hadn't been on the list of things I'd hoped for in a mother.

I pushed open the door to the Bean and stepped in, holding my breath a little, not sure of who knew what and how they would react. But no one seemed to notice me, or if they did, they didn't stare or point or anything, much to my relief. My mother followed me inside, looking around curiously. I stopped to breathe in the familiar smells and the warmth. Pete saw me immediately and raised his hand in a wave, which set me a little bit at ease.

I waved back and got in line, pretending to study the menu even though I knew it by heart, hoping not to make eye contact with anyone else.

"I'll get us a table," Fiona said.

"There aren't any," I said, and it was true. Every table was occupied. "The place is full. I shouldn't stay long anyway."

Fiona raised amused eyebrows. I noticed how perfectly shaped they were and wondered if witches had to use makeup, or if they could just blink and get their face set perfectly and their skin as smooth as they wanted it.

That might not be a bad power to have, come to think of it. "I'm sure I'll be able to find us something. Will you get me a tea?"

I really didn't want to sit here. I felt exposed, waiting for someone to come at me with the scarlet *M* for *Murderer*—or worse, handcuffs. On the other hand, I didn't want to look like I was running away or hiding. On the third hand, I didn't want my mother teleporting anyone else into another dimension. I wrestled with the decision for a lot longer than it called for, then just gave in. "What kind of tea?" I asked.

"Surprise me," she said. "I'd love to try something new." She turned and swept to a table in the back corner. I joined the line that snaked around the front of the café, keeping one eye on her. I lost sight of her for a moment, behind the people coming and going, but when my field of vision cleared, I saw her sitting at an empty, clean table.

I didn't even want to know.

"Hey, Vi."

A tap on the shoulder had me turning. My eyes almost popped out of my head at Syd balancing two coffees and a bag of pastries a bit precariously. Wherever she'd come from, she'd been up and at 'em early, which is unusual for Syd on a good day, and downright unheard of when Presley was sick.

"Hey," I said, letting my breath out in a *whoosh* and grabbing her in a hug, nearly knocking the coffees out of her hand. I was relieved to see her. Part of me had been worried my mother had banished her to some witchy dungeon somewhere just to free up her apartment. I wish she had moved out cranky Mrs. Owens down the hall instead of picking my friend. "How are you? How's Presley?"

"Jeez. Easy," she said with a laugh. "It's not like we haven't seen each other in years. She's fine. Look, I wanted to tell you I'm sorry I was kind of out of it last night," she said. She glanced around, a bit surreptitiously, I thought. "How are *you* doing? Have you heard anything else?"

"I'm fine. I'm just so happy to see you." I resisted giving her another squeeze. "So where are you? How did this happen? And *when*? I mean, we were at your apartment last *night*." I waited expectantly for an explanation.

She cocked her head, giving me a long, searching look. "I'm right here. How did what happen? And we were at *your* apartment last night."

"You moving out of our building," I said, exasperated. What else would I be talking about? It was kind of the elephant in the room.

Sydney frowned. "Vi. Are you sure you're okay?"

"I'm fine," I said impatiently. "But I want to know how you moved out in the middle of the night."

A worried look passed over her face. "Vi. I know it was awesome being across the hall but we aren't far away. And we love our new place. It's a lot bigger. I needed the space for Presley. Plus the noise factor is way better, not being here in the middle of the busiest area in town. We talked about this when we moved out." She looked concerned. "Don't you remember?"

I watched her closely for the slipping gaze, but she was looking straight at me. "When did you move out, Sydney?" I asked.

She leaned in closer, conspiratorially. "I have a great doctor that I've been seeing for anxiety, if you need his name."

I recoiled a little at the suggestion. The last thing I needed was to be medicated on top of everything else. "I'm fine. I don't need a doctor." I did not want to turn this into a conversation about my mental health, especially when I was worried about it myself. "You still didn't answer me. When did you move again?"

There was a suspiciously blank look in her eyes. "Recently," she decided vaguely. "Anyway, it's all good. You still need to come over and see the place. I'll call you later. I have to open the shop. Please let me know what else I can do to help you with . . . you know." She blew me a kiss and hurried away, leaving me staring after her.

CHAPTER 27

"Hey, Violet. Whatcha havin'?" Ben, the college kid who worked for Pete, waited for me to place my order. I realized I had reached the front of the line during my odd encounter with Sydney, and everyone was waiting for me.

I blinked and refocused, pushing Sydney out of my head. "I'll have a vanilla latte with soy. And a tea. Do you have some kind of funky tea?"

Ben looked at me, puzzled. "Funky? We have chamomile, green, black, and raspberry. Pete, you got more tea?" he called over his shoulder. "Somethin' funky?" He lifted his shoulders, communicating to Pete that he wasn't exactly sure what that meant.

Pete raised his eyebrows at me over his latte machine, a silent question: *Are you okay?* "I have a passion fruit tea that people love," he said.

"I'll try that." I avoided the real question, because I wasn't sure how to answer it.

"You got it," Ben said, snapping his fingers and grabbing two cups. "Cream and sugar for the tea?"

I looked at him blankly. "Um . . . I don't know." Should I know? Was there some kind of mother-daughter telepathy that should tell me if my mother liked cream and sugar in her tea? If there was, I hadn't been able to tap into it yet.

Ben stared at me, waiting for my answer, a small frown furrowing his eyebrows together. Behind me, I could hear people shuffling restlessly.

"No. Nothing for the tea." I paid and moved to the other end of the counter to wait for my drinks, near where Pete managed the espresso machine, creating coffees with a deftness and grace that I envied. I focused on the steaming machine and tried to breathe.

"What's going on?" he asked, keeping his voice low. "I heard about Carla and . . . everything. How are you holding up?"

"I'm fine," I said, pasting on a fake smile. "Thanks for telling Todd, by the way. We'd been out of touch most of the day yesterday."

Pete shrugged. "Not a big deal. I was just wondering why he wasn't with you, so I asked if he knew what was going on."

"Yeah. Well, thanks. Hey, by the way, did you see me drop my scarf in here yesterday?"

He frowned. "Your scarf?"

"Yeah. I had a fluffy pink scarf on that I lost somewhere yesterday morning." At least word hadn't gotten out about that piece of the crime scene yet. Pete certainly didn't seem to put the two thoughts together. Although he was looking at me strangely, as if wondering why I was worried about a scarf when I clearly had bigger problems. I felt tears choke the back of my throat. I couldn't take it if the people I'd come to love thought I was an awful person.

I had to prove them wrong.

"Well?" I pressed. "Did you see it?"

Looking chagrined, he shook his head. "I didn't, Vi. I'm sorry. It was so busy in here I never got out from behind the counter."

"It's okay. Figured I'd ask." Maybe it had fallen off in the street somewhere. But I felt like I would've noticed that. It hardly mattered, though. Wherever I'd dropped it, someone had scooped it up. Who? The killer? Or had a random and well-meaning person done so and put it somewhere hoping I'd come back for it, and the killer grabbed it later? I shivered. It was so creepy to think I'd been in the midst of a killer while I was doing my usual morning routine. Picking up my morning coffee. Walking down a street I'd walked a million times—half a block from where I lived. Maybe walking past that person at some point during my day.

I hated the thought of it.

Pete placed two cups on the counter and called for Jamie to come pick them up. "So who's your friend?" he asked casually, nodding toward the corner where Fiona sat watching the people around her as if they were the most fascinating specimens she'd ever seen.

I'd been expecting the question—Pete didn't miss a trick and would surely have seen who I came in with—but I still cringed when it came. It was no use lying about it. If Fiona had really moved to town, which I was still trying to wrap my mind around, the truth would come out soon enough.

"That," I said, examining my fingernails—my purple polish was chipped in a few places—"is allegedly my mother." I risked a glance at Pete to see his reaction and immediately a weird sound filled my ears. Like static, kind of like that weird sound I'd heard on and off yesterday, but louder. I shook my head to clear it, but it only seemed to get louder. I tried to focus on Pete through the noise.

His eyes widened. "Your mother? Seriously . . . ?"

"I know. Long story." I rubbed my forehead, closing my eyes for a second.

"Wow. That's big. Were you expecting her?"

I smiled, a little. "Not for about twenty-seven years."

He frowned as he placed my latte and my mother's tea on the counter in front of me, but didn't ask. He flipped another cup off the stack and poured some milk into it for the next drink on his list. "If you ever need to talk," he said. "I'm a good listener."

"I know you are. Thanks, Pete."

"Call if you need anything," Pete said. "I'm serious, Vi."

I nodded my assent and picked up my drinks. Before I made my way back to Fiona, I looked back at him. "Hey. Have you seen Todd yet today?"

He shook his head.

I wondered when he'd turn up. As I went to join Fiona, I couldn't help but notice the trail of glitter on the floor that led to her table. I thought of that old fairy tale, "Hansel and Gretel," that my dad used to read me—the children following the trail of breadcrumbs to the evil witch and ultimately, to their death.

Now that was a cheery thought.

CHAPTER 28

Fiona looked like she was enjoying herself when I sat down and placed her cup in front of her. "These people are precious," she said with a little smile. "That one over there?" She pointed at a woman somewhere behind me. "She just told her friend that she thinks her boyfriend is cheating on her and how she hopes she can get his attention again."

"Why is that precious?" I asked, incredulous. I turned to look for the girl, craning my neck to see who my mother was talking about. Instead I saw Anna Montgomery, the art-store proprietor, sitting by herself two tables away, scrolling through something on her iPad. I thought of Syd and the paint party last night. Natalie's husband, Andrew Mann, sat at the table next to her. He was with a man I didn't recognize who wore a rumpled suit. Their heads were bent together looking at some papers. I caught a glimpse of a spreadsheet.

Charlie's words rang through my mind. What had Andrew and Carla's relationship been? I didn't know Andrew well, but Natalie adored him, and he'd seemed nice the few times I'd met him. I wondered if they were equal partners, or if Carla was the majority stakeholder. My gut told me Carla would always want to hold the balance of power. Had he been tired of living in her shadow? Or was the idea that he killed her as preposterous as the idea that I killed her? It struck me that this was a bit like a witch hunt.

Fiona chuckled, and I shifted my focus back to her to see what was funny before continuing to look for her poor victim. "Why? Darling. If a man cheats on you, the only way to handle that is to take drastic measures." She leaned in close to whisper in my ear. "Of course it's easier for us to handle something like that than these Lulus, but still. There are ways."

Of course there were. And I was pretty sure I didn't want to hear about them.

"That one right there," Fiona said, obviously getting impatient with my neck-craning. She pointed a long French-manicured nail down the middle of the café. I saw her now. The red eyes gave it away. She had frizzy strawberry-blond hair, too short to be pulled into a ponytail but somehow she'd made it happen, and tons of freckles. I pegged her for midtwenties. She huddled into an oversize black parka, pushing pieces of a muffin around on a plate dejectedly. Her friend across from her looked concerned. She kept rubbing her arm.

Maybe I should offer to bring her to my store, find her a crystal that would help her see the relationship more clearly and figure out how to stand up for herself. I started ticking through stones in my mind, trying to tune into her aura from where I sat. But there were too many people between us and too many emotions swirling around, and I couldn't pinpoint hers well enough.

Fiona watched me, amused. "Our power doesn't simply mean we can turn people into toads, dear. It goes much deeper."

Before I could ask what she meant, the front door opened and the guy with the crazy hat from town hall yesterday stepped in, making me forget momentarily about other people's problems. He held a bunch of flyers up in the air like he was delivering a critical message to the town.

"Good morning," he announced, and his voice was commanding enough that the chatter in the café subsided as everyone turned to look. Behind the counter, Pete's eyes darkened.

"I want to make sure everyone knows about the peaceful protest we're holding tomorrow down by the riverfront," he said. "I hope to have everyone's support as we work to convince the powers that be that this railroad bridge project will come at the detriment of this beautiful town and its natural resources. We'll meet down by the water at three o'clock and we'll stay as long as necessary. Please join us." He began threading his way through the tables, handing out flyers as he went, that ridiculous hat bobbing over his head. He paused to scratch at his scruffy goatee between tables, and the synapses in my brain finally started firing enough for the dots to connect.

This wasn't just the guy from town hall—Rain. This was also the guy from the alley with Syd.

He made his way around the café, and when he got to my side, he noticed me right away. "Hey, Violet! Nice to see you again."

I mumbled something and shrank down in my seat. Last thing I needed was to be associated with this guy too.

A snicker had started somewhere in the café and was getting louder. I pinpointed the originator as a guy in the corner. He was dressed in a leather jacket with chains dangling off the sides, dirty jeans, and a surly demeanor.

"Hey," he called out. "No one here wants to hear your save-the-planet BS, okay? We need *jobs*. People will have work when that project starts."

"Yeah, then what about the jobs that are getting displaced when they take our office building down?" a woman waiting for her drink countered. "The whole thing is ridiculous. I'll come to your protest," she told the hat guy, reaching for a flyer. "Keep up the good work."

"Oh, gimme a break, lady!" The naysayer stood abruptly, knocking his cup over. Coffee sloshed off the side of the table and puddled on the floor, but he didn't seem to notice. "You and your suit friends wouldn't know a hard day's work if it hit you over the head. You're all a pampered bunch of whiners. And you." He took a few steps and shook his finger in Anna Montgomery's face. "You need to be careful about where you're scattering your glitter. Someone's gonna fall and break their neck!"

Anna stared at him. "That is *not* my glitter," she said coldly. "And talk about being self-centered. You shouldn't need to find work at the expense of our planet."

I wanted to hide under the table. Anna was getting blamed for Fiona's glitter litter, and Fiona certainly didn't look like she was about to step in and take the blame.

But glitter was the last thing on anyone else's mind. Voices started to chime in to the argument, adding to both sides and raising the energy level of the room to heated, heading toward frantic. Rain looked satisfied, as if he'd accomplished exactly what he came for. Fiona looked enthralled.

Pete, however, did not. He threw his rag down and came around from behind the counter, sticking two fingers into his mouth to create the most ear-shattering whistle I'd ever heard. "Enough," he said once the room had quieted. "This is a safe place for everyone. No one gets attacked here. And no one comes in here to advocate for a cause without asking my permission first," he said, sending a withering look toward Rain, who shriveled a bit under his gaze. "Out," he said, pointing toward the door.

"Sorry, dude," Rain said. "Didn't mean any harm. Peace out." Flashing the peace sign, he headed out the door.

"And you," Pete said, turning to the biker guy. "Apologize to her"—he pointed at the woman at the counter—"and then clean up your mess." He threw his wet rag at the guy, who also looked properly chagrined. Pete was probably the only guy I knew who could get away with disciplining his patrons like this. But no one wanted to be blacklisted by Pete. His coffee was too darn good.

"Sorry," the guy muttered without really looking at the woman, then bent to sop up the puddle of coffee.

I swore Pete was going to go back at him and tell him to apologize like he meant it, but after a second he let it go and went back behind the counter.

Everyone else went back to their conversations, the room still buzzing a bit. Everyone, that is, except Andrew Mann, who slipped out the front door. I watched curiously as he hurried after Rain, finally catching up with him. He started talking animatedly, waving his hands around.

First Syd, now Andrew. Who *was* this guy, and what was his connection to the people in North Harbor?

CHAPTER 29

Fiona lost interest in the crowd after the show was over, which was just as well since I really had to get to work. In unspoken agreement, we both rose and pulled our coats on. "Well, that was fun," Fiona said after we stepped out onto the sidewalk.

I shot her an incredulous look.

"What?" she asked, the picture of innocence.

"Anna's getting blamed for the glitter," I said. "Do you think you should stop doing that?"

"Darling. This mortal life really has had its effects on you. We'll have to work on that," she said, squeezing my arm. "Everyone can use a little glitter in their life. They'll be fine."

It was no use arguing with her. And I had to go. I still hadn't heard from Josie about the smell, but since I hadn't seen any tape or signs restricting access to my shop when we'd passed earlier, I figured it was okay. Which was good, because I had two private consults today, and Natalie was coming in later so we could finalize our details for the healing circle.

Which we clearly needed, given the environment in Pete's café a few minutes ago. It was kind of unheard of to see the angst reaching inside of The Friendly Bean—it wasn't named that just for the heck of it—and it had shaken me a bit. Between worries about the economy and the growing problem of our planet being compromised, people were vested in the outcome of this vote.

As for me, I'd only dipped my toe into learning about the pros and cons, although I was leaning toward opposition. On the other hand, if the current bridge was unsafe, that was a problem too that needed a solution. The train line was a critical piece of our county's infrastructure, and if it became disabled, it wouldn't be a good thing for anyone.

In any event, the town was violently divided, and things were only heating up. The vote to go or no-go on the project was going to a special referendum next week, so things were ramping up as each side got louder and louder in their quest to be heard. Natalie and I wanted to do something to try to heal the community in advance of the vote, and we'd decided on this healing circle. We were going to hold it in the yoga studio, complete with meditations and singing bowls and generally just a plea for everyone to remember who we were and that we all wanted only what was of the highest good for the town.

Unfortunately, a lot of the planning had fallen onto my plate. Normally I wouldn't mind, but given the state of my life at the moment, it was just one more thing to do. We had flyers up at the yoga studio and my shop, and word of mouth in our circles was huge, but we needed to do more publicity.

"Are you going to work now?" Fiona asked.

I nodded. "What are you going to do?"

She shrugged. "Go tidy up my place a bit, and then I'll

probably go out and get to know the town," she said. "I'll stop by your shop later."

Please don't, I thought, but I didn't say it out loud. "Have fun," I said instead.

"I'm going to take the long way around," Fiona said. "I could do with a walk. See you later." She bussed my cheek and then headed toward the next block. I was surprised she hadn't insisted on coming to see my shop, but maybe she meant what she said about giving me space. Whatever it was, I was relieved.

I waited until she rounded the corner before I turned to head toward the shop. My first appointment was in thirty minutes. But Todd's silence weighed heavy on my mind, on top of everything else. I didn't think I'd be able to concentrate until I talked to him. Maybe he hadn't tried to call or text this morning because he thought I was mad after last night.

Still, that annoying little voice whispered in my ear. *Shouldn't he be cutting you a little slack given what happened? Why isn't he marching down to the police station, telling them how insane they all were for thinking you're a killer?*

"Because no one does that," I said out loud, earning a surprised glance from a woman hurrying past me on the sidewalk. Oh, screw it. I turned and started walking in the direction of Luck o' the Irish. He was probably there now, since he usually went in early to start setting up for the lunch crowd.

But the place was silent and the doors were locked when I got there. I cupped my hands around my eyes and peered inside, but no lights were on. I blew out a breath and turned around, leaning against the door for a moment. And swore I caught a glimpse of platinum-blond hair with streaks of color disappearing around the corner next to the bar, into the side alley, one of the ways into the courtyard. The courtyard where Carla had been killed.

I stood up, on alert. I recognized Mazzy's hair immediately. What was she doing here? I started walking in the direction I'd seen her vanish, when I heard my name.

"Violet!" I turned to find Natalie rushing to catch up with me. She wore her typical yoga pants tucked into a pair of black fuzzy UGGs, and a gold puffy coat. Her yoga bag was slung over her shoulder, and she carried a bottle of kombucha in one hand. Her hair was pulled up into its usual bun on top of her head. She'd just gotten done with a class. A class I probably should've gone to, given that Zen would likely be hard to come by for a while. I was really glad that my mother had already left, because while I didn't know if Natalie's yoga pants were Lululemons, she still would've had a lot to say.

"Hey, Nat. I was about to text you to see what time you were coming over."

"I was just heading to your shop," she said. "You on your way over?"

I nodded. "I have an appointment in about twenty minutes. I was hoping to catch Todd first, but . . ." I let the words trail off.

Natalie eyed me. "What's going on? Something wrong with the two of you?"

There was no way I was going to get into what had happened last night. And if she hadn't heard that I'd been questioned in Carla's death, I wasn't going to volunteer the information.

"No, I just haven't talked to him much the past couple days." I started walking toward my shop. She fell into step beside me, but stayed silent, which surprised me. My friends were kind of on the fence about Todd. I'd never quite figured out why. But usually Nat would be eager to tell me all the things I should do when he stepped out of line, but she seemed preoccupied today.

Then again, I guessed everyone was.

"So what do you think of the whole Carla thing?" she asked finally.

It had been inevitable, but I'd hoped we could talk about anything else. "Crazy," I said. "I mean, it seems surreal. Things like that don't happen here."

"I know. It's scary," Natalie said. "I was in the studio yesterday evening too. Meditating. The whole place was dark and I had the curtains shut and music on. I lost track of time. I was supposed to meet Andrew. He was out putting up posters for the healing circle for me, and I was late. Had no idea what was going on right outside, until later when I left and saw all the police." She shivered a bit. "Imagine? It could've happened right behind me."

I couldn't. The yoga studio backed up onto the court-yard where Carla was killed. It wasn't like it had been some seedy alley in the bad part of town. It was right here, a place we all walked past a million times a day.

"I can't imagine what Andrew must be feeling," I said, trying to sound casual. "How awful, and it must have caused a lot of business angst too."

Natalie's face fell. "He's so stressed. When the police came to talk to him last night . . ." She trailed off. "But he doesn't want me to worry, so he's trying to hide it. And to think he was probably one of the last people to see her alive." She shuddered. "It worries me. I mean, what if it was a customer? You've heard those stories about realtors being lured to their deaths by some sicko."

That was a terrifying thought, but also the thought about Andrew maybe being the last one to see her alive had caught my attention. "The police don't think there's a danger to the general public, though," I said. "By the way, I saw him at Pete's this morning. Hey, what are his thoughts about the bridge project? Was he on board with it? I know Carla was."

Natalie's head snapped up defensively. "Why?"

That reaction I wasn't expecting. Why was that a loaded question? "I'm just curious. There's a guy organizing a protest who's running around town wearing a model of the bridge on his head. I saw Andrew talking to him earlier, that's all. I figure he must be between a rock and a hard place, with Carla's position and yours."

Natalie frowned. "Of course he's opposed. Anyone with any concern about our environment would be. Andrew doesn't really get involved in the town politics side of things, especially with Carla. He stayed out of all that stuff. He only cares about the business, and he's not as interested in the hoity-toity perception as she is. Was," she amended with a wince. "He really just wants to do well and put people in houses they love."

I kept my mouth shut. I knew for a fact that Andrew's job was the reason she'd been able to quit her corporate job to become a yoga teacher. And they had a fancy house in the next town, right on the water. It must be a lot of pressure for him to keep up with their lifestyle. So he had to be somewhat interested in the big-money aspect.

We turned the corner and stopped in front of my shop. "Can you come back around two and we can work on the circle?"

Natalie checked her own watch and appeared lost in thought. Then she nodded. "Sure. I have a few things I need to do this morning anyway. I'll see you then." She headed back in the general direction of the yoga studio.

I watched her go, wondering why she'd gotten so defensive about Andrew and the bridge project.

CHAPTER 30

I unlocked the door to my shop, my gaze falling on the *North Harbor Day* wrapped in plastic on the ground. I hesitated, then stooped to pick it up and headed inside, flicking lights on as I moved through, pausing to sniff every few steps. I didn't smell anything at all. False alarm? Or had whatever it was been resolved because of Josie's quick action? I checked my phone again. She hadn't replied.

She'd be along soon enough. Guess I just had to wait.

I went to the counter to drop my purse and the paper. I wasn't going to read it. That lasted half a second before I picked it up and yanked the wrapper off, my eyes drawn immediately to the photo of Carla Fernandez above the fold, smiling out from behind her nameplate at one of the town council meetings.

Local councilwoman dead, the headline read. The sub-head said, *Brazen killing in public courtyard leaves residents on edge.*

A sidebar article showed a somber photo of the remaining council members gathered last night behind the mayor as he made a statement about the "swift and fitting justice" the killer could expect.

I flipped the paper over abruptly. I didn't think my stomach could take reading the rest of the article, terrified to see my name in print as a "person of interest." *Brazen killing*. I realized my hands were shaking and closed my eyes, took a few deep breaths to steady myself. I had to go along today like nothing had happened, at least in my world. I couldn't let anyone think I was disturbed by the visit to the police station. I hadn't done anything wrong. Now I needed to make sure I acted like it.

I took a deep breath and went out back to check my messages to see if any of my appointments had canceled. But when I got to my desk, I nearly jumped a foot when I saw a pair of yellow eyes blinking at me from on top of my desk.

"How did you get in here?" I asked the black cat, trying to calm my hammering heart. What was with this cat? How was he getting into all these places—all *my* places, specifically? If he belonged to someone, they really needed to start taking better care of him.

He regarded me with a slow *blink, blink* of those eyes. I guess if I expected him to answer me I was in for a big letdown.

"Okay, well. I guess you can stay. It's warmer in here than outside," I said. I wondered if I should think about bringing him home with me permanently. Monty might hate it. But how awesome would it be to have a black and orange cat pair? Maybe this was the Universe telling me it was time to get myself a black cat since I'd always wanted one.

Although now was probably not the time to think of

that. "Right," I said. "I have an appointment." I left him sitting on the desk. On my way into the main room of the shop, I paused and looked back.

My desktop was empty, except for the piles of papers I still hadn't gone through.

He's a cat, Vi. What do you expect? My little voice chided me. *He jumped down and is hiding somewhere until you leave. That's it.*

I saw a woman waiting at the door and hurried over to unlock it. My first appointment, and thank goodness, she was the real deal, not another Mazzy.

I threw myself into the consultation. As I got into my routine speaking to my client, I started to feel almost normal again. In this moment, there was no Carla, no murder, no Fiona. And no police. When my client left forty-five minutes later with her stones and a tearful thank-you, I felt like my place in the world had been righted. She was going to be fine. I could feel it. And I would be too. I'd needed this.

I checked my book for my next appointment. Not for an hour and a half, which gave me time to unwind and clear my energy field for the next person. And usually the best way for me to do that was by working with some stones. I went out back to get one of the boxes from my as-yet-unpacked shipment and came face-to-face with my new friend, the black cat.

We regarded each other for a moment. I blinked first.

"So what can I do for you?" I asked him finally.

He blinked, slowly. I was pretty sure it was a he. Just a feeling I got.

"Do you need a home?" I asked.

Another long, slow blink.

"Did Fiona send you? Are you some kind of witch

posing as a cat to spy on me?" I asked. Sadly, I was only half kidding.

I could've sworn he gave me a scornful look.

"Then how do you keep getting inside?"

He wasn't interested in conversation. He leaped gracefully off the desk and came over to twine himself around my legs. I reached down to pet his sleek body. His fur felt like velvet. He looked like one of those true Halloween cats, the ones you see in all the depictions of witches on brooms with their arched black cats balancing next to them.

The comparison didn't escape me.

I lugged the box out front and used a box cutter to slice it open. It was filled to the brim with stones wrapped in Bubble Wrap. I turned some music on and started unpacking, reveling in the brilliance of each stone. I'd placed this order from one of my favorite suppliers at a recent gem show, and as usual, the product didn't disappoint.

As I worked, I saw out of the corner of my eye people stopping outside. Potential visitors checking the place out before committing to walking through the door, I assumed, turning to look. And was shocked to find a guy with a camera and a woman with a notebook speaking into a microphone.

As much as I would love to believe they were there to cover my shop, I had the sinking sensation that this might be about Carla. Clearly word had gotten out that I was the person who'd been dragged down to the police station last night, in the aftermath of her unfortunate demise. That sinking sensation in my stomach made me want to run for the back room and hide, but that didn't last. Instead I felt angry. This was crap. And the police needed to get their heads out of their rear ends and work on finding the real killer before my reputation went down the drain. Not that I wanted anyone else to go through what I did, but why hadn't they dragged Andrew down there if he had been the last known person to see her alive?

I set down the stones in my hand and went to the door. Before I even registered what I was doing, I'd thrown it open, startling them out of their conversation. I saw a glimmer in the reporter's eye as she realized it was me and snapped to attention.

"Can I help you?" I asked.

She flashed a dazzlingly white smile at me. "Ms. Mooney?"

"Yes," I said.

She kept the smile in place. "So nice to meet you. We were hoping to get a quick comment from you relating to the death of Councilwoman Fernandez." She shoved a microphone in front of my face at the same time I saw the red light flare on in the camera. It was still filming.

"I have no comment. Please leave." I turned to go back inside.

"Oh, come on," she said, her voice taking on a cajoling tone. "You've spoken to other media. It's only right that you give our viewers the story too."

I turned back, indignant. "I have *not* spoken to any media!" What was she talking about?

"It's got to be shocking," she went on as if I hadn't spoken. "To know that someone was murdered in cold blood right in front of all our noses, in broad daylight, has to be unnerving. Is it making you think twice about being a business owner in town?"

I tried to keep a neutral expression on my face. I was well aware of how they could cut this footage to make me look bad. "I'm confident the police will get to the bottom of this quickly," I said. "I have no worries about North Harbor being a safe place. I firmly believe this was a one-off incident."

There. That should shut her up. I turned again to go back inside, but the reporter's voice followed me. "So you think someone was targeting Ms. Fernandez?"

Just go inside, Violet. No comment is the best comment.

I pushed open my door.

"Is it true that you and Ms. Fernandez were on bad terms?" she persisted. "That you two had gotten into a very public argument not long before she was killed?"

I paused, closing my eyes and counting to ten so I didn't say something I'd regret. Once I got to ten, I took a small amount of pleasure picturing their camera smashing into a million pieces on the ground, then, feeling much better about my answer, I turned around.

At that exact moment the camera fell from the strap around the cameraman's neck, smashing on the pavement. It probably shouldn't have broken into so many pieces given the height it fell from, but it must've hit at just the right angle. The three of us watched it fall, almost in slow motion, the cameraman's cry of dismay lodging itself in my consciousness.

The three of us looked at each other. "Jeez, Matt," the reporter said, an edge in her voice. "How did that happen?"

"I . . . have no freaking idea," he said, sounding crestfallen as he bent to assess the damage.

The reporter looked at me, clearly torn between pinning me down for a quote and dealing with the fact that she couldn't get my response on film.

"I have no comment," I said with a sappy sweet smile, then slipped back into my shop, locking the door behind me. Part of me felt some satisfaction in the mishap. The other part of me felt kind of sorry for him. Journalists didn't make a ton of money, and now he'd need to buy a new camera.

And a third, quieter part of me wondered, How on earth *did* that happen? The camera's descent had been almost exactly what I'd pictured in my mind.

CHAPTER 31

My next client was a teenager named Alice who'd saved up her babysitting money for a personalized crystal consult. She confessed with a nervous giggle that she was going to school late today just so she could come in to see me. Alice had concerns about her grades, which she called average, and dating, which she said she wasn't having much luck with. But as soon as she sat down in front of me and allowed me to tune in, I could feel an overwhelming sadness enveloping her. I don't think she even realized it was there.

I did love a challenge.

I chose a pink lemurian seed crystal, a citrine, and an aventurine to help combat her depression and promote feelings of happiness and improved communication, and threw in a pink opal to help with her relationship and self-love. I could tell she was feeling better even before she left the store, and felt a huge sense of satisfaction that I'd helped someone today.

Josie had come in while I was busy with Alice, and

had picked up where I'd left off earlier unpacking boxes. "Morning," I said, making my way over to her. It seemed like ages since I'd seen her last.

"Morning, sweetie." Josie rose and wrapped me in a hug. I let the familiar scent of patchouli settle over me and thought I could stay here forever. "How are you holding up?" she asked.

"I'm fine," I mumbled into her chest. Guess she knew.

Josie stepped back, holding me at arm's length. She was a lot taller than me, so she had to look down to see my face. "Really?"

I shrugged. "I think so. How did you hear? About . . . me?"

"The police chief's wife was at the event I went to last night," she said. "Everyone knows Connie has a big mouth. Plus she was friendly with Carla, so she made it her business to know what they were doing about it."

I was always surprised at how much Josie knew about everyone in town, although at this point I shouldn't be. But something else she'd just said bothered me.

"What event were you at last night?" I asked.

"The paint party for the rescue league. At Anna's," she said.

"Really? I thought you were watching Presley last night since Syd went to that?"

Josie shook her head slowly. "Syd wasn't at that event."

I frowned. "Are you sure?"

"Positive. There were only about twelve people, so it wasn't like I missed her in a crowd. Why?"

"No reason," I said, brushing it off. I needed to sort that out in my head. Why had Sydney lied about where she'd been last night? Did it have something to do with that Rain guy?

"Anyway, don't get me wrong, no one deserves to be murdered, but that woman was a classic troublemaker. And no one in their right mind who's ever spent five seconds with you would ever think you'd kill anyone," Josie went on. "They were just checking a box to show that they're on top of things. Don't give it another thought, Violet."

I hoped she was right. But since I'd decided my mother was also right about me not sitting back and letting myself get steamrolled for this crime, I knew I needed to be proactive about making sure the cops were sniffing up the right tree. I needed to get myself eliminated as a suspect. Josie would help.

I checked my watch. My next appointment wasn't until after lunch, and no one was in the store at the moment. Now was as good a time as any, I figured. "Jos. I need your help. And I need to talk to you about something."

Josie studied me for a moment, then pulled out the chair I used for my consults. "Sit," she said.

I sank down into the chair. Josie perched against the counter facing me.

And the black cat appeared from out of nowhere, winding his way between our legs.

"Hey." Josie pointed. "Who's that?"

"I don't know. It's been following me around since yesterday morning. Showing up in my apartment and here."

Josie frowned. "Really," she said.

I nodded and wondered if I should talk freely in front of this cat. What if . . . *God, Vi. Get. A. Grip. All this talk about magic is getting to you.*

"I'm not sure how he or she keeps getting in. Hey, by

the way, what was the deal with the smell? You never said anything else about it."

"Oh, that." Josie brushed it off with a sweep of her hand. "False alarm. A recipe gone wrong next door. You know how it goes over there." The pub next door didn't have the best reputation for food. I was a little annoyed that my shop had been closed down because of it, and made a note to go talk to the cook when things settled down. I sat across from her, clasping and unclasping my hands.

"So what do you want to talk about?" she asked.

"I need to figure out who killed Carla. I need to get them to stop thinking it's me," I said. I braced myself for the same protests as Sydney had voiced, but Josie didn't say anything for a full minute—just watched me. I shifted uncomfortably under her scrutiny. But when she spoke, she didn't tell me I was crazy, or to leave it alone. "Tell me what happened yesterday," she said instead.

Grateful she was at least letting me talk, I went through my day yesterday after I'd left my store—the trip to town hall, my long nap, the cops showing up at my door and asking me to come to the station. She listened impassively until I paused abruptly at the point where I was left in the interview room alone. I had no idea how she would react to this.

"And?" she prompted.

I sighed. "Now you're really going to think I'm crazy."

Josie smiled. "Try me."

I described the experience as best I could. As I talked, I remembered how vividly I experienced being in my grandmother's chair, smelling her scent on the blanket draped over the back. My voice faltered, once again on the verge of tears. I wasn't usually a crier. I'd barely even cried at my dad's funeral.

"I don't know what happened. I must've blacked out," I said, avoiding her eyes. "It was crazy. But then . . . the cops came back and seemed to think I hadn't been in the room, so that freaked me out too." I risked a glance at her to see if she was completely weirded out by me at this point. Her face hadn't changed.

"And then?"

I hesitated long enough that Josie reached out and put her hand over mine. "Vi. Whatever it is, you can tell me. I can't help if I don't know."

She was right. I took a breath. "They let me go and Gabe told me someone was here to pick me up. My mother, he said." I waited. Josie was the only one who knew the real story about my mother taking off when I was a kid. She also knew my alternate version of the story, though she'd never commented on that.

Josie sucked in a breath and sat back. "Go on."

"So I walked out into the lobby and these two women were out there. One allegedly my mother, the other allegedly my sister. Can you believe that?" I shook my head. "Just like that, after almost thirty years."

"That's wild," she said. "So what happened?"

I'd expected more from Josie when I dropped this bombshell. She was way too calm about all this. "I thought at first that he'd made a mistake. I mean, how would she have known to come to the police station, of all places, even if it really was her? So I tried to just leave, but she stopped me. She wanted to talk. It was kind of crazy talk."

"Crazy how?"

I looked around the room, trying to figure out how best

to answer her. I trusted Josie with everything. She'd been my friend and mentor since I was a kid. I also didn't want her to think I was nuts. My eyes fell on the cat, sitting at our feet. He watched me too, his eyes as piercing as Josie's. Apparently he was also eagerly awaiting the answer.

When the silence threatened to stretch on, she sighed. "Vi. Are you going to share, or do I need to keep pulling teeth by asking a million questions?"

She was right. I was wasting our time. Time that I might not have.

"Do you believe in witches?" I asked abruptly. I waited for her to laugh, or at the very least, to ask me if I was feeling well.

Instead she said, "I believe in strong, powerful women who understand their connection to the earth, and who know they are natural healers. Sometimes those women have . . . powers that other people don't have. Is that what you mean?"

I had no idea if that's what I meant. My mind automatically went to the pointy hat and striped tights, which I knew was silly and pure Halloween marketing, but other than that I had nothing with which to associate the word.

"I don't know. She said she's a witch," I said, throwing up my hands. "And that I'm mostly a witch. Three-quarters witch, to be exact. Apparently my dad was half a witch. And Grandma Abby was a witch." That still blew my mind. "That she found me because my necklace that Grandma Abby gave me broke. It apparently had a spell on it that kept her from finding me." I risked a glance at Josie. She would know what to do, how to handle this. If she didn't run screaming from the building, or call an ambulance to take me to the psych ward.

But she didn't do either of those things.

"Well? Is that not the most ridiculous thing you've ever heard?" I demanded finally when she still didn't say anything.

Josie still said nothing. Her face was unreadable. I wasn't sure if this was a good or a bad sign, but my patience was wearing thin.

"Josie. Say something. You're kind of freaking me out, staring at me like that. I wasn't even going to tell you because I didn't want you to think I was crazy enough to believe it—"

"Violet," Josie interrupted. "Calm down."

She waited until I had lapsed into a fretful silence. "Now, let me show you something." She reached into her pocket and pulled out her phone, spinning it around so I could see the screen. As I watched, all the apps dissolved in front of my eyes—it was left with just a blank screen. She tapped with her index finger.

As I watched, wide-eyed, the blank screen turned into a picture of a bedroom. A child's bedroom. One that I had to admit I would've fancied if I'd had a child—or been one. Not any of that sickly sweet pink that graced so many kids' rooms. Instead, the room was done in an array of purples, from lavender to deep violet. The fabrics ranged also, from soft, fuzzy-looking pillows on the bed to a puffy down comforter to velvety curtains.

I glanced at Josie, curious. "Cool, but how did you get your phone to—"

"Shh," Josie said. "Watch."

Frowning, I refocused on the phone. And my eyes widened as I watched a woman walk into the room, holding a redheaded child, maybe four years old, by the hand. Instinctively, I reached up to touch my own hair and leaned closer to the phone, my heart starting to pound in my chest. I only had a side view from where they were standing, but I swore I recognized that dress. A purple tutu that I'd worn nearly nonstop during one point in my childhood. There were so many pictures of me in that dress that the image of it was seared into my brain. My dad used to tease me that they could barely get it off me to wash it. And that braid. I'd worn my hair that way too. Without thinking, I reached out a finger to touch the screen as the child ran off camera and returned holding a teddy bear against her chest. I could see her face clearly now, and man, did she look a lot like me.

I shifted my attention to the woman. Her hair was long, halfway down her back, a light brown shot through with blond. Light bangs brushed her forehead. I couldn't see all of her face at the moment, so I waited in rapt fascination for her to turn my way.

And when she did, I gasped out loud.

A younger version with different hair, sure, but it was Fiona. There was no doubt.

My eyes flew to Josie. "What is this? Where did you get this?" I picked up the phone. Immediately, the picture disappeared. I shook it, frustrated, but the normal Apple apps had returned. "What app was that?"

"Vi," Josie said gently. "It wasn't an app. I'm showing you a scene from your childhood."

"But how can you . . ." I sat back, feeling that dizzying rush again that had become all too common in the past couple days. I tried again. "What do you mean?"

Josie leaned forward and rubbed the stone on one of her rings. That staticky sound filled the room again, and I watched, awed, as two of my large raw amethysts literally levitated and moved to the other side of the room.

My gaze traveled from the rocks back to her, not quite believing what I was seeing.

"I'm a witch, Vi," she said quietly. "I've known who

you were this whole time. And I know Fiona. She is, unequivocally, your mother. And I know it's hard to get your arms around that, but you have to trust me." She leaned forward and took my hand again, but hers was grasping now. Urgent. Her eyes were dark and serious. "And you have to trust her."

CHAPTER 32

I don't know what shocked me more—the idea that I was a witch, or the idea that Josie was. And that she knew Fiona. And that she somehow had a video of me as a little kid, probably before videos were even a thing.

What the goddess was going on here?

"I know it sounds crazy, Vi." Josie still held on to my wrist, a little harder than necessary. "But you have to listen to me. Trust Fiona. I'm not going to pass judgment on the family drama, but she's always loved you. All of them did. They just . . . disagreed on how to do it best."

"But," I began, and was interrupted by the bell on my shop door jingling. I muttered a curse as Josie pushed off from the counter.

"I'll take care of it," she said. "Think about what I said."

"You didn't really say anything," I muttered. I waited until she was engrossed in the customer, then I went out back, pulling the curtain so I had privacy. Then I paced.

I hadn't felt this agitated last night when my long-lost

mother had appeared on my doorstep. This seemed like more of a betrayal. Josie had known this crazy story this whole time, if it was true. Which also meant my beloved grandmother, and my father, had both lied to me about the biggest defining moment in my childhood. It seemed like everyone around me had been keeping secrets from me my whole life. And it felt really lousy.

I still wasn't sure about trusting Fiona, even on Josie's instruction. I was a pretty trusting person, but this whole thing just felt weird. And how could I trust someone who walked out on me and didn't return for twenty-seven years? I had to unpack that baggage when there was less going on. In the meantime, there was a murder to solve, and something else Josie said had me on alert. I had no idea why my mind chose to focus on this piece among everything else she'd just thrown at me, but it was the one I could actually, maybe wrap my head around.

She hadn't babysat Presley last night.

Which in and of itself wasn't a huge deal. Syd could very well have some backup babysitters for when Josie had other plans. No, it wasn't only that.

She'd said Syd wasn't at Anna's paint party. And since she was there, she would know that for a fact.

So why would Sydney lie about that? Unless she'd been up to something she didn't want anyone knowing about. It could have something to do with that guy Rain, and she was embarrassed about it for some reason. Maybe she thought aligning herself with a rabid environmentalist wasn't good for business. But why lie to me? I wouldn't say anything about her personal life.

No, it would have to be something pretty serious for her to lie about it.

And some serious things happened yesterday.

I pushed the thought out of my head as fast as it came

in. What was wrong with me? Syd hated Carla, sure, but she was as likely a killer as I was. Was I that desperate to save myself that I would throw my friend to the wolves?

My phone rang, jolting me out of my thoughts. I glanced at the number and sighed, both annoyed at the interruption but glad to see that it was Carissa Feather, one of my contacts from the local metaphysical community. She was a multitalented musician who did drumming circles and also played singing bowls. I'd hired her to play them at the healing circle. I hoped she wasn't canceling on me—it would take me forever to find a good singing bowl person. I picked up, trying to force some normalcy into my voice. "Carissa. Hey. Are we still on for the circle?"

"Of course we are! And what timing. This is amazing, Vi!" Carissa's voice bubbled through the line, completely overpowering me. Her personality was so big there was often little room for anyone else when she was around. It was good when she was putting on a show, but in regular life it could be overwhelming.

"I'm sorry, what's amazing?" I asked. I could picture her on the other end, sitting in her studio with all her singing bowls, her mass of blond hair piled on top of her head, feather earrings brushing her shoulders.

"That woman's murder! Listen, there's a new medium in the community. Her name is Lilia Myers. She moved to town about a month ago. I heard she's good. We should invite her to the circle. Maybe she can get in touch with Carla's spirit and find her killer? That would bring a ton of people in! Are you charging for entry?"

I felt the blood drain from my entire body. For a moment I couldn't even find words, but I knew Carissa would probably take that as affirmation that she was on the right track. "Carissa. What are you talking about?" I stood and moved to the other side of the room. "That's insane.

We can't let that happen. Do you have any idea how . . . *inappropriate* that is? Do *not* invite her. Promise me. And no, we aren't charging! This is a healing circle."

Carissa huffed out a breath. "Inappropriate? If the cops haven't arrested anyone by then the whole community is going to be up in arms. This is a healing circle. How much more healing could it be to find a killer?"

"Carissa." I closed my eyes, willing my patience and usual good nature to make an appearance. "I am not falsely accusing anyone of murder based on a medium's message. That's not something to mess around with. And it gives us all a bad name if it goes awry, no?"

"We wouldn't be falsely accusing anyone," Carissa argued. "A name may not even come through. But imagine if it did? And she was right? We'd be heroes. They'd make TV shows about us."

"No, they'd make TV shows about her. And I'm not looking for a TV show for anyone at my expense. This is Natalie's and my gig and we're not inviting a medium. This is a healing circle, not a freaking séance." I cringed, thinking of Carla's accusations about a séance the day she died. Little did she know she might become the subject of one. "Got it?"

"Oh, Violet. You're such a killjoy sometimes," Carissa scoffed. "You know it's going to come up."

"I don't care if it comes up. We can add it into the healing circle as something we need to address in order to help the community. Otherwise, we aren't talking about it," I said through gritted teeth. "And if you even utter a word about this medium to anyone, I'll cancel the whole thing. Understood?"

Silence on the other end. Then, "Fine," Carissa said, huffing a bit. "I'll see you Friday."

Maybe I was getting better at the assertive thing. I disconnected and took a big breath, then tossed my phone on the desk. I looked around for the black cat, but he or she was nowhere in sight.

I had to get out of here. I needed to find Syd and clear this up. Sitting here speculating wasn't helping either of us. And I wasn't the type to ignore the elephant in the room. I wanted to get him safely home to where he belonged.

I grabbed my coat and bag, shoved the curtain aside, and strode through my shop. Josie was still with the customer. I could see her looking at me in my peripheral vision, but I ignored her and made for the door.

Just as I reached it, my door opened and Rain, the model-bridge-head guy himself, stepped in. He paused in front of me and shot me a brilliant smile.

"Hello, Violet. I really wanted to check out your shop." He looked around, nodding approvingly. "Tell me, from where do you source your stones?" He lifted his eyebrows at me, clearly hoping to get into an environmental discussion.

I wasn't in the mood. And since I took my job and my shop extremely seriously, of course I paid attention to where I got my stones. Crystal sourcing was an extremely controversial topic, and one that didn't get much attention—or thought—from consumers as a general rule. But for people like me, whose living depends on the quality of my products, making sure I had quality stock was a no-brainer. I'd been doing detailed research on geology and mineralogy for years, and I'd become quite familiar with mining practices in every region from which my dealers bought stones. Additionally, when I purchased, I took into account the lapidary practices in each—the way the stones are cut, polished, and generally handled—as well as the socioeconomic situations in certain countries. I had a small stable of people from whom I bought stones, all of whom I trusted implicitly.

But I resisted snapping at him, because it struck me that I could potentially tease some information out of him about Sydney. I forced a smile. "I have a small group of trusted sources, in some cases the mine owners themselves. If you're interested in a particular stone, we can certainly discuss its origin."

He blinked at me. Obviously he hadn't expected me to have a ready answer to that. "Oh. Well, good for you. I hear you do one-on-ones?"

I nodded.

"Can I get one?"

That, I wasn't expecting. "You want a consult?"

He nodded.

I did a quick tuning in to see what his energy was like. Not surprisingly, it was off. I could feel confusion, defensiveness, and some level of anger vibrating in the air around him. I focused on a spot in the center of his forehead, looking for a glimpse of his aura and, not surprisingly, saw dark browns and muddy greens above his head. Deception and something about relationships. The right side of him was surprisingly absent of color, which told me there was a large, abrupt change or some kind of transformation going on.

He still waited for an answer. The low hum of Josie's and the customer's voices provided the only backdrop.

"Sure," I said. "Have a seat." I pointed at the chair I'd recently vacated.

Rain went over and sat. Josie shot me a curious look, but said nothing.

I came over and sat across from him. "I'm going to tune in to your aura and your energy," I explained. "I already got a good picture of yours when you came in, but I'll do it more consciously. After that, I'll ask you to tell me a bit about what's going on."

Rain nodded, appearing fascinated.

I did another scan of his aura. This time I got a glimpse of violet on his right side, which made sense. This side was all about what the person was calling into his or her future, and violet represented things like collective knowledge and wisdom, and also someone who could think globally. It fit with his profession.

"What's your chief complaint?" I asked.

He thought for a moment. "Family," he said finally.

I felt some sympathy for him, given my own struggles. I definitely got it. "Secondary?"

He flushed a little and mumbled something about a relationship that was sort of a relationship but not really and he needed to figure it out. Clearly he didn't want to talk about it, but it was fine—I didn't need my clients to talk to assess their needs.

"One second," I said, and got up to peruse my cases.

I was immediately drawn to Botswana agate, a beautiful bluish-gray stone. The antidepressant stone. After another moment of focus, rose quartz came up. A beautiful heart-chakra healing stone. Hematite for grounding. And finally, agate, to heal emotional trauma and transform negativity.

I collected the stones and brought them to Rain with a velvet pouch, presenting them with a flourish. "Your prescription."

"Cool." He reached out and touched the agate.

I explained each one to him and how to use it, then placed them in the bag. He accepted it gratefully.

"This is awesome. Really. Can I give you a hug?" I was too surprised to say no, so he did. "This means a lot. Thank you, Violet."

"Anytime." I watched as he turned to go, then slapped himself in the forehead.

"By the way. I didn't see any of my protest flyers here that I gave you yesterday. Would you be able to put some up?" He reached into his backpack and pulled out a stack. "I really want to make sure people know about the protest tomorrow. It's gonna be epic."

"Sure," I said, taking the flyers from him and glancing at them. I hadn't even paid attention to them yesterday.

Meet at Wildflower Park at 3 p.m. Wednesday to protest the UNETHICAL bridge project that will ruin North Harbor's environmental footprint for years to come!

Underneath was a picture of the current railroad bridge, along with a crude drawing of where the new bridge would go and what would be destroyed in the process, with more bold letters and arrows pointing to certain spots in or near the river. Childish at best, but it got the point across.

"I'll put some on the board and keep them at the counter. Is Sydney helping you distribute them?"

He narrowed his eyes, but not before I saw something dark pass through them. "Who?"

"Sydney. The woman you were with in the alley last night near the police station." I smiled pleasantly.

His expression changed to one of deep concentration. "The alley. Ah, yes. Nice girl. I heard about her tiny house and was hoping she could tell me more about it. I want to buy one in the next year or so. Great information." He saluted me. "Thanks for the awesome reading, and for your help with the protest. I hope to see you there."

And he turned and walked out the door.

CHAPTER 33

I watched him go, the contradicting lies bouncing around in my brain like one of those ping-pong-ball arcade games on steroids. Syd said she'd bumped into this guy on the street while she was on her way home from the paint party, and he'd needed directions. A party she hadn't even been at.

Rain said he'd been asking Syd about her tiny house. If that was true, it meant he knew her at least a little bit. Enough to know she operated her business out of a tiny house. Granted, it could just mean he'd heard about it from someone, or even gone to the door and met her while he was looking for protest-minded people.

But there seemed to be a lot of lies surrounding Syd's evening. Which reminded me that I'd been on my way to talk to her and had been derailed.

Luckily Josie was with another customer, so I didn't have to offer an excuse. I hurried out the door, pulling my hat out of my bag and tugging it over my hair. I had a different scarf on today, a turquoise one with silver threads shot through. It wasn't as fluffy as my pink one, but it would have to do. I pulled it around my face and cut through the alley to the back of my building, then crossed the street to Charlie's barbershop and the infamous parking lot.

Syd's "house" was there, parked as usual. I had to admit I had no interest in tiny homes—or owning any home for that matter, aside from my grandma's. I was plenty happy renting an apartment. But Syd's was adorable. It looked like a little tree house nestled in an urban jungle. The wood paneling was rustic enough to give you a sense of being at an upscale camp. She had star-shaped lights strung up around the roofline, and a sign in the shape of an old-fashioned dress fastened to the door that proclaimed you were about to enter *Yesterday*.

Inside was just as lovely. There was one long room when you stepped inside where she kept most of her clothes, and one room in the back reserved for accessories—shoes, scarves, jewelry. The small bedroom area was part dressing room and part specialty room, reserved for her vintage wedding dresses and evening gowns. Aside from a bathroom, a tiny section she'd curtained off for her office, and a tiny kitchen area that doubled as a play and nap space for Presley, that was the whole house. The experience was amplified by the tasteful decor. Syd had a knack for creating an old-time, classy vibe infused with eclectic, present-day touches that gave you the impression you were suspended delightfully between two worlds, and could choose the one into which you wanted to step, and stay.

I went up the front step and twisted the handle.

Locked. I knocked, wondering if she'd just closed to eat lunch or something, but only silence came from within.

What the heck? It was as much like Sydney to be closed during the day as it was like me to be. Unless Presley was still sick. But she hadn't mentioned that this morning. I pulled out my phone and fired off a text.

Where are you?

I pocketed my phone and went up to Charlie's door. When I got closer, I saw that he'd already seen me. In fact, he stood in the window and watched me.

I pushed the door open and stepped inside. "Hey, Charlie."

"Miss Violet," he said with a nod. "Need a haircut?" One side of his mouth lifted in a grizzled smile.

"No, thanks. I'm looking for Syd. Do you know where she is?"

He shook his head slowly. "Hasn't been to the shop today, not that I've seen."

"Really." She'd told me this morning she was on her way here. I looked back outside at the tiny house, but she hadn't magically appeared. "And you haven't talked to her?"

"Nope. She doesn't report in to me, usually."

"Do you know what time she closed up shop yesterday?" I asked.

Charlie thought. "Not really sure, to be honest. I know she was gone when I left. It was a slow day so I went over t' your boyfriend's place."

He'd been to the bar? "You did? Did you talk to Todd?"

He shook his head, but didn't elaborate.

"What time did you go over there?"

Charlie grabbed a broom that rested against the wall and began sweeping up some stray hair left over from a cut. "Dunno. Sometime around four, probably."

"You saw Todd?"

"Yup."

"Was he . . . alone?"

Charlie stared at me. "He was workin'. There were other people workin' too, so I guess he wasn't alone."

Not what I meant, but I let it go. "And Syd was already gone?"

"Think so."

"Did she mention she had plans last night?" I asked.

Charlie stopped sweeping and used his palms to anchor the broom handle, casually leaning on it. The door banged open, and a UPS guy came in, huffing a bit, and dropped a giant box. "Here you go, Mr. Klein. That's a heavy one. Want me to put it somewhere else?"

"Nah, leave it, young man. I'll get it," Charlie said.

The guy waved and left, letting the door bang again behind him.

Charlie shook his head. "So noisy. My ma woulda belted me if I let doors slam like that. Now. I'm not Miss Sydney's social director, Miss Violet. There something you want to be asking her instead of me?"

I flushed. "I guess. Once I find her."

"I'm sure she'll be around soon. You're welcome to wait," he said, shrugging. "Now. You done grillin' me so I can ask you something?"

"Sure."

"Who was that lady with you this mornin'? She was a looker." He nodded approvingly.

I took a deep breath, weighing my response. Finally I figured, what the heck? "That was my mother."

"Your mother?" Charlie's eyes almost popped out of his head. "Well, then, girlie, you have some good genes."

"Watch it, Charlie." I was in no mood to hear about how sexy my mother was. All Charlie needed to know was that he wasn't her type.

He held up his hands defensively. "Hey, you can't blame a guy for admiring the ladies. I've been widowed for a long time, but I'm not dead yet."

"I know, I know. Sorry," I said, remembering that he could be useful as far as information gathering went. I glanced around the barbershop. There was one other person working at the far end of the room, a guy nearly as old as Charlie. He and his client, a middle-aged guy getting a shave, were engrossed in conversation.

"She new to town?"

I nodded. "Just visiting." I hoped.

"Ah. Well, sorry to bring up the murder in front of her. She'll probably be wondering if this is a proper place for her little girl."

"Yeah. Speaking of . . . that, have you heard anything?" I asked.

Charlie shrugged. "Like what?"

"Like any progress on the investigation?"

"Now how would I know that, Miss Violet?" He laughed. "The cops aren't down here telling me anything."

"Come on, Charlie. You get around," I said.

"What, you think I'm a tip line or something?"

"No, but you hear everything in here," I said. "I know she had a reputation around town. People have to be talking about who would've gone as far as killing her?"

He studied me, those watery eyes sharp and alert. I got the sense that Charlie didn't miss a trick. "Why are you so interested, anyway?"

It was only a matter of time before people found out I'd been questioned. I was actually surprised Charlie hadn't heard yet. Or maybe he had, and wanted to see what I'd say. "The police are asking me questions. They think I did it."

He stared at me for a second then burst out laughing. "You? Are ya kidding?"

"No, but . . . why is that funny?"

He waved a hand as if I were a gnat flying around his head. "You're a good girl, Miss Violet. Everyone knows that."

"Not everyone," I said. My throat was choking with tears again.

"Eh." Charlie gave another wave of his hand. "They're just grasping. Not sure where to start. Why they didn't have that fella she works with down there straightaway I can't guess."

"Andrew?" I asked.

He nodded.

"They did question him. Natalie told me." This was the second time he'd mentioned Andrew. Did Charlie know something? "Why?" I prompted. "Other than the business-partner angle, of course. Did they not get along?"

Charlie thought before he answered, grizzled fingers playing with the strings on the apron he wore. "They tolerated each other because there was money to be made. But I heard there was trouble in paradise over there lately. Fights and the like."

"Over what?"

"Not sure, really," he said. "I get my information from my clients. Sometimes it's accurate, sometimes . . ." He tilted his hand from side to side. "But I'm sure the fighting part is true. I can't imagine having to spend any time around that one without wanting to kill her, whether ya could actually do it or not."

It was an interesting answer. I wondered if there was more to the Charlie/Carla disagreement than Syd's house in his parking lot. I decided to ask.

He was quiet for a moment, then he sighed. "Nah. Just don't like her politics and her idea that she was the only one knows what's good for this town." He puffed his chest out a bit. "We were here long before her and we'll be here long after her. In the end, she really didn't know what was best for any of us."

He bent down and hoisted up the box the UPS guy had left, seemingly effortlessly, and disappeared out back.

CHAPTER 34

Charlie's words played in my head as I stepped outside. I'd known from Syd he didn't love Carla, but his animosity toward her seemed to run deeper than a parking lot clash. I made a mental note to ask around. Although at this point I wasn't sure who to ask. I wondered if Charlie knew Rain too. I was dying to know the real story about this guy.

I tried Syd's shop door again in case she'd snuck in while I'd been occupied, but it was still locked. Frustrated, I turned to go. But when I walked around the side of the house, I remembered the back door, and how Sydney told me once that she left it unlocked during the day because she was terrible at remembering her keys when she ran out, and because it faced Charlie's shop, she didn't worry too much about people just walking in.

I went over and climbed the two steps, twisting the knob. It opened.

I looked around again to see if Charlie was watching me from his window, but I didn't see anyone. So much for Syd's theory there. I could just go in and wait for her.

I didn't really want to go back to the shop right now anyway. I had no idea what to say to Josie, and I didn't even think I wanted to talk about any of it at this point.

Decision made, I pushed the door open and poked my head in. "Syd?" I called.

Nothing.

I stepped inside. I was in the accessory room. This little house was actually really cute. I wandered through, enjoying being in there with no customers so I could get a feel for it. I tried to imagine Monty and me living in one, able to move around wherever we wanted. Although we'd need a truck or something to tow it, and I wouldn't have the first clue how to deal with that—and logistics like that didn't sound terribly appealing.

I went into the main room and browsed through some of the merchandise, eyeing an ornate gold necklace with a gorgeous turquoise stone in the center. I made a note to ask Syd about it—if it was authentic, where she'd found it. Then I went into the little space Syd used as her office and sank down into her chair. She wouldn't mind if I waited in here. I hoped. Plus, I needed some quiet time where no one knew how to find me.

I checked to see if she'd texted me back—she hadn't—and put my cell phone on do-not-disturb. I sat back in her desk chair, closing my eyes, willing my brain to sort out some of the information overload that had come in over the past fourteen or so hours. Had it really only been that long since my entire world flipped?

First, Carla's murder. That was my biggest problem right now, family drama aside. When I stopped and got really quiet, I still had a hard time reconciling the woman shouting at me in the café and the image of a lifeless body lying in a courtyard. I don't think I'd actually processed the fact that she was gone. And that someone had killed her. Strangled, I would venture to guess, even though the police didn't specifically say that. How else would my scarf have been so incriminating? I made a mental note to see if I could get confirmed information out of Gabe. It seemed like he was kind of on my side, anyway.

So I was an obvious person to home in on because we'd had such a public . . . discussion. But I had no doubts I was one of many who could be asked the question.

The cops had spoken to Andrew. Not surprising. They'd have wanted to know if Carla had been in the office most of the day, who she'd spoken to, who she had appointments with. Maybe there was someone she'd been showing properties to who had been angry with her about something. Like they hadn't gotten preapproved for enough money to buy the fancy house they wanted. Not that it would be her fault, but you never knew how crazy people could get when they wanted something. Especially if she'd promised it to them.

I wondered if Andrew would talk to me. He didn't know me that well, but he knew I was Nat's friend. Maybe I could go see him and position it as, *we both got questioned about this, we need to put our heads together and really think of some possibilities here*. Maybe Andrew would remember something else as the shock wore off. And he had to be just as invested as I was in finding out who killed his business partner.

Buoyed by the idea of action, I looked around for a piece of paper so I could write down the questions I wanted to ask Andrew. But Syd's desk was a heck of a lot neater than her apartment, and there wasn't much on her desk, aside from her monitor, keyboard, and a mouse sitting on a mouse pad with her shop logo on it. A mug holding some pens. A stack of mail, neatly sliced open in the same place with an opener. Whatever correspondence was in them had been tucked back neatly into the envelopes. A couple of pictures of Presley, one of her on a swing in the midst of its flight, her long blond hair flying behind her, the other of her hugging a big black dog.

There was also a planner. Maybe that would tell me where she was and when she was returning. I flipped it open, ignoring the guilty feeling tugging at my brain. I didn't usually snoop through my friend's things. But technically, I was just looking for a piece of paper and a sense of when she was coming back, since she hadn't answered my text. So I wasn't really *snooping*.

I opened the planner to today's page. The only notation was a diagonal scroll from twelve thirty to approximately two that said simply, *Lunch*.

I glanced at my phone. It was only one fifteen. I flipped to yesterday's page. Same notation, same amount of time. No way to know if she actually had a lunch meeting, or if she just noted the time as personal time. No other appointments yesterday. Like the paint party at Anna's that I now knew she hadn't gone to. Or a clandestine meeting with Rain.

Hissing out a frustrated sigh, I opened the top drawer of Syd's little desk. A jumble of paperclips, rubber bands, old receipts, pens. Now this was more like the Sydney I knew. Also, I didn't want to put my hand in there for fear something would bite me. Knowing Syd, it hadn't been cleaned out since, well, ever.

I went to the next, larger drawer. It was full of order slips, invoices, and other paperwork. Not much else that I could see, and I didn't want to go digging any more than I already was. I went to the other set of drawers—was it really this hard to find a Post-it note?—and opened the top drawer. It was filled with candy, almost to the brim. A virtual trick-or-treat drawer. Thinking of my own misplaced Lindt truffles, I scored a mini Milky Way bar, grabbed a small box of Milk Duds for later, and moved on.

The bottom drawer had, finally, a pad of paper. There was writing on the top couple of sheets. I pulled it out and flipped to an empty page, tearing it at the top-line perforation, then shoved the pad back into its place. I put the paper on the desk and reached for a pen. When I did, I inadvertently hit the mouse and the computer screen flickered and came to life.

I glanced at it, then did a double take.

It was Syd's Facebook page. Which was not strange—Syd was really into social media. I remembered her telling me recently about how she was using Instagram as her main platform for her business these days, and how I should be using it more. Instagram stories, specifically. And how Facebook was a necessary evil—people looked for your presence on there, even if it wasn't attracting the same followers as Instagram.

In any event, this looked like her personal page. Which wasn't enough on its own to catch my eye. We were friends on Facebook, so I saw her stuff all the time—photos of Presley, status updates about her meals, and posts about new items at her shop that she could cross-post on her business page.

It wasn't any of that catching my eye. It was the message that bloomed at the bottom of the screen that almost gave me a heart attack.

I told you to stay away from my family. If the cease and desist wasn't enough, I can go further. If you want to speak, I'll see you at five forty-five.

The sender was Carla Fernandez.

It had been sent yesterday at 4:13 p.m. Syd had read the message but hadn't responded. And she'd left it up, as if she'd left in a rush after receiving it. I remembered what Charlie said, that Syd hadn't been in yet today and that she'd left early yesterday. But I'd seen her twice since then. Last night, which was anything but normal, and this morning, when she'd seemed perfectly normal. Aside from the not-knowing-when-she'd-moved thing.

I stared at the words, willing them to make more sense in my brain. With a shaking hand, I scrolled up to see the rest of the thread. As if it weren't enough that they were communicating at all, I got another shock when I realized this had been going on for a couple of months. Short, cryptic messages on both sides, beginning back around Thanksgiving.

From Syd: *You have no right to treat me this way. What you're doing is unfair and probably against the law.*

From Carla, a few days later: *I'm telling you for your own good. Do not contact me again, or you'll regret it.*

Then a few weeks ago from Syd: *Hopefully this changes something. I'll wait for you to tell me when we can speak.*

The last one, before Carla's message yesterday. What was she hoping changed something? I scrolled back down to the bottom, reading the new message again. Syd hadn't answered her, but maybe that was on purpose. The police had specifically asked me where I'd been between five thirty and six. But it looked like Carla had another appointment during that time. And if they were checking Carla's social media feeds, it wouldn't be long before they found this message.

And if Syd had met her, it was right smack during the time when they seemed to think she'd been killed.

CHAPTER 35

This was crazy. My best friend wasn't a killer. This was some weird coincidence that they were supposed to meet. It was probably just a thing about her shop, and I was blowing it all out of proportion.

I checked my phone again. Sydney hadn't texted me back. I couldn't sit in here forever. Plus, I didn't want her to know I'd seen this until I could make some sense of it. I pulled my coat back on and hurried out the back door the way I'd come.

And almost ran right into Charlie, who was on his way up the steps.

He raised his eyebrows at me. "Miss Violet. I thought you left," he said.

"No, I . . . I was going to wait for Syd, but I haven't heard from her," I said, turning sideways so I could slip past him. "And I have to get back to my shop."

He nodded, still looking at me curiously. "She called and asked me to lock up for her. She won't be back today."

"Oh. Well then, it's good I'm leaving." I forced a smile. I didn't want to get into it with Charlie. "See you," I said, and fled out of the parking lot.

I turned the corner into the alley that would take me back to my street and stopped to lean against the building, letting my breath out in a whoosh. Why was Carla messaging Sydney? What family was she supposed to stay away from?

And where the heck *was* Sydney, anyway? I thought about going to her house and demanding answers, but thanks to my mother, I didn't even know where she lived at this point. I was out of luck. Which seemed to be my current state of existence.

Frustrated, I started back toward the shop. But I wasn't in the mood to go back, which wasn't like me at all. Usually there was no place I'd rather be. Today, to be in there pretending to hold the key to other people's problems—well, I felt like a fake. I didn't have a good handle on my own problems.

I pulled out my phone to text Josie and ask her to cancel my afternoon appointments and realized I had a voice mail. Todd. Finally. I felt a rush of relief and pressed play.

"Vi. Listen, I'm sorry about last night." His voice sounded distant, far away. "I didn't mean to upset you. And hey, is that really your mother? It's another crazy day at the bar, but maybe we can talk tonight." A pause, like he didn't know what to say. Then, "Call me later."

Not exactly what I wanted to hear. He hadn't said much of anything. Didn't even ask if I was okay, after everything that happened. I felt angry tears sting my eyes and furiously blinked them away. I'd be darned if I was going to cry over this. Over any of it. I had things to do. Like clear my name. And possibly Sydney's.

And I needed to start with Andrew Mann.

* * *

North Harbor Realty's office was located in one of the oldest buildings in town. It was also one of the most expensive buildings to lease, which I'm sure was the point. I texted Josie as I walked the short distance to the office, then put my phone away and stepped into the lobby, scanning the directory. Fourth floor. The only business listed.

I took the stairs.

The office encompassed the whole floor. The floors weren't huge, but there were two whole office spaces that they'd taken over. I went to the main door, hoping for signs of life. The frosted glass made it impossible to see inside. I pushed the door and it opened. I stepped in and looked around. Sell sheets of various expensive properties lined the waiting-area walls. I moved closer to take a look. A waterfront property in Roger's Field, which was a village within North Harbor, was listed for $1,595,000. Yikes. No wonder Carla was so serious about her work. Lots of money to be made. I wondered how they divvied it up, or if it all came strictly from their respective commissions.

I heard a low voice coming from down the hall, fixed with a lot of pauses. On the phone, perhaps. I couldn't tell if it was Andrew, and I had no idea if they had other staff. No one else was around.

I went into the little waiting area and perched on the edge of a chair, glancing down at the pile of reading material stacked on the gleaming wooden coffee table. A few newspapers, still in their wrappers, lay on top of some recent *People* and *Us Weekly* issues. I moved them aside to get to the magazines, but a photo facing me from one of the papers caught my eye. I bent closer to look at it.

It was me. In my shop, behind the counter, bending to retrieve a stone. The photo wasn't great quality—and not the most flattering angle—but it was obvious. And from the outfit, it looked like it had been taken . . . yesterday.

I ripped the plastic off the paper and unfolded it. The *Fairway Independent*. I'd never heard of it. The caption under the photo read, *Full Moon proprietor Violet Mooney selects crystals for a customer*.

There was a small article accompanying the photo. The headline: *Rise in fake psychic healers puts Fairway County officials on alert*.

What was this crap? I went to the story, but my eyes fell on the byline. My mouth dropped.

By Mazzy Witherspoon.

Seriously? Blood rushed to my face. This was why Mazzy was in my shop? To write nasty things about me and accuse me of being a storefront scammer psychic? So much for awakening her spiritual side.

I realized the voice down the hall had gone quiet. I shoved the paper in my tote bag and stood up, taking a couple steps down the hall.

"Hello?" I called out.

A second later, Andrew's head poked out of one of the offices. "Yes? Oh, hey, Violet." He stepped out, closing the door behind him, an inquisitive look on his face. I noticed the bags under his eyes, the hair that stood up in tufts as if he'd been running his fingers through it. He wasn't dressed like he was seeing clients either, if his faded jeans and flannel shirt were any indication. Maybe he'd come in just to get things in order. Whatever that meant. "What can I do for you?"

"I'm sorry to bother you. I know it's . . . a crazy time but I need to talk to you," I said. I wasn't sure how he was going to react to this impromptu interview. The only times we'd really interacted had been during one or another of Natalie's events. He'd always seemed a little aloof to me, but he could just not be good with crowds.

"Of course. What's up?" Then his eyes widened. "Is Natalie okay?"

"She's fine," I assured him. "At least I think so. I haven't seen her since earlier this morning."

Which reminded me. She was due to come back to the shop today, and I was probably not going to be there. Shoot.

He visibly relaxed. "Want some coffee? Water?" Without waiting for an answer, he moved toward a little kitchenette off the hallway.

"Water's fine," I said. "Thank you."

I watched him grab a mug and put a pod of coffee in a coffeemaker. He hit a couple of buttons, then leaned against the counter while the coffee brewed. I couldn't see what he was staring at, but my guess was the wall.

He came back with a bottle for me and a mug for himself and motioned to the chairs lining one of the walls. I sat in one, and he pulled another over so we were facing each other. He perched on the edge of his, holding his mug with both hands like a safety blanket. Not only did his eyes carry excess baggage, they were red-rimmed and a little puffy. "Sorry," he said. "I guess I'm a little jumpy after . . . everything. So what's going on?"

"I don't blame you," I said sympathetically. "How are you doing?"

Andrew jerked his left shoulder in a shrug. "Fine. I can't quite believe it yet. I'm just trying to make sure I take care of some of her clients who were close to buying." He motioned vaguely behind him toward the offices. "I don't know what else to do, really."

I nodded. "I get it. After my grandmother died I had no idea what to do. I still don't, some days."

His gaze fell to the floor, and he studied his boots.

I wasn't really sure how to start this conversation, so I decided to be straight. "Look. I'm sorry to barge in like

this, but I wanted to talk to you about Carla. You may
know that the police . . . have been talking to me. About
her death."

That got his attention. "You? Why on earth would they
be talking to you?"

"Because people saw us having words the morning she
died," I said.

Andrew thought about that, and one side of his mouth
lifted in a smile that wasn't quite amused. "If that's the
only reason, you're good. Carla has—had—words with a
lot of people. She didn't mean anything by it."

The heck she didn't. But being argumentative wasn't
going to get me anywhere. "Yeah, I took it at face value,"
I said. "But Nat said the cops came to talk to you too, and
I thought it might be, I don't know, helpful if we put our
heads together and thought about alternatives to give the
police." I paused, but he didn't say anything, just continued looking at me.

I waited.

Finally he said, "The cops weren't questioning me as a
suspect, Vi. They were asking me as the person who
probably spent the most time with her, all things considered."

"I didn't mean to suggest," I began, but he cut me off.

"I already gave them all her client lists and any other
people I could think of that could've had a problem with
her, from a business perspective. I didn't get involved in
her politics or any of that. Not my thing."

I shifted uncomfortably in my seat. I was far from an
expert interrogator, and I got the feeling this wasn't going
well. Plus I was getting a weird vibe in the room—a
heavy, dark cloud, depressive and hopeless, settling over
us. It felt suffocating. I knew the feeling. I'd been living
with it. Grief, strong and all-encompassing.

I focused on taking a few deep breaths. "Was she here all day yesterday?" I asked.

"She had appointments in the morning. We were here together for a bit in the afternoon, then I left around five. I promised Natalie I'd help her with some publicity for your healing circle."

"Thank you," I said.

He looked at me a little strangely.

"So did she mention having an appointment with anyone yesterday evening?" I asked, trying to sound casual.

"She didn't, but that didn't mean anything. We didn't keep tabs on each other." He kept his gaze steady on me. He hadn't taken a sip of his coffee yet. A muscle jumped near his eye. "Why are you asking all this? I've already been over this with the police. Are you working with them all of a sudden?"

I flushed. "No. Like I said, they questioned me pretty extensively. I feel like I need to think up some other options for them, in case they get too stuck on one thing. You know?"

"Ah. So you're being Nancy Drew."

I didn't like his tone. "I'm looking for an answer. That's all."

Andrew raked his hand through his hair, adding to the untidy tufts already standing straight up. "An answer," he repeated with a harsh chuckle. He stood, abruptly, coffee sloshing over the rim of his mug. "I'm afraid you're not going to find an answer here. Despite what people would have you believe, there were no problems in this office—not with money, not with clients, not with anything. We had—have—the best reputation in the county for placing people in high-end homes. And I'd really appreciate if you didn't start looking for trouble where there isn't any. This was either someone with a deep-seated grudge that had been festering, or truly a random act of violence. Let the police do their jobs, okay?"

I sprang to my feet, defensive. "I didn't mean—"

But he cut me off and went to the door, holding it open. "I have to get back to work," he said.

I grabbed my bag and stepped through the door, but paused on the threshold. "Andrew. I know you're as invested in this as I am. We should be helping each other," I tried again.

But he wasn't hearing me. "It's out of our hands, Violet."

And he closed the door. I had to jump back to avoid being hit with it.

CHAPTER 36

Well, that hadn't gone as planned. I leaned against the wall and rubbed my temples. Andrew definitely hadn't liked me asking questions. He was probably going to march straight home and tell Natalie all about how her friend had come snooping around, trying to find a scapegoat to save her own skin.

I wasn't making friends today, that was for sure.

I adjusted my hat back on my head and took the stairs down to the first floor. I was walking out just as Rain was walking in. How many times in one day was I going to see this guy?

Rain, however, brightened when he saw me, like I was an old pal he was delighted to bump into. "Hey, Violet! Got my crystals right here," he said, patting his pocket.

"Great," I said, trying to slip past him. I really wasn't in the mood to chat.

But he blocked my exit. "You here for the nail salon?" he asked, nodding at the directory on the wall behind me.

"What?" I glanced behind me. I didn't even know what else was in this building. But there was a salon on the second floor. "Yeah," I lied, shoving my hands in my pockets so he couldn't see my clearly-in-need-of-help nails. "You?"

"Just running some errands. So I'll see you tomorrow, right?" he asked.

"Yep. Can't wait," I said.

He grinned and pointed his two index fingers at me, thumbs up, like he was aiming a gun. "I knew I could count on you." He hit the button for the elevator. The door opened immediately. He winked at me as it slid closed behind him.

I watched the button light up above the elevator as it rose, stopping on the fourth floor.

At North Harbor Realty.

I swallowed hard. Why was Rain going there? He didn't look like he was in the market for a million-dollar house. Yet he had been talking to Andrew this morning at the Bean, so they had to be acquainted somehow. But if it wasn't related to the bridge—which Natalie hadn't seemed to think Andrew had cared that much about—then what?

I thought about going back up, but figured Andrew would throw me out this time. But what if he was in danger? This guy had, for all intents and purposes, appeared out of nowhere. The environmentalist thing could all be an act. Maybe he was some crazed killer who went after wealthy or well-off people or something. Andrew wasn't wealthy, but he might not know that.

I couldn't live with myself if someone else died.

Decision made, I found the stairwell door and climbed the four flights. I paused before opening the door, listening hard. Silence. I pushed the door open a crack and peered out. I had a clear view of the office door. No one was visible. I slipped out of the stairwell and approached the door. Taking a deep breath, I pulled it open as quietly as I could. Thankfully there was no bell or buzzer when someone came in here, unless there was a silent one that rang in the offices.

I could hear voices down the hall. It sounded like the office door was closed, though. Rain was talking—I'd gotten to know his voice after today—but even with the volume he used, the words were muffled. I crept as close as I dared, staying against the wall, and tried to hear.

Unfortunately, I only caught every few words. But the ones I did hear were worrying. *Financial mess* particularly. And *cops will want to see . . . records.*

I strained my ears to try to catch more, but Andrew was soft-spoken, so whatever he was saying in return was lost on me. But I couldn't wrap my head around why Rain was here having any kind of conversation with Andrew about financials. I guess Nat was right, and whatever they were talking about wasn't bridge related. Maybe they had some other business deal going that was separate from any of this? But then why would the cops want to see anything?

I was startled out of my thoughts when the office door flew open. Without thinking, I jumped through the nearest door, which happened to be the bathroom. I stood behind the slightly ajar door, holding my breath and praying that no one needed to go before they left.

Luckily, the footsteps went straight past my hiding place. A second later, I heard the front door open, then whoosh closed. I stayed put, listening for any sound.

More footsteps, then the sound of running water. Andrew was getting more coffee, by the sounds of it. Hopefully he hadn't drunk enough that he needed to use the bathroom. I waited what seemed like the longest five minutes ever until I heard footsteps retreating, then a door down the hall softly closing. I waited another fifteen seconds, then peered around the corner.

All clear.

I stepped out of the bathroom and crept down the hall, letting myself out as quietly as possible. I took the stairs again, hoping I'd given Rain enough lead time. The lobby was empty when I exited the stairwell. I wasted no time hurrying outside.

Back out in the cold, it occurred to me that I could've tried that whole teleporting thing again to get me out of the bathroom once it became clear I'd heard everything I was going to hear. I wondered if it would've worked if I was actually counting on it.

I ducked into the parking lot next door and reached into my bag for my phone. It was still on do-not-disturb, so I hoped Syd had texted back and I'd missed it. But when I checked messages, still nothing. I shoved the phone back in my bag and as I did so, I remembered the newspaper I'd also stuffed in there. I yanked it out, stopping in the doorway of the next building to flip open the paper.

I almost blew right past the above-the-fold article, since it had to do with Carla's death. But I caught the words *possible financial troubles* and *alleged unethical business practices* and that slowed me down. I thought of Rain's words—*financial mess*. I went back to the beginning and read.

The infamous Mazzy had written this article too. North Harbor must be her beat. It was vague—and not well written, in my humble opinion—but it hinted at trouble within the realty office. The article outlined Carla and Andrew's business and the types of homes they sold, pretty much parroting the literature I'd seen at the office. But then it mentioned a "source" who tipped this reporter off to potential financial distress within the company. She didn't draw a conclusion to anything, or mention specifically what type of distress, but the intimation was clear—

that something going on at the office had led to her death. The final paragraph told me Andrew Mann had been unavailable for comment and police were still investigating.

A grainy photo of the courtyard area surrounded by crime scene tape accompanied the article.

I pondered this mysterious source. Carla's soon-to-be ex-husband? Charlie said he was out of the country, but maybe he'd returned. He had to be her next of kin. But in my heart I knew the answer. This had something to do with Rain. But I just couldn't seem to make the pieces fit.

I flipped the paper and skimmed through the other article, which appeared below the fold—not as big news as Carla, but big enough to make the front page—and felt my blood pressure go up almost instantaneously, forgetting about Carla for the moment.

It was a load of garbage, and pretty badly written too. *The Fairfield Independent* must be so small and desperate its editors didn't seem to care if their reporters were actually qualified. The article claimed that storefront psychics and people claiming to be all sorts of healers were popping up in droves all over the county, and scamming desperate people out of their money. Officials from the various towns were coming together in an attempt to crack down on the practices, Mazzy claimed, with hopes of driving these fraudulent businesses somewhere else— or out of business entirely. One of the names sounded familiar to me. I racked my brain and then realized: Lilia Myers. The psychic Carissa Feather had mentioned.

There was even a way-out-of-context quote from me, from when Mazzy had asked me if crystals really worked, or something like that. I'd explained the crystals had incredible energies and promoted great healing, but people had to do their own work too.

She'd quoted me as saying, "They're nice, but people

have to fix themselves." So this is what that other reporter lurking outside my door had meant when she said
I'd spoken to other media.

By the time I finished reading it, I was so hot I forgot I
was standing outside in thirty-degree weather. I read it
again, then noted the small text in italics under the story:
Mazzy Witherspoon can be reached at . . . and it gave a
phone number and email address.

Before I flew completely off the handle, I forced myself to stop and think. I wanted to ream her out for this
hideous piece of tabloid journalism, but I also wanted to
know who her source was for the Carla article. There had
to be some sort of trade-off I could offer. Or maybe I'd
just threaten to sue her for slander, or libel. I wasn't exactly sure which but figured one of them would fit. This
could be a direct hit to my reputation, if anyone actually
read this garbage.

I guessed the direction I took would depend on how
open she was to a conversation. She'd probably be on the
defensive if I identified myself, just given the content of
the article, so I decided to try a different tack to ensure I
got a response.

I pulled out my phone and dialed the number at the
bottom of the article.

She answered on the third ring. "Mazzy Witherspoon."
Her voice was distant, as if the speaker was too far from
her mouth, and there was a lot of background noise.

"Yes, I'm calling about your recent story in the *Fairway Independent*," I said, trying to send my voice up a
couple of notches. We'd only spoken once, so she likely
wouldn't recognize it anyway, but why take the chance?

"Yes," she said, her voice warming slightly. "How can
I help you?"

"I have a tip on another one of these terrible fraudulent
people," I said, working some distress into my voice. "I

just handed over my grocery money for the week and I'm devastated."

"What is the business, ma'am?" she asked. I could hear pages rustling, as if she were looking for a clean sheet in her notebook.

I hated being called *ma'am*. "I'd rather not say over the phone. If you'd like to meet me I can give you more details. Better yet, I can point the place out," I said.

"Sweet," Mazzy said. "Where?"

I gave her the name of a diner on the outskirts of town—a place I hardly ever went. I didn't want to bump into a million people I knew. "Twenty minutes okay?"

She started to protest, then changed her mind. "Sure. Yes. I'll be there."

I disconnected, satisfied with my performance. Now Mazzy and I could have a real heart-to-heart.

CHAPTER 37

I cut through the alley to my car and slipped into it, cranking the heat. While I waited for it to warm up, I thought of texting Josie to tell her what I was up to. Then changed my mind. I didn't feel like reporting in to anyone today. I was probably being childish, and deep down I knew Josie had been only a bystander to whatever family drama had played out all those years ago, but still. She'd kept this from me for so long, and it hurt.

I tried Todd again. Voice mail. I gritted my teeth and waited for the beep. "Got your message. I think we need to talk," I said. "When are you done at work? Oh, and I'm fine, thanks for asking. I haven't been arrested. Yet." I ended the call and tossed my phone into my console. Then I pulled out of my parking space and headed to the diner.

Seven Points Diner's biggest selling point was its '50s-throwback persona. The building itself was built to look

like the silver car-like diners of that time frame, and there
was so much food on the menu I wondered how any kind
of cook could wrap his or her head around it. Or make
any of it really good.

I made it there in seven minutes and commandeered a
booth right near the front. After nineteen minutes, a beat-
up silver Volkswagen Jetta zipped into the lot, parking
haphazardly in two spots. Mazzy emerged almost before
the car stopped and rushed inside, glancing at her watch.
Her multicolored hair was in desperate need of some hair-
spray to tame down the static. She wore jeans, a North
Face jacket, and a pair of black leather motorcycle boots
I found myself admiring until I remembered who was
wearing them. I wondered what kind of fiction she'd
been in the middle of creating when I summoned her
away.

I watched her eyes do a quick scan of the diner, then
land on me the moment the front door slammed behind
her. I pasted on a sweet smile and waved gaily. I had for-
mulated a plan on the way over, so I was ready.

She wasn't. Score one for me.

Eyes narrowed, she skulked into the diner and poured
herself into the seat opposite me. She didn't entirely look
human as she did so. The thought flitted through my mind,
uninvited, and I tried to brush it away. But I couldn't stop
thinking about the image—or lack thereof—I'd seen in the
mirror when she was in my shop. She reminded me of
some kind of giant snake, slithering around. I shivered in-
voluntarily.

"Are you my anonymous tip?" she asked with a sneer.

I nodded. "Sure am. What gives, Mazzy? What are
you up to? Did Carla Fernandez put you up to this?"

Mazzy threw back her head and laughed. It was a
booming sound that didn't seem like it could even come

from someone as small as her. "You're blaming a dead woman?" she asked when she got hold of herself. "That's awesome. No, I'm just reporting."

"I guess you could call it that," I mused. "When you work for a tabloid, you have to dress it up somehow. But, I might be able to be convinced not to sue you or your paper for libel." *Libel: a written or published defamatory statement.* I'd looked it up when I'd arrived to make sure I had the right term.

Mazzy frowned, shifting around in her seat. I could see the wheels turning in her head. If I was right, she was ambitious enough to want a job at a serious paper. Even the threat of a lawsuit like that could be a career killer, especially for a young reporter who had no proven track record.

At least I hoped that was how it worked.

"You have no grounds," she said, but she sounded less certain now.

"I think I do," I said. "I've already spoken to my lawyer." A white lie, but it did the trick. "You took my quote out of context, you weren't forthcoming about why you were in my shop, and this could hurt my reputation." I could see the waitress approach from the corner of my eye and shot her a look that said, *Don't even think about it.* She backed away.

I could see Mazzy calculating all her options before she folded her arms across her chest. "What do you want?"

"I want to know who tipped you off to the financial troubles at Carla's real estate practice."

Her eyes widened. "I can't give up a source."

I shrugged. "Okay. I'll call my lawyer, then." I grabbed my bag and started to slide out of the booth.

She muttered something that sounded like a curse. "Wait!"

I paused and looked back at her expectantly.

"Are you gonna tell where you got his name?"

His. I sat back in the booth. "Nope."

"How do I know that?"

"Guess you'll just have to trust me," I said with a wink.

She hated me. It was written all over her face. The feeling was kind of mutual. I could see her waging one more internal battle in her head, which she subsequently lost. With a giant sigh, she admitted defeat. "It was that guy. The environmentalist, Rain. No last name, at least that he'd given me."

So I was right. Not that it made me feel much better. It just opened up more questions. "Did he say what his connection was?"

"He said he was a 'family insider.'" She shrugged. "It worked for me. He said he could get me proof in a few days so I could write a follow-up."

This was getting weirder and weirder. I stood. "Thanks, Mazzy. One more thing."

Her jaw set, but she waited.

"You're going to print a retraction. At least about me and my store."

"No way," she started, but I waved my phone at her.

She cursed again under her breath. "Fine. Whatever."

"And you'll print my real quote? I'm happy to repeat it for you. Or maybe I should email it to you," I decided. "Just to alleviate any room for error."

"Sure. Whatever. Email it. Are we done here?"

"We're done. A pleasure doing business with you. Oh, and do me a favor? Don't ever come to my store again."

CHAPTER 38

I took great pleasure in strolling to my car, taking my time, upper hand played. Little twit. But forget her. What she'd told me, on the other hand, was sobering enough to take away some of my satisfaction. I got in and cranked the heat, thinking about what I'd learned. Or rather, what new questions were in front of me.

All of this kept coming back to Rain—some scruffy guy who wore weird hats to make his point, who seemed to love the planet more than people. Who'd shown up in town out of nowhere and claimed to have family ties to Carla, enough to know about her financials. But if he had family ties with her, wouldn't he be worried more about her death than the railroad bridge? It made no sense.

To make it more complicated, Sydney had fibbed about her conversation with him—I knew she had in my gut. And Sydney had been communicating with Carla, her sworn enemy, via Facebook message. And Andrew Mann knew him, well enough to invite him into the office.

I needed to know who this guy was. Obviously his

name wasn't really Rain. But I didn't have a lot to go on otherwise. So what kind of family ties could he have with Carla? Charlie mentioned she was getting divorced. She couldn't be seeing this guy, could she? He had to be half her age. I didn't know how old Carla was, but old enough that this guy could be her son.

Her son.

I sat straight up with a small squeal. Was Rain Carla's son? Did Carla have a son? Carla was of Latino descent, but I'd never seen her husband. Rain was light skinned, but he could very well be of mixed race. I fished my phone out of my bag, shutting off DND, and checked my messages. No reply from Sydney. Josie, however, had texted me, wondering when I was returning. She wanted to talk more. I didn't.

I opened my browser and Googled "Carla Fernandez North Harbor CT family" and searched images.

The only recent pictures were of her alone, in various settings including on the council bench. But there was a picture from three years ago of her at some gala event, all dolled up in an evening gown, laughing. I enlarged the photo and studied it. Her hair was down, and it was long and straight. She'd been a pretty woman when she wasn't being nasty. It really was too bad.

Shoving away the melancholy, I shifted my focus to her husband, breaking into a smile. A blond guy, identified as Thomas Grella. Bingo. She hadn't taken his name, but I could see why. Carla Grella didn't have the best ring to it, especially for a politician. I scrolled the rest of the images, but there were none of Carla, her husband, and a son. I tried another Google search, this time looking for "Carla Fernandez North Harbor CT son" and waited for results to load.

I checked images first. A lot of solo images of Carla again. I scrolled through, past pictures of her alone, pic-

tures of other Carla Fernandezes, and found nothing. I
checked the other results. A lot of unrelated items for the
first bunch of pages. I almost gave up—I wasn't known
for my patience—but then on page nine, I hit the jackpot.

A short blurb from the *North Harbor Day* from seven
years ago that read:

> *Miguel Fernandez, son of esteemed councilwoman
> and local business mogul Carla Fernandez, has been
> arrested in Boston, Mass., for disturbing the peace
> and assault. Fernandez was picked up outside of the
> Bijou Nightclub, where he was reportedly having an
> altercation with another man. He's currently held on
> $50,000 bail.*

Miguel Fernandez. No kidding. I wish there'd been a
photo accompanying the article so I could see if I was
right. But my gut was telling me I was on to something
here. Now all I had to do was prove it.

And if Rain was Miguel Fernandez, therefore meaning
he was Carla's son, he definitely didn't seem that broken
up about her death. Which was pretty suspicious in and of
itself.

Maybe I could talk to him at the protest tomorrow and
see if I could get him to confess his real identity. If he
wasn't chaining himself to the side of the railroad bridge
for the next forty days. But first, I needed to see if anyone
knew about this guy. If he'd grown up here, people had
to. And what about the police?

I needed to talk to Gabe. He at least didn't think I did
it. Maybe he'd listen to my theory.

But when I got to the police station, I lost my nerve. I
didn't really want to go back in there. I reached for my
phone and dialed the non-emergency number.

"North Harbor PD," a guy's voice barked.

"Yes, hello. I'm looking for Sergeant Merlino."

"One minute." He put me on hold.

I held my breath, hoping Gabe was there. A minute later, he picked up. "Merlino."

"Gabe. It's Violet Mooney."

"Vi, hey. What's going on?"

"Do you have a few minutes?" I asked.

"Sure I do. Where are you?"

"Outside, but I don't want to come in."

A pause, then, "Okay, I'll meet you at Pete's in ten."

I parked my car back in my lot and walked down to Pete's. Pete wasn't behind the counter. He may have left for the day, since he got in so early. And the place wasn't busy, which suited me just fine. I found a table in the back, avoiding the one Fiona had taken over this morning, and pulled out the Milk Duds I'd scored earlier. I was starving.

Gabe slid in opposite me a few minutes later. "Coffee?" he asked, jerking a thumb at the counter.

I shook my head.

"Be right back." He went to the counter and returned with a small black coffee. "Okay. What's going on?"

I cut right to the chase. "Does Carla Fernandez have a son?"

He nodded slowly, but said nothing.

"Is it Rain?"

Now Gabe grinned. "How'd you figure that out, Vi? You want a job?"

I sat back, satisfied with myself, but more concerned about what that meant. "Are you guys looking at him? I mean, for someone who just lost his mother . . ."

"Whoa, hold on." Gabe held up a hand. "I don't know a lot about that family, but some of the guys on the force have been around a while. They remember the kid when he was younger, before Carla banished him out of state. Said he'd given her a lot of trouble, and they became estranged when he left."

"For Boston?"

"No idea."

"He got arrested there seven years ago," I added.

He raised his eyebrows, impressed.

"Don't be," I said. "It was a fairly easy Google search. But why are they questioning me when he suddenly shows up in town and she ends up dead? Especially if they didn't get along and the fact that she's dead seems to not even be a blip on his radar?"

"Vi. You know I can't give you details about the case. But trust me when I say, they are pursuing everyone they think deserves pursuing."

I sat back and let my gaze drift around the café. No one seemed to be paying attention to our conversation, and no one was sitting close enough to hear us. "None of the reporters have figured this out yet?"

Gabe shrugged. "Guess not. And it's not up to us to reveal his identity. At this point. As long as he cooperates."

"Is he dangerous?" I asked.

Gabe frowned. "I don't honestly know. He seems to be all about peace, love, and tackling climate change, but I haven't spent any time with him."

"Sydney has." I hadn't known I was going to say it until it came out, and then I realized that was why I was worried. If this guy was dangerous and Syd was affiliated with him in some way, enough that she was lying to me about it, then what if he was a danger to her? Those messages with Carla made a bit more sense now—at least the part about leaving her family alone.

Which meant Syd knew Rain before he'd shown up in town a couple of weeks ago, and Carla knew it.

"What do you mean? How do you know that?" Gabe asked.

"I saw them in the alley the other night. Next to the police station, after I left. When I asked her about it, she brushed it off, saying he stopped her for directions. I felt like she was lying but had no idea why." I leaned forward. "Can you help me make sure she's okay?" I didn't mention the Facebook messages. I wasn't about to tell the police anything that would make them suspect my best friend had killed Carla.

Although the timing of that meeting troubled me. But if they had seized Carla's computer or other device, chances were good they'd seen the message anyway.

Gabe looked troubled too as he thought about what I'd said. Finally he nodded. "Let me see what I can do."

"Thanks," I said, relieved. "You'll let me know?"

"Yeah."

"Hey, one more thing," I said.

He waited.

"This might sound odd too, but . . . Charlie?"

"What about him?"

"What's his deal? I know he can't stand Carla," I said. "And I'm starting to worry that everyone I care about are the biggest suspects in this thing, myself included."

"Wait. You think *Charlie* killed her?"

"I don't know." I filled him in on the cease and desist Carla had thrown at Syd. I was willing to bet Charlie had gotten a similar one, since it was his property. "And when I talked to him after, he just . . . well, there was really no love lost there."

Gabe was silent for a few minutes. Then he said, "Did you know Charlie was in Vietnam?"

I shook my head.

"He was. He and his best friend, a guy named Eddie

Mathers. Eddie had a market here in North Harbor all his life. Real old-school market. People loved it."

I waited. I could sense there wasn't a good ending to this story.

"Eddie rented his shop. From the town. And when certain . . . people decided they wanted to make this town more high-end, they started raising rates on all the properties they owned, hoping to drive out some of the old-timers."

"And Eddie got driven out," I guessed.

Gabe nodded. "My dad knew Eddie well from being on the force here most of his life. I remember he was really upset about it. That market was the whole reason Eddie had held it together after the war, and once his wife died it was all he had left. And it got ripped out from under him."

"What happened to him?" I asked.

"He moved to Florida. And then killed himself less than a year later."

I gasped. I wasn't expecting that.

Gabe nodded. "Charlie never got over it. It happened about five years ago, right around now, actually. So yeah, he has no love lost for Carla. Would you?"

"I wouldn't," I murmured.

"Now. All that said, I don't think Charlie has the strength to do anything like that."

I perked up. "Like what?"

"Like strangling . . . shoot. You cannot repeat that," he said, pointing at me.

I stared at him. "Strangled? Like with my scarf?" My hand was on my throat. Guess my powers of deduction had been right.

Gabe didn't answer, but I could read his face. I was right. She'd been strangled with my scarf.

"Don't worry, Vi. We're going to get it solved. Okay?" He rose to go. "Hey, by the way. That girl. Your sister?"

Uh-oh. What had Zoe done? She hadn't cast a spell on anyone, had she? "What about her?" I asked warily.

"She sticking around? With your mum?"

It took me a second, but then I had to laugh. Gabe thought my sister was hot. Little did he know.

"Yeah," I said. "I think she's sticking around for a bit. I'll introduce you next time I have the opportunity."

Gabe grinned. "Thanks." He grabbed his coffee and left the café.

I thought about what he said. I liked Charlie too. I definitely didn't want to think of him as a murderer. And that story was definitely super sad. But Gabe was wrong about one thing, though. The way I'd seen Charlie haul that UPS box around, he had a lot more strength than it appeared on the surface.

CHAPTER 39

Wednesday dawned sunny but freezing. The sort of day that made you think you wanted to venture outside, but once you got there you found you'd been sadly mistaken. But today, we had no choice.

It was protest day.

And I guessed it was going to be a doozy of an event, especially given the climate around town. The people who were for the bridge project had started making claims that Carla had been killed over it, and even more finger-pointing was occurring. The cops had held a press conference again last night with a tight-lipped mayor standing next to them, who was clearly unhappy about all this press and the lack of resolution. The cops didn't say much aside from the fact that they were tracking down every possible lead and promising that the case was their first priority.

Despite that, there'd been a story on the news right after the press conference—the woman reporter outside my shop yesterday had reported on it—going into great detail about the project, recapping which town official had been on which side, and playing sound bites of some of Carla's very best comments. It gave me a jolt to see her alive and well, with her biting tone and sure-footed demeanor. The reporter had been live at the park where the protest would be held. I couldn't help but wonder if the same cameraman had filmed the piece. If he'd gotten a new camera yet, or if he'd been sidelined by the . . . accident.

While I supposed anything could be true about Carla's murder, I wondered about this motive. Carla had been "for it" in the way a politician was for something that would appease his or her main supporters who were for it. I'd never gotten the sense that she felt overly strongly about this bridge. No, I definitely thought she cared more about which shops were allowed to grace our downtown, and whether or not séances were being conducted, rather than how we addressed an old railroad bridge. But of course people would be watching for her position, so she had to say something.

But for the life of me, I couldn't figure out who else was a viable suspect. The people on my list were: Sydney, Charlie, Andrew. And now Rain, given his identity. I couldn't bear to think it was Syd—any of them, really, except Rain—but that meeting time haunted me. As well as why she was trying to make contact with Carla.

But Andrew? Natalie would be devastated. And probably in financial trouble. I couldn't bear to think of that either. And Charlie, with the tragedies he'd lived through. His daughter. His wife. His best friend.

I hated to think of any of it.

I got out of bed and pulled a hoodie on over my jammies. I loved my building but it was drafty in the winter. We needed new windows. I looked around for Monty and saw him in his tree, tail swishing as he watched some action outside. No sign of the black cat. No sound from across the hall.

I'd avoided Fiona yesterday, after my conversation with Josie. I was still trying to process everything Josie had told me. And also decide how I felt about her knowing all this and never telling me. Nothing. Not even a hint, not when I'd poured my heart out to her about my mother and how I'd felt knowing she'd walked away from me so young.

How do you keep a secret like that?

Anyway, I knew I couldn't avoid Fiona for long, but I wanted to process some of this a bit more first. Although she'd likely show up at the protest.

Heck, maybe she could melt the snow so we could get around better.

But before all that, I had to spend some time at my shop. My business was taking a beating this week, and I couldn't continue to not pay attention. Instead of canceling them, Josie had handled two of my consults yesterday and I was grateful, but I would rather have been in the right mind-set to do them myself. I resolved to do better today.

I went to the kitchen to make coffee. And stopped, my mouth dropping open.

My entire kitchen counter was covered in breakfast. Like, real breakfast. Steaming eggs with spinach and a side of sliced avocado. A plate of smoked salmon. Buttered toast. A pot of coffee. A pitcher of green juice.

Still gaping, I inched closer and caught a movement out of the corner of my eye. I turned and nearly jumped a foot when I saw Zoe sitting at my little table. She wore a long black sweatshirt dress with a tangle of scarves wound around her neck. Today, her Converse sneakers were green. She grinned and waved a piece of toast at me.

"Morning," she said, around a mouthful. "I thought you might be hungry. Took a guess at what you liked." She shrugged. "Whaddaya think?"

"What do I think?" I sank into the other chair. "Where did you get all this? And how did you get it in here without my hearing you?" Unfortunately, I thought I already knew the answer.

"I just whipped it up," she said with a wink. "Help yourself."

It did smell good, I had to give her that. I rose to get a plate, but Zoe sighed and held up a hand. With a snap of her fingers, a full plate appeared in front of me. She observed her work and nodded approvingly. "Getting better," she said, more to herself than me. "Coffee is tricky. I usually spill it. Want to try?"

"Uh—"

"Oh, just give it a go," she said impatiently. "Stop treating these powers like they're a burden. Trust me, it's freakin' *fun*."

I knew she wouldn't let up, so I closed my eyes and concentrated on envisioning a full mug of hot coffee in front of me, much like I'd thought about the reporter's camera falling and breaking.

I opened my eyes when I heard Zoe gasp. "Wow. First try? And you did that well? I'm impressed." She nodded.

I gazed at the perfectly full mug of coffee and felt a stab of pride. I looked at her. "Want one?"

She nodded. I did it again, delivering her a mug. She lifted it and touched it to mine. "Cheers, sis."

The word sobered me, and my gaze dropped to my plate. I was starving, but I felt like a major blockage sat between my mouth and my stomach.

"I take it you aren't thrilled that Fiona and I . . . dropped in this way," Zoe said after taking a sip.

I shifted uncomfortably in my seat. "It's not that. I'm

surprised, is all. Did Fiona send you over here this morning?"

She shook her head. "She actually said to let you be. That you'd come to us when you were ready."

"Then why did she relocate my best friend and move in across the hall?" I demanded.

"Because she wanted to keep an eye on you. And she wanted to help," Zoe added, not acknowledging the anger I knew had come through in my voice. "Like taking away your chocolates."

I stared at her. "She did that?"

Zoe nodded. "Chocolate weakens your powers. It's forbidden in our world."

"You're kidding." *One more reason to stay out of that world,* I thought. "Todd brings me chocolates all the time."

Zoe's eyes narrowed at that. Then, "She thinks this murder thing could be serious, Violet."

"No kidding," I said, unable to keep the sarcasm away. "I think if anyone is accused of murder you can deduce that it's serious."

"It's not just that," Zoe said, shaking her head. "She's worried that there's more to your grandmother's death. I know you don't want to hear that. I'm just telling you what I've heard."

"What does that even mean?" I asked, exhausted again. "As much as I don't want to admit it, Grandma Abby died of old age. I never thought she could either, for different reasons obviously, but I guess that's not realistic, right?"

Zoe pressed her lips together. "From what I hear, that's not exactly true."

"What's not?"

"That she died of old age. She wasn't really supposed to."

I stared at her. "You've lost me."

"Look. I don't know the details, but it's been on Mother's mind. And she's worried about you."

"She's worried about my grandmother dying too young? She didn't even like her."

"It's the way she died," Zoe corrected. "Like I said. You'll have to ask her about that. I'm not really sure how it works."

This was a bit much for me. My head was doing that spinning thing again. To take my mind off it, I ate some avocado.

Zoe ate some eggs. "Look. I get that we disrupted your life and all that. And that you really don't know what to believe about Mother. But I gotta tell you, a day didn't go by that I can remember when she didn't mention you."

I took a sip of my coffee, trying for cool, but my hand trembled. "Really?"

Zoe nodded. "I have no idea what happened with your grandmother, or any of that, but she never forgave her for keeping you two apart."

I poked at my avocado with my fork. "If she's such a powerful witch, why didn't she just override the spell, or whatever witches do?"

"I see you need a crash course in witch etiquette," Zoe said with a giggle. "You can't just override certain things, especially things like whatever they had going on. Or I suppose you could, but it would cause a war. Especially between those two. It went way deeper than just the two of them. And they had to work together on the council."

"So let me get this straight." I put my fork down and looked at Zoe. "Fiona is a super powerful witch, but another equally powerful witch—"

"Actually, Abigail was more powerful," Zoe interrupted. "Mother doesn't like to admit that, but it's true. I mean, she was a lot older. Mother knew it too. It's what made it so hard when she had to see her all the time."

"She saw her all the time?" I shook my head, trying to keep up. It seemed so insane that Fiona saw my grandmother regularly, but Grandma Abby never spoke about it to me. It was like she had this whole other life I knew nothing about. "Okay. So a powerful witch who she used to be related to put a spell on her to stop her from finding me."

"Related to by marriage," Zoe corrected. "And the spell was really just on the necklace. Which was on you. So it was more about you than her. Sorry." She winced. "Go on. Ask me whatever you want."

"What's this council?"

"They both have seats on the Magickal Council. The kind of seats that you come by because you're part of a long line of witches in special families." She gestured to the plate of eggs. "Are you gonna have some? It's getting cold."

I took a bite of eggs and salmon, barely tasting it. "So they both sat on this council and never fought it out about me?"

Zoe shook her head slowly. "Forbidden topic. It's like the whole elder thing, you know? And Mother can be volatile, but she understood that if she started a feud with the Moonstones, the results would reach way beyond her family problems. I heard Grandmother—our other grandmother, Fiona's mom—talking to her about it many times. Warning her, in fact."

My other grandmother. That thought hadn't even crossed my mind yet. I had a whole other branch of family, of whom I had no real concept. I wondered what my other grandmother looked like. All I could picture was Endora, Samantha's eccentric mother in the classic TV show *Bewitched*, and I started to giggle.

Zoe stared at me. "What the heck is so funny?"

That made me laugh even harder, and soon I was snorting, tears running down my face as I contemplated how my life had ended up at this moment, and if there were any spells I could learn to go back a few days and create a whole different story.

Zoe waited until my apparent fit was over before she spoke again. "I know it all sounds a little nuts," she admitted. "But Vi. It's all true. And I've never seen Mother as happy as the moment she knew the spell over you had been broken."

CHAPTER 40

After Zoe left, I showered, got dressed, fed Monty, and headed out to my store. I didn't know if I felt better or worse after Zoe's visit and our talk. I certainly didn't want to think about what she'd said, about there being more to Grandma Abby's death. I had to put that aside for the time being.

I needed to focus on my work, at least for a little while—until it was time for the protest. I wondered if Gabe had tracked Syd down. Or if she would show up at the protest, or at Pete's this morning. I hoped Presley was okay and that wasn't the reason for her radio silence. But it wasn't like her to drop off the face of the earth.

The first time I met Syd, it was at Pete's right after she showed up in town two years ago. We were both waiting for our coffees, and she'd casually asked me where people went dancing around here. Of course I had no good answer for her because I didn't dance and had no clue, but somehow we'd struck up a conversation anyway. Despite our differing priorities (me—yoga, Syd—food) and different opinions about all things woo-woo, we had become good friends.

But when I really thought about it, I knew next to nothing about Syd. She'd told me she used to live in Chicago, but hadn't really said what brought her here. She never mentioned family, or Presley's dad, and she hadn't dated anyone that I've known about since moving here. I knew she flirted with Pete, but I had no idea if she really liked him or what. She'd made a vague mention of her mother once or twice and said they didn't speak much. She hadn't mentioned her dad. I wasn't sure if she had other family. She'd never volunteered the info, and I hadn't asked.

I really didn't know much at all. I'd never wondered why before, but now it seemed incredibly important.

When I got to Pete's, she wasn't there. Fiona, however, was, holding court at the table she and I had commandeered yesterday, with people crowded around her. I could hear her tinkling laughter while I waited in line. It made me feel worse. Here she was apparently having a grand old time and making friends, and I was conflicted as ever about all this. I got my coffee and slunk out. I'm sure she saw me, or felt my presence, or whatever, but I didn't feel like socializing.

I unlocked my store and got ready for the day. No appointments today, I saw after checking my book. *It may be just as well,* I told myself. I needed some brain space to untangle some of these convoluted threads weaving their way around Carla and her death. So I figured I'd focus on some busy work. Boxes with new stones were still waiting for my attention. I lugged a couple out into the main store and spent some time rearranging the display in the front window with amethyst and rose quartz stones. I'd gotten some lovely large, raw pieces in my last shipment and figured they would help send positive vibes out into the town. And hopefully, back to me.

I was so engrossed in what I was doing that I barely glanced up when the door chimed.

Then I did a double take. The last person I expected to see there stood in my doorway. "Syd!" I jumped up and went over to her, not sure whether to hug her or yell at her for making me worry. "What are you doing here?" She never came to my shop. I didn't take offense to it, really—it just wasn't her thing.

"Hey." She gave me a weak smile, letting the door slam behind her. "Sorry I've been out of touch. I know you were trying to get me yesterday. I . . . wasn't feeling well."

She didn't look well. It had been only twenty-four hours since I'd seen her, and she looked like she'd lost weight. Her face was pale and drawn, hair pulled back in a messy bun. She wore no makeup, not even her trademark lipstick. Syd was a huge proponent of lipstick making everything better, even if you did nothing else. "Don't worry about it. Come in."

I was dying to start firing questions at her, but figured that would freak her out. I was getting pings of energy off her the closer I was to her, and I could feel fear, confusion, and despair.

"I actually thought, um . . ." She glanced around as if looking for the right words. "Can you help me?"

"Of course. What do you need?"

"Crystals, maybe? I don't really know. You know me, I don't usually want stuff like that, but I've been feeling lousy and thought, what's the harm?"

I tried to cover my shock at this request, but probably didn't succeed all too well.

Syd took my hesitation to mean this was a bad move

on her part and took a step back toward the door. "But if you're too busy—"

"I'm not busy at all," I said. "I would be honored to help you."

Relief softened her face. "Thanks. Really."

"Of course." On impulse, I locked the door and flipped the sign closed. "For some privacy," I said when she sent me a questioning look. "Now, what's going on? Is it Presley?"

She chewed on her lip. "Not really. It's just . . . a lot of things. I'd rather not go into detail, if that's okay."

No, it's not! I need to know what the deal is with you and Carla's son, I wanted to scream, but I swallowed it. She must really be desperate, to be coming here for this kind of help. Her science mind wouldn't stand for this on a normal day. I covered my impatience as best I could. "It's totally fine. Sit." I pointed her toward a chair.

I pulled my chair up in front of her. While she got comfortable, I concentrated really hard on tuning in. If my mother was right and I had some kind of magical power, maybe I could amplify what I already did, reading people. I focused a soft gaze just over her head and saw a rainbow of greens—dull and muddy, lime, dark and stormy and almost black. And a yellowy tinge too, which troubled me—it usually meant emotional blackmail.

Whoa. I sat back, trying to process this. Syd's typical aura was usually red or magenta, both strong, creative, independent, happy colors in aura-land. These colors were all about conflicting emotions, relationship trouble, and overall relationship negativity.

What did all this mean?

"What?" she asked, alarmed by my silence.

I shook my head. "Just concentrating. It's how this works. I'm going to get you some stones, okay?"

She sat back, still clearly uncomfortable, while I got up and did my thing. My hands went automatically to three stones: Rose quartz. Hematite. Agate.

Three of the four stones I'd given to Rain. I wasn't much for coincidence.

I brought them over to Syd, along with a small velvet pouch. "Okay," I said, beaming a smile at her. "This is what we have." I explained the healing properties and how to use them. "You can keep them in here if you don't want to wear them. Also, you can put them under your pillow at night to help cleanse your energy."

She examined them a bit doubtfully. "And these are going to fix things?"

"They're going to help your energy, and they'll help with any blocks you have." I pulled my chair closer to her and squeezed her hand. "Let me know if I can help. If you want to talk. Okay?"

Syd nodded and slid off her chair. "I will. Thanks, Vi." She blew me a kiss, looking a little more like herself. "I gotta go. See you later?" Without waiting for a reply, she unlocked the front door and slipped out.

I watched her go, frustrated that I hadn't gotten any real answers. But there had to be something to the matching stones. And I knew exactly who would know—Josie.

CHAPTER 41

After Syd left, I flipped my sign back to open and looked outside, wishing for Josie to materialize. Although I couldn't blame her if she didn't. I hadn't reacted well yesterday. I didn't want there to be bad blood between us. I'd be lost without her. The last couple of days had been so off, and without my regular confidants I'd felt even more untethered.

I forced myself to get back to work, convinced she'd show. And less than fifteen minutes later, she did. I sprang up to greet her with a hug as soon as she stepped through the door. She looked surprised, but hugged me back. She held on for a moment longer than necessary, then pulled back and studied me. I opened my mouth, but she shook her head. "No need," she said. "We can talk when you're ready."

"Thanks, Jos," I said, but she waved me off.

"Now. What's on the list for today? By the way, you missed Natalie yesterday."

I winced. "Was she okay?"

"She seemed distracted." Josie grabbed some paper

towels and glass cleaner and began wiping down cases. "I think she's worried about her husband being so close to this murder. And what it could mean for their income. By the way, I heard that Carla's funeral will be private."

"Really?" I wondered if it was because of Rain.

Josie nodded. "Very quick and hush-hush. Her almost-ex flew back, and they're doing the service tomorrow."

I mulled that over. "Did Natalie say anything about Andrew? I went to see him yesterday."

Josie paused midspray. "You did? Why?"

"I don't know. I wanted to talk to him about Carla. See if there was anyone he could think of who was upset with her and maybe unstable enough to do this."

"And?"

"And nothing. He didn't want to talk about it." I took a deep breath. "But he was talking to Rain."

"The protest guy?" Josie asked.

I nodded.

"Hmm," Josie said, going back to her wiping.

I couldn't hold back any longer. "Josie. Do you know who Rain really is?"

She looked up at me, something darkening her eyes. "Who?"

"He's Carla's son."

That got her attention. Her movements stilled. "So that's what I was feeling when I saw him," she said, almost to herself. "But he doesn't seem like he's upset at all."

"I think they were estranged." I told her what I'd gleaned from Gabe.

"There's something else," I said after a moment. I didn't usually discuss my clients' specific troubles or requests with anyone, but this was an extenuating circumstance. "Syd came in this morning."

"In here?" Josie asked.

I nodded. "She wanted crystals. Said she wasn't feeling well and had a lot of things on her mind. Have you seen her?"

Josie shook her head. "Not since Monday. That was the last time I watched Presley. She didn't need me yesterday."

"I went to her store yesterday to wait for her. I saw a Facebook message. From Carla."

Josie turned slowly, her eyes sharp. "Go on."

"From the day she died." I told her what it said, as well as how far back the messages went. "And Sydney hated Carla. Well, *hate* is a strong word, I guess."

"No, she hated her," Josie said. "I tried a few times to tell her that wasn't going to get her anywhere but she couldn't see past it. You don't think, Vi . . ." She let the thought trail off.

"Maybe there's a deeper reason for Syd to hate her than any of us know. I think there's something going on. With Syd and Rain. And Carla didn't like it. There's another thing," I said. "The crystals I gave her. The prescription was nearly identical to what I gave Rain when he came in yesterday."

Josie frowned. I could see her trying to fit these pieces together and coming up short.

"It fits, but I'm missing a piece," I said. "I saw Syd with him in the alley near the police station. The night Carla was killed. She denied knowing him, said he asked her for directions, but I knew she was lying. So does it mean anything, when two people get the exact same stones?"

"Definitely," Josie said. "It's a personal connection, for sure. I've seen it many times. Husbands and wives, mothers and daughters. You think they're dating?"

"I don't know. Why would Carla care if she'd effectively disowned her son?"

When it hit me, I gasped out loud. "What if Syd's pregnant? And Carla thought they were going to try to get money from her?"

Was that what the meeting was about? And what if that meeting had gone terribly wrong? "What if Carla tried to hurt Syd," I whispered. "And she had to defend herself?"

CHAPTER 42

By the time two thirty rolled around, the shop had hit a lull. I didn't feel bad about leaving.

"You okay if I head out? I want to put in an appearance at the park," I said to Josie.

"Of course. I got it."

"Were you planning on going?" I asked.

"No. I think there's enough conflict right now without adding fuel to the fire," she said with a small smile. "You go ahead."

I shrugged into my coat, wrapped my scarf around my neck, and adjusted my new slouchy hat on my head. "I'll let you know if I find out . . . anything." We'd both stopped trying on theories about Syd and Carla, because neither of us liked what we were coming up with.

I hurried outside and down toward the bridge, which would lead me over the river and into the park. I could already see the protesters gathering. There was quite a crowd, and I could see hats like Rain's bobbing off a lot of heads.

Something told me this was going to be a long, cold afternoon.

But the food trucks were lining up. Winter was hard for them, and they seized on every opportunity to get some business. Of course they'd be all over this. I scanned the offerings as I got closer. Potatoes from Heaven was front and center. I hoped I had enough appetite after this to get some fries.

I'd just arrived at the park entrance when Zoe literally materialized right next to me. "Hey, sis. Figured I'd join you," she said.

I pressed a hand to my pounding heart. "You need to stop doing that. People will see."

Zoe threw her head back and laughed, her long black hair falling down her back. "And they'll do what? Stone me?"

Despite myself, I had to laugh. I kind of hated to admit it, but I liked her. She was sassy and willful and didn't seem to care what anyone thought. Complete opposite of me.

She reached in her bag and pulled a hat that looked a lot like one of mine out and plopped it on her head. "I borrowed it. Hope you don't mind," she said when she caught me looking at it.

"Not at all. Help yourself," I said dryly.

"Thanks!" She beamed. "So are we gonna chain ourselves to something?" She nodded in the direction of a line of protesters holding lengths of rope and apparently trying to work out some kind of mathematical problem about where they could tie themselves.

"No idea." I scanned the crowd and paused when I saw a shock of platinum hair streaked with green and blue. Mazzy. "I'll be right back."

"Sure," Zoe said. "I'm gonna get some fries. I've been hearing amazing things about them."

"Great. Have fun." I slipped into the crowd, trying to

keep my eye on her, and in the process I bumped right into Sergeant Haliburton.

"Sorry," I began, then realized who it was and flushed. "Oh. Sergeant."

He smiled, but it didn't quite reach his eyes. "Ms. Mooney. You're against the bridge project?"

"I, uh, yeah, I guess so," I stammered.

He arched his eyebrows. "That didn't sound very convincing."

I shrugged. "I just wanted to see what was going on. Are you against it?"

He smiled. "I'm here in a public servant capacity. My opinions don't matter. I just want to make sure everyone stays civil and safe."

I didn't know what to say to that, so I remained silent.

"Quite a crowd," he remarked, looking around.

"It is." I tried to slip past him, but he stopped me. "Ms. Mooney. Did you happen to see your friend Sydney Santangelo the night Ms. Fernandez was killed?"

I stopped dead and turned to stare at him, hoping the dread wasn't apparent on my face. "Syd? Yes. Why?"

"Do you remember where and when?"

"She was home," I said. "Her daughter was sick."

"What time did you see her?"

"I don't recall offhand," I said. "But I believe she was home most of the night."

"She left work around"—he pulled out a notebook and scanned through some pages—"four. Any idea where she went from there?"

I shook my head. I wished I knew.

"Okay. Thank you very much. Enjoy the protest," he said, and walked away.

I huffed out a breath and started moving again in the direction I'd last seen Mazzy, but I couldn't pinpoint her hair anymore. "Damn," I muttered, looking around. I couldn't see her.

But I saw Andrew Mann, down by the water, speaking with Rain. Again. And Rain looked like he was running out of patience. Rain had a megaphone in his hand, like he was ready to start the proceedings. But Andrew was doing a lot of talking, while Rain kept looking around, as if he was bored or trying to get away. So what were they talking about? More financials?

"Vi!" I turned as Natalie made her way to me. "You seen Andrew?"

"Hey, Nat. Yeah, he's right there." I pointed at where he stood with Rain, still talking urgently.

She folded her arms and watched, not saying anything. But she didn't look happy about it. She seemed tightly wound as it was, which wasn't like her.

"You okay?" I asked.

"Me?" She glanced at me then back at Andrew. "I'm fine. Just needed Andrew for something."

"Okay. Sorry I couldn't be there yesterday, but did you and Josie get everything else done for the circle?"

Natalie nodded, but I could tell she wasn't really paying attention to me. "Yeah, I think we're good. I'll talk to you later, Vi." She squeezed my shoulder and walked away in Andrew's direction.

I watched. He saw her coming, turned back to Rain, and said one more thing. Rain regarded him with an insolent smirk, then turned away and walked back toward his line of protesters, who dutifully waited for him to start the show. Natalie said something to Andrew. He didn't look happy. And he didn't answer her, just shook his head and walked away, leaving her staring after him. I watched her swipe at her eye and felt helpless for my friend. I wondered what was up with those two. Natalie was usually so happy, but today she looked downright miserable.

Meanwhile, Rain was starting the show.

"Hello, North Harbor!" he shouted into his mega-phone. "Thanks for coming out on this chilly day, and I'm sorry we're starting late. But hey, hopefully you had a chance to eat some awesome food from the food trucks! How about those fries? Let's hear it for Potatoes from Heaven!"

A cheer went up from the crowd. Rain went on for a few more minutes about the protest, the project, how bad it was for the environment, how he dedicated his life to making sure the planet was taken care of because it was the only one we had, etc., etc.

As he talked, I let my gaze travel around the crowd. I'd lost sight of Zoe earlier and didn't see her anywhere. I wondered if she'd stuck around. I caught sight of Ginny Reinhardt, one of Todd's waitresses. She waved and made her way over to me. My heart sped up a bit. I'd been meaning to talk to Ginny, try to get some info about Todd, but I wasn't sure this was the place or time.

"Hey, Vi." She gave me a hug when she reached my side. Ginny was a hugger. Didn't matter if you'd seen her five minutes ago or five days ago, she gave you a hug like it was the first time in a long time. "Having fun?"

"Not really," I said. "It's too cold to have fun out here."

"For freakin' sure. I just figured I'd pop in between shifts." Ginny worked at the deli in the morning, doing the breakfast shift, then at Todd's in the afternoon/evening. "This guy is something, huh?" She motioned toward Rain, who was now tying people together in some sort of con-voluted knot.

"Yeah," I said.

"I can't believe he's still doing all this after what hap-pened. You'd think he'd stop out of respect." Ginny shook her head. "I don't get along with my mother that much either, but I'd definitely stop flaunting that if she died."

My head whipped around. "You know who he is too?"

Ginny laughed. "Doesn't everyone? It's the worst kept secret in town. Carla thought no one knew since he looks so different now, but a lot of people remember him."

"So she didn't like that he was home?"

Ginny shook her head. "Not from what I gathered. She complained a lot about it in the bar."

I frowned. "Carla came into Todd's bar?"

"Oh yeah. You didn't know that? She was a regular. Both her and Andrew. They had a lot of business meetings there."

Something else my boyfriend had never mentioned. Not that it would've been newsworthy before she'd zeroed in on me.

"Hey, I gotta go," Ginny said suddenly, squeezing my arm. "We'll talk later?" Without waiting for an answer, she headed across the park.

I lost sight of her when she went behind a crowd of people. When I saw her again, she was huddled next to a tree. Talking to . . . Mazzy?

CHAPTER 43

I stayed at the protest until I couldn't feel my fingers anymore, which was about an hour. People had slowly started leaving anyway. And after Mazzy and Ginny had finished their conversation—another shock to my system—I think Mazzy had left, because I hadn't seen her again.

I reached my shop, grateful to be back, and shoved at my door. Locked. What the heck? I thought Josie was going to be here. I cupped my hands around my eyes and peered inside. Didn't see her. With a sigh, I dug my keys out of my purse. I hoped everything was okay. It wasn't like Josie to just bail like that.

I pushed open the door and stepped in, turning lights on. And immediately was hit by a stench so disgusting my stomach actually turned. Pinching my nose, I tried to breathe through my mouth and figure out where it was coming from. Was this related to the smell from Monday? Had the guy next door screwed up some other recipe and I was paying for it again? Was this why she'd closed? I wondered why she hadn't texted me.

I pulled out my phone and tried calling her. Straight to voice mail. "Crap!" I disconnected and shoved the phone in my pocket. "Like I need this," I muttered, venturing deeper into the store, trying to figure out where the smell was the strongest. "I can't open with the place smelling like this." But what the heck was it? I'd honestly never smelled anything like it. It didn't smell like anything that would come out of a kitchen, even as a mistake.

I Googled *What does it smell like if something died in your walls?*

While I waited for the page to load, I peered behind the cases in the middle of the store. Nothing. I walked to the far end and sniffed. Definitely didn't smell better, but it didn't seem like ground zero either. I glanced at the webpage, which wasn't helpful at all, giving me examples of smells ranging from rotten eggs to "the rotting stench of death." I was about to throw my phone. If I knew what the rotting stench of death smelled like, I wouldn't have to ask.

I turned to go out back, a little apprehensive of what I might find, when I saw something sticking out from behind my counter. Holding my phone like a weapon, I moved closer.

And saw a black leather motorcycle boot lying on its side. I crept closer and realized it was attached to a leg.

I moved around for the full view and stared in horror. I wasn't sure if something was wrong with my eyes, or if I was suddenly seeing things with a witch filter on them, or what the heck was happening, but there on the floor behind my counter was Mazzy. Sort of. I mean, I could see her, but I could see her in almost a holographic form. The outline of her. The hair. The clothes.

But she looked dead. And there was a giant sticky mess on the floor that reminded me of the slime from the *Ghostbusters* classic.

Jumping back, I tried not to drop my phone due to the violent shaking of my hands. I had no idea who to call. Todd? I wasn't sure he'd answer. Sydney? No, she had her own problems. And what would I tell either of them—that I had kind of a dead body in my shop? And some unidentified slime?

Fiona would know. But I didn't have time to run to the apartment building, and I didn't know how to summon her otherwise. And maybe I didn't really want to involve her anyway, on second thought. The police? Yes, that's what I should do. Call the police.

I dialed 911, whirling around when I heard my door open. I'd forgotten to lock it. "No, no, no, I'm sorry, I'm—what are you doing here?" I demanded when I saw Zoe in the doorway, holding a paper boat of french fries.

"I came to see your place and to bring you some of these amazing fries, since you barely ever eat." She eyed me. "What's up?"

"Nothing. You should go. Not you," I said, realizing the dispatcher had answered and was asking my emergency. "Uh. I'm at 873 Water Street. The Full Moon." I lowered my voice to a whisper, turning away from Zoe so she wouldn't hear. "There's a body." I hung up, even though she was still trying to ask me questions.

But Zoe had stepped into the shop, clearly on alert. "Violet. What's going—uh-oh." She sniffed the air, her face contorting as the smell hit her.

"I know. It's probably toxic. You should go."

"No way. I need to call Mother. Oh, crap," she said when she reached my desk and saw Mazzy.

I locked my door and flipped the sign, torn between waiting outside where everyone who passed would know something was wrong and waiting in here with . . . whatever that was.

"The cops are coming," I said. "You really don't need to be involved in this, Zoe."

"Vi," she said urgently. "You don't need the cops for this."

I snorted. "I don't need the cops, but I need Fiona? What is she going to do about it? Perform a magical cleanup?"

"I can do that too, darling, but first I need to figure out what's going on here," Fiona said in my ear, and I almost jumped out of my skin. I looked at Zoe.

"What?" she asked with a shrug. "You think I need a phone?"

I threw up my hands, then turned to the door, distracted by the sound of sirens. Less than four minutes. Record time. I didn't know that for a fact, of course, and they were around the corner, but probably news of a body got them moving. I'd been dreading seeing Denning or Haliburton, but when the car pulled up to the curb, lights flashing, I was relieved to see Gabe step out of it. A minute later, another car coming from the other direction joined him at the curb.

"Oh, darling. Tell me you didn't call them." Fiona sighed reproachfully. "We'll be right back." She grabbed Zoe's arm, and the two of them disappeared. I waved at the puff of smoke they'd left behind and tried to kick the glitter away with my shoe as Gabe and the other cop came to the door.

I didn't know the other guy. I unlocked the door and motioned them inside.

"Vi. Are you okay? What happened?"

"I don't know. I was at the protest and left Josie here. When I came back, she was gone and I found . . ." I swallowed.

"Where . . . ?"

I pointed. "Behind the counter."

"Stay outside and make sure no one comes in," he said to the other cop—a young guy with a shaved head and a worried look on his face. The cop nodded and went back outside, planting himself in front of my door.

When Gabe got to the counter, he paused. Peered behind it, then looked at me, his eyes curious. And a little worried.

"Thought you said there was a body?" he asked.

I nodded, coming over to him. When I looked, I could still see the shimmery outline of Mazzy on the floor. It made me queasy. "Yes. What do you think that is?" I pointed.

He looked from me to the floor again, then back at me. "Maybe you should go home. Get some rest. The past few days have been really rough on you," he said. "But Vi. Seriously, you're lucky it was me who answered the call."

I stared at him, completely confused. "But," I said, then trailed off. "But don't you see that?" I tried again.

Gabe sighed. "Look, Violet. I'll take care of it. I'll say someone passed out and you panicked. But be careful what you're calling us about, you hear?" And he walked out the door, leaving me dumbfounded and once again on the verge of tears.

I watched him go, feeling like I'd just gotten surprised by a giant ocean wave that had knocked me under. When I turned again, a crackle and a loud pop filled the air, then Fiona and Zoe appeared in a shower of glitter right in front of me. "Now are you ready to listen to me?" Fiona asked, her eyes dark.

CHAPTER 44

"Listen to you?" I asked in disbelief. "I don't have any idea what listening to you has to do with anything. There's a body right there"—I pointed at Mazzy, horrified to realize her image was fading even as we spoke—"and the police can't seem to see it. Now they think I'm messing with them, on top of everything else they think I've done this week. Care to tell me what any of this has to do with you?"

Fiona swept around the counter, as regal as if she were a queen, her long cape brushing the floor and sending the glitter scattering even farther. "This," she announced, pointing at Mazzy, "is a witch who's been Genied."

Well, at least she could see her. But wait. Mazzy was a witch too? "Genied?" I repeated.

"Genied." She nodded. "Worse than killed."

"Worse than . . . Fiona." I rubbed my temples with my knuckles, wishing desperately for some aspirin. Or a drink. "You do know that makes no sense to me, right?"

She rolled her eyes. "I figured as much. Another favor

Grammy did for you in the name of humans," she muttered.

"Fiona." I hadn't even seen Josie standing behind her until just now. "Tell her what it means and save the commentary."

I gaped at her. "When did you get back? And where were you?"

"I was with Fiona," Josie said. "I closed up the shop and went to see her. We needed to talk."

"You can explain to her later," Fiona said. "Violet. This woman is a witch. Her name is Mariza Diamond. She's an investigative reporter with ties to both human and magickal news outlets. She uses a pen name for her work . . . over here."

Mazzy the reporter, playing both sides. "Magickal news?" I shook my head. "Okay. So?"

"So, someone obviously didn't want her reporting on something," Fiona said grimly. "So they followed her here and Genied her. It's a particularly brutal form of magickal kidnapping. She's basically turned into a pool of slime and put in a bottle, where she's destined to spend the next two hundred years unless someone finds out who did it and can break the spell. It's not sanctioned by the Magickal Council," she added, as if that made it any better. "It's actually a very rogue, criminal act, punishable by, well, we won't get into that now."

I didn't miss the look Josie had sent her to shut her up, but I let it go.

"The point is, whatever she's doing here, someone doesn't like it. Which means you're in danger."

"Me?" I pointed a shaking finger at my chest. "But why? She came in here to see my shop a couple days ago. She wrote a nasty article about me and I called her out on it. She was supposed to print a retraction and stay away from my shop. But she wasn't happy about it, so apparently she snuck back in to, I don't know, try to find out some other bad thing to write about. I have nothing that secret going on in here that any kind of magickal criminal would be interested in, I can assure you." I looked down at the floor again. The holographic image of Mazzy was almost completely faded, leaving only a sticky, slimy mess and that putrid stench in its wake.

Fiona joined me to gaze down at the floor. "Terrible," she murmured. "I wouldn't wish this on my worst enemy. It's very hard to find the exact person who committed the act. In my lifetime, only one person who'd been Genied was returned to their proper form."

Josie stepped up, flanking me on the other side. "I agree," she said. "This certainly seems like extreme lengths for a council seat."

"Exactly my thoughts," Fiona murmured. "I'm not quite sure what's occurring, but it isn't good."

"Wait. One person? Out of how many?" I interrupted.

Fiona shrugged. "About as often as murders happen in your world, my dear."

I cringed, thinking of Carla. "Not many. At least not that I'm used to."

"Come now," Fiona said. "I've been reading the papers. In any event, Violet, my point is I'm concerned about you. This, happening here in your shop, is a warning."

"Oh, for the love of—" I stomped my foot on the floor. "A warning about what? This is all nonsense. Absurd nonsense that I don't have time for. Did you do this?" I pointed at the mess on the floor. "Is this your idea of trying to scare me into believing you? Did you send Mazzy here in the first place to spy on me, then set it up to look like whatever your fictional horror story is so I'll be scared into trusting you?"

Zoe let out an audible gasp and pressed herself against the wall. Josie covered her face with her hands.

Fiona's eyes darkened to the point of twin storms. "Fictional, eh?" she said in a deadly cold voice that actually gave me shivers. She waved her hand, and my blinds slammed shut around me. Waved it again, and the lights went off. A third time, and a giant screen appeared in front of me, a bit smaller than something you'd see at the movies, but not much.

"You think this is fiction?" She swiped at the screen with one ring-clad finger. Images of women being tortured flashed in front of me. Medieval tortures, from the looks of it, but the images went so fast I couldn't get a grip on them.

"Or this?" She swiped again. These I recognized. Images of the Salem witch trials—women being hanged, burned at the stake, waiting at the gallows.

"Or this?" A third swipe and I cringed, recognizing a story I'd seen about a woman burned alive in a Middle Eastern country not that many years ago, accused of witchcraft.

"And this," another swipe, "really is fiction. But this is how they depict us now. To take our power away."

I stared at the screen and the images of old, ugly witches with warts on their noses and wrinkly faces cackled over a smoking cauldron.

"You can't let them push you around like this. These bad witches, they are trying to make you vulnerable. They found a way to overtake your grandmother. And they're using this," she waved her hand around again, bringing the air to life around me with snaps and crackles, "this human life, to do it. This is not your priority," she said, stepping up to me so we were nose to nose. "Wake up, daughter. This is bigger than you. And if you don't step up and take control of your life, and let me help you, this"—and now an image of Mazzy's slimy remains filled the screen—"this could be you. So go ahead and Lululemon your way into a noose. Or a Genie bottle. The choice is yours."

And with that, she passed her hand in front of her face and disappeared. Another *crack* and the blinds snapped back into place, the lights came back on, and all that was left of her was her signature pile of glitter puddling around my feet.

CHAPTER 45

I stared at the glitter on the floor, then at Josie, hoping she'd shake her head at the drama of it all and tell me to get back to work—body hologram on the floor notwithstanding.

But she wasn't smiling.

I was getting the feeling this could be serious.

"So you think she's for real?" I asked casually.

"Oh, sweetheart, she's for real," Josie assured me. "If there's one thing about Fiona, it's that she doesn't mess around. There's plenty of drama, but it's real drama, not pointless drama."

It stung a little, hearing these casual references to how well they knew each other. A reminder that people I'd trusted had kept me in the dark. I looked around for Zoe, but she was gone too. Fiona had probably taken her with her.

Josie read the look on my face and came over to take both my hands. "Listen. I know you're upset about all this. I can't blame you. All I ask is that you reserve judgment until you know the whole story, and that you try to put that on the back burner for the moment because your mother's right. There are more serious things to contend with at the moment."

I didn't necessarily agree—they both seemed like serious contenders for attention and processing—but I was hardly in a good position to argue. I pulled my hands away, eyes trailing to the sticky goop on my floor. "So is this related to Carla?" I asked, waving a hand at the mess.

Josie's eyes followed mine, lips pursed as she studied the floor. "I can't say with certainty, but my instincts tell me no. That your mother is right, it's bigger than that. Carla is a human problem. No offense," she added at the look on my face. "I know that's the only world you've ever related to. But there's more to our lives than the human world. Which is why your mother was so frustrated with what happened. With your family."

"So why didn't you step in?" I demanded, the question that had been weighing on me all this time finally escaping my lips. "You knew me. You knew Fiona and Abigail. Why didn't you talk to them? Or at least tell me?"

"Because it doesn't work that way," Josie said. "I know how hard it is for you to understand, in our human world of 'see something, say something.' But you see how she turned out?" She waved at Mazzy's rapidly disintegrating form. "Meddling in another family's affairs in our world is no joking matter."

I couldn't quite wrap my mind around that. "But don't you know how to get around all that? Aren't you able to figure out if something is connected, like Mazzy and Carla?" I was still frustrated. "With all these *powers* you guys have?" I couldn't keep the sarcasm from the word *powers*, though I did try to tone it down some.

Josie just smiled, albeit a little sadly. "It doesn't really work that way, my dear," she said gently. "We all have the powers we're predisposed to. We can develop other powers along the way, also, but all of it takes practice. And being a witch doesn't mean we are all-seeing, all-knowing beings about everyone and everything. We have to work at our expertise just like everyone else. It just so happens we have a different sort of expertise than the people with whom you've been spending your time.

"The magic we hold is part of our being. It's been passed down to us through generations of our mothers. Which is why female witches are more powerful than male witches. And our world is a world where women lead, and everything is better for it. But some people don't want women to lead. And they see an opportunity to stop it."

"Who are these people?" I asked finally.

"Another family of witches," Josie said. "They're largely male dominated, and they are desperate to have a foothold in some power. They see your grandmother's death as a way in."

"What family?"

"The Sagebloods," Josie replied. "They aren't . . . well, I'll let you draw your own conclusions."

I thought about that. "Is she serious about my grandmother?" I couldn't bring myself to say the words. *Had someone killed her?*

"She's looking into it," Josie said finally. "Very carefully. But Vi. You need to let her help you. Even if Carla isn't related to this, you need her help with . . . this." She motioned to the floor. "You know, that smell I smelled on Monday? It was her that was here, wasn't it?"

I nodded.

"She'd already been tagged for this," Josie said grimly. "I always had a nose for that kind of thing. I wish I'd been here. I could've warned her. They were waiting for the right time."

"I felt something when she was here. Heard something," I corrected myself. "I heard it throughout the day Monday. With Mazzy, with Fiona and Zoe when they showed up. And I've been hearing it on and off ever since. A staticky sound. What does that mean?"

"You were starting to open up," she said. "To the witches around you. People experience it differently at first. Sometimes it's a vision. Other times it's a sound."

"I saw it too," I said, suddenly remembering. "I saw her in the mirror and she was just a shape. Formless. It's hard to explain."

But Josie snapped to attention at that. "You experienced both? Violet, that's amazing. Most people don't. That means . . . well, we can talk about it later. But it's powerful. And maybe that's why you're in someone's sights."

That kind of gave me the creeps. Maybe I did need to listen to Fiona and take her seriously and let her help me figure out what was going on here with this sort-of dead witchy reporter. But right now, whether she liked it or not, there were mortal things that needed my attention. I needed to figure out who killed Carla before it got pinned on me. I needed to see what Sydney had to do with it, if anything. And for the love of everything holy, I needed to get my shop cleaned up and opened before I was out of a job and an income.

But first, I needed to go to the one person who always had the answers to everything.

"I'll be back," I said to Josie. "I have to take care of something. Then I'll clean this up." I waved at the floor, wrinkling my nose at the smell and the mess.

But Josie shook her head. "I'll have someone come in and deal with this. It's not a traditional cleaning job," she said. "It takes, well, magic."

"So you have to call in some witch cleaning service?" I asked, only half kidding.

But she nodded. "Yes. I'm sure I can get someone in today. Don't worry. These people aren't far away, Vi. I would ask Ginny, but she only does it on weekends."

"Ginny Reinhardt?" I was stunned.

Josie nodded with a small smile. "You haven't realized it, but you've been living among your community all along."

CHAPTER 46

I let the shop door slam shut behind me, leaving it to Josie to lock. I was a little curious about this magickal cleaning company, but maybe I was better off not knowing. I'd had enough surprises. Like Ginny. Next thing she'd be telling me Pete was magickal or something absurd like that.

Ginny knew Mazzy. It was all starting to make sense now, if they were both magickal. I wondered how much Ginny knew about this feud between these families.

When I let myself into my grandmother's house twenty minutes later, I stopped for a moment, closing my eyes, just breathing in the familiar scents. They were fading, of course, but still there, on the fringes of every room, seeping into the walls. I moved to the living room, noting the chair I'd shown up in when I'd transported myself from the police station. It looked exactly as it had then, the white throw blanket over the back of it, but it could easily have been my memory.

I went into the kitchen to fire up the kettle. It was still sitting on the stove. There was actually water left in it, as if Grandma Abby had been about to make herself a cup of tea. My eyes blurred as I emptied out the water and re-filled it from the sink. The shock of her death was still as real as it had been when I'd gotten the news. Her friend Helena had called me, her voice broken and wrecked, and told me Grandma Abby had passed away in her sleep. That it had been peaceful.

But there was no warning. She hadn't been ill. She hadn't even had a cold for as long as I could remember. She was going to come to my shop the next day and spend some time. She said she wanted to see me in ac-tion, maybe get some new stones, just be near her grand-daughter and be proud.

I'd been so looking forward to that visit. We hadn't had one, a quality one, in a while. My fault. I'd been too busy with my shop, and my life. I knew Grandma Abby would wave away these regrets, tell me to stop being silly, that I was young and vibrant and had a life to lead, for goddess's sake, and that we spent loads of time to-gether.

But we hadn't, lately.

I brushed the tears away, set the kettle on the stove, and turned on the burner. I hunted through her cabinet for her favorite chamomile tea, and put one of the silky bags into a mug to wait for the water. Then I leaned against the counter and thought about my grandma as a witch.

I couldn't even get a picture of it in my head. While I wasn't picturing her like the pointy-hatted hags riding a broomstick with their black cat across a full moon, like the images Fiona had shown me, I had to admit I wasn't sure what to make of the concept. I understood more than most people, given the circles I ran in. The metaphysical world was a wide one, and I encountered a lot of different beliefs. I knew enough about things to be dangerous. I knew paganism, Wicca, and witchcraft, while intertwined, did not have a singular meaning, and it was way more complicated than that. I knew some people considered tarot cards "witchy." As a fledgling tarot reader, I knew that was a short-sighted assessment, and tarot had nothing to do with religion. I knew about mediums.

But what I'd seen and experienced the past couple days, well, that was something else entirely. That was magic. It was the stuff of movies and fantasy novels, and I was expected to just sit back and believe it while nodding and smiling at my new mother.

Anger flared in my chest as I thought of it. The teakettle began a low whistle, jolting me out of my head. I poured the mug, set the kettle back on the burner, and walked through the house. At the bottom of the stairs, I paused. I'd told myself I was coming here for comfort and familiarity, to be close to my grandmother again. But I'd known all along what I was going to do.

I took a breath and headed upstairs.

Someone had made Grandma Abby's bed.

Had to have been Helena. She was the one who had found her, after all. I couldn't imagine what a shock it must've been for Grandma's oldest friend to arrive for their daily coffee date and find an empty kitchen, never mind the shock of her subsequent search of the house. She would've known Grandma hated an untidy house. I wondered if she'd gone to the hospital with Grandma's body, or if they'd even bothered taking her to the hospital. If not, Helena would've stayed and gotten things to where Grandma would've wanted them.

Helena had tried to call me a couple of times since the funeral. I hadn't called her back yet. I'd told myself I needed to be in the right headspace, and things had been too busy. Really, I knew I'd been avoiding it because it would make it real in a way a wake and funeral just didn't.

I stared at the bed for a few minutes in fascination. I'd

been thinking of it as a weapon all this time—like it was the thing that took Grandma Abby from us. But it wasn't the bed's fault. And here, in its presence, well, it was just a bed.

I took a deep breath and moved into the room. I wasn't sure what I was looking for, or what I'd even find. I just knew it had been an unspoken rule as a child to never go through Grandma's things. And as I got older, it had never been a question of whether the rule had changed. Not that I'd ever felt she was keeping things from me, just that she valued her privacy.

Had it been because she never wanted me to find out her secret?

I thought about Helena, and the group of women Grandma had spent all her time with. There were six of them, and they did everything together. I remember as a child watching from my bedroom window on certain nights as they all gathered and made their way to the field behind our house, loaded down with bags of supplies. Some nights when I couldn't sleep, I would kneel with my chin on the windowsill and watch them walk through the grass, barefooted and arms linked, up over the hill in the backyard until I couldn't see them any longer.

I'd been so curious about what they did, and so desperate to go. I'd asked Grandma Abby about it a few times, and she'd hugged me and told me maybe when I was bigger.

"We go out to look at the moon," she'd said. "There are certain days when the moon is very powerful, and it can help make you more powerful. We like to go outside and soak that in."

As I got older, she'd taught me everything about the moon and its cycles. I'd learned that the nights they gathered were on the new moon, and again on the full moon. Once, they'd brought me, but I got the feeling they'd changed up their normal practice because I was there. Not wanting to intrude on their special times, I hadn't asked again. And as I got older and learned the moon, I developed my own connection. I respected it. It's why I called my store *The Full Moon*—both as a nod to Grandma Abby and because I'd come to love and respect the cycle as much as she had. Now I understood that maybe there was more to their evenings in that field than just a social gathering. Were Helena and Grandma's other friends witches too?

They had to be, I decided. Even though she had her feet in this world, it seemed she kept her other world close. I wondered why my dad had chosen to turn his back on that world.

I left her room and went down to my old room. It was still the same too. Grandma Abby told me she'd keep it for me, in case I ever needed it. And that being here, being home, would fix everything.

Being home would fix everything.

Buoyed by that, I moved into my room and began going through my drawers. Nothing in the dresser, as I'd left it. My nightstand, though, still had some of my original crystals. Some old journals. Someday I'd have to sit and read them.

I moved to the closet. Empty, except for some old clothes that definitely needed to go to Goodwill. But on the top shelf, which I was almost too short to reach, I struck gold.

I pulled down a book. An old-school book, like something out of a museum, with embossed gold lettering on the front. But it was in some other language, because I had no idea what it said. I went to open the book, but I couldn't lift the cover.

I stared at it, frustrated. Maybe it was so old the pages

had all stuck together. I pulled at it as hard as I dared, not wanting to wreck it.

But it wouldn't open.

I wanted to throw it across the room, but I resisted. Then I noticed a piece of paper sticking out of the top. I pulled, and it came out easily. I almost couldn't handle it when I saw Grandma Abby's familiar, flowery script. The paper looked old, like she'd written the note a long time ago.

Dear Violet,

If you've found this book, then what I've tried to shield you from per your father's wishes has found you, and I'm not around to stop it. But don't worry, my love. This isn't the worst life you could have. You'll find the answers you need in this book, but only once you have embraced your destiny. I can't wait for the day I see you again.

Love, Grandma Abby

I blinked and read the note again. The book had answers, but I couldn't access them because I hadn't embraced my witchiness?

Was she *kidding* me?

CHAPTER 47

I must've fallen asleep on my old bed, because I awoke to the sound of my phone ringing. I reached for it. It was still in my pocket. No wonder my hip was sore.

It was Todd. "Hey," he said.

I tried to clear the sleep from my voice. "Hey."

"Want to have dinner tonight? It'll have to be a quick one. On my break."

I frowned. What kind of an invitation was that? "I don't think so," I said. "Maybe tomorrow, okay?"

"Vi—"

"I'm kind of busy right now. I'll call you tomorrow," I said, and hung up. I needed to figure out some of these other problems before I could let myself get too worried about Todd.

I swung my legs off the bed. I'd gotten the best sleep I'd had in days in the—I checked the clock—half hour I'd sacked out on my old bed. I tried the book again, but it still didn't open. Guess I wasn't any closer to accepting my destiny.

I put it in my tote bag, along with the note, and headed

back downstairs. My head felt a little clearer, although I still had no good answer about who Carla's killer was.

I wondered if my shop was cleaned up yet. Or how to approach Fiona.

In the end, I decided I was starving. I'd skipped lunch and hadn't even gotten any fries after I left the protest. I locked up the house, got in my car, and headed back to North Harbor. I'd pop into the deli and get a sandwich, then go face up to whatever had happened in my shop.

When I got to the deli, I saw Ginny Reinhardt sitting alone in a booth in the back. I checked my watch. It made sense. She'd probably finished her shift here and was eating before she went to work at Todd's bar. Without thinking, I went back and slid into the seat across from her, shrugging off my coat as I sat.

She looked up, surprised. "Hey, Vi."

I studied her face. She didn't look distraught or anything, which meant maybe she hadn't heard about Mazzy yet. They'd seemed friendly enough at the protest for her to be sad about what happened if she knew it. Even if she didn't know about what had happened to Mazzy, maybe she could tell me why Mazzy had been in my store.

"You know Mazzy Witherspoon," I said without preamble.

She looked surprised, then wary. "Yeah. Why?"

"How do you know her?"

When Ginny hesitated, I sighed. "Come on, Ginny. I know you're a witch."

Relief put a smile on Ginny's face. "You do? Which means you know—"

"Yeah." I cut her off. "I can't talk about that now. I need to know about Mazzy. She was in my store today. After the protest."

Ginny frowned. "What do you mean?"

"So you didn't hear?"

She was staring at me now, and she looked frightened. "Hear what, Violet?"

"That she's been Genied," I blurted out, then flinched and looked around, dropping my voice. "In my store."

Ginny's face had gone so pale I thought she might pass out right in front of me. "Ginny?"

It hadn't really occurred to me until that moment that it probably wasn't a good idea to break the news like that. To me, the concept didn't mean much, despite Fiona and Josie's grim description of it. It still seemed like something out of a sci-fi novel. But I learned pretty quickly that it was all too real for some.

"What do you mean?" Ginny's voice had dropped to a whisper. Her hand clenched the side of the table like she was clinging to a life raft.

"I'm sorry," I said. "Josie and Fiona said she'd been Genied. And the police couldn't see anything." I wasn't sure all of that made sense, but she seemed to grasp exactly what it meant. Without a word she grabbed my arm and pulled me out the back door of the deli, not even giving me a chance to grab my coat.

She stood there for a moment, leaning against the door, obviously trying to collect herself before continuing this conversation.

Shivering, I hugged myself. When I thought I might freeze before she spoke again, I broke the silence first. "Do you think it has something to do with her BS article that I called her out on? I told her to print a retraction. Was it about that?"

"Wait a minute. What article?"

"The article in *The Fairway Independent*. About fake psychics and energy healers."

"She was working there too? She really wanted to be a famous journalist," she said softly. She didn't seem to feel the cold at all. I think she was kind of in shock.

"Ginny." I grabbed her arms. "Focus. Where else was she working?" I remembered Fiona saying she worked in both realms.

"For the *Magickal Minute*. In the . . . other realm. And I think that someone didn't want her writing about you," Ginny said grimly.

"What was she writing about me?"

"I'm not sure, but my guess is an exposé on who you are, now that the barrier between you and our world is broken."

"But why?" I asked, exasperated. "Who cares?"

Her expression was a mixture of *How-can-she-be-this-clueless?* and some level of pity. "Because you're the heir apparent, Violet. And some people who really want to see the balance of power shift don't want that."

I leaned against the wall, forgetting all about the cold. It was one thing to hear this from Fiona, and even Josie. But to hear it from Ginny, who had no skin in this game that I could see, made it seem more real.

"So who would've done that to her?" I asked.

Ginny bit her lip, shaking her head. "I don't know. And that's what makes it really scary."

I let that sink in, then grabbed her arm. "Let's go in. We're going to freeze out here."

She followed me back to the booth and sat, still seemingly in a daze. I felt bad for her, but there were still things I needed to ask her.

"Did Todd know Mazzy?" I asked.

Something passed over Ginny's face that I didn't like one bit.

"She came into the bar sometimes," she said.

"And?"

"And what?"

"And was there something going on between them?" I asked bluntly.

Ginny's eyes widened, and she shook her head vehemently. "No. No way, Vi."

"Then why did he lie to me about knowing her?"

She frowned. "When did he do that?"

"Monday morning. The first time she came into my store. He was there. I swear they knew each other, but he denied it."

She shrugged. "You'd have to ask him that. I'm not in his head," she said.

I took a deep breath. I'd been avoiding asking this question, but I couldn't hold it off any longer. "Was Todd at the bar on Monday night?"

I didn't know if she would be straight with me. She worked for Todd, after all, and my guess was that she made a crap-ton more money at the bar than at the deli slinging grilled cheese sandwiches and omelets.

But the question didn't seem to throw her off. She thought about it. "He was working," she said finally. "I know he had a meeting off-site. I don't know who with," she added before I could ask. "But it was slow, so it was only me and one other guy on. Two people called in sick and he didn't bother getting replacements."

I leaned forward. "Slow?"

She nodded. "Really slow. Only a few people all night."

"Do you remember who was in?" I remember Charlie telling me he'd been there that evening.

She thought some more. "That guy who worked with Carla was in there. I remember that. He looked so down and was drinking a lot."

"Andrew?" Something about that seemed off to me, but I couldn't pinpoint why.

"Yeah. I remember thinking he never came in that early to pound down some beers."

"Like what time?"

"Around five, I think. He left an hour, hour and a half later? In a big rush like he'd just remembered he was late for something."

"What about Charlie?" I asked.

"Charlie Klein?" Ginny shook her head. "No, haven't seen Charlie in a while."

"You're sure," I said slowly.

"Positive. Hey, Vi?" She grabbed my hand.

"Yeah?"

"Mazzy . . . wasn't a bad person. She was just really ambitious." Her eyes dropped to the table again. "I'm sorry she was giving you a hard time."

"It's not your fault, Ginny. And hey," I said, trying to sound positive. "Fiona said if they catch the person who did it and get them to reverse it, she'll be okay. Right?"

Ginny looked at me like I had three heads. "Right," she said, but didn't offer anything else.

Still, I could tell there was more to the story.

CHAPTER 48

Thursday felt like snow.

It had been three days since Carla's murder. Four days since my life had turned upside down. And whatever answers I'd found had just brought up more questions. And there was apparently some bad witch out to get me. I felt a little shiver as I stood at my window that morning overlooking my town. Was I in danger of being Genied too?

Of course, I couldn't let that worry me. I mean, it still sounded rather absurd when I thought about it. But that puddle of slime on my shop floor . . . I shivered a little.

But I couldn't let that sideline me. My poor business had taken a beating this week, but I was determined to right things. And the healing circle was tomorrow night. I was really looking forward to it, despite everything.

As I was leaving, I realized I hadn't seen the black cat lately. I wondered if that was because he'd found his home, or if there was another reason.

I walked down to Pete's, lost in thought, and didn't notice Rain until I nearly bumped into him.

"Sorry—oh, hey, Violet!" He smiled at me, as if nothing at all was wrong or out of the ordinary.

"Rain. Just the guy I wanted to see," I said.

"Oh yeah? What's up?"

"We need to talk," I said. "At my shop. Now."

He glanced at his watch. "I can't right now. I have to—"

"Wrong answer," I muttered. I focused on his wrist, concentrating really hard on the watch. To my delight—and his shock—the watch flew off his wrist, bouncing off the pavement.

He stared at it, then at me. "What . . ."

"You should see what else I can do," I lied. I wasn't really sure what else I could do, but there had to be something. "Coming?"

He trailed behind me as I about-faced and marched to my shop. When we got there, I said a silent prayer that no one else had been Genied and that the smell was gone, and pushed the door open, taking a careful sniff. Nothing. Thank goodness for magickal cleaning services.

"Come on in." I waited until he'd stepped in, then closed and locked the door behind us. I led him to my back room and pointed to a chair set up at my little card-reading table.

He sat. I pulled up my seat across from him.

"You're Carla Fernandez's son," I said without preamble.

He winced a little, then nodded. "Your past is never really hidden, is it?"

"Not when you come back to your hometown," I said, exasperated.

"Well, I had business here," he said. "No choice. And I figured I'd try to do some good while I was here." He motioned to his hat. "My way of giving back and trying to offset any damages."

"What kind of business?" I asked. "Did it have anything to do with Sydney?"

Now his face went white. "She told you?"

I inclined my head in what could have been a nod, but said nothing.

"Look. Whatever she told you, I'm not a bad guy." He waited expectantly.

"Okay," I said.

"I'm serious, Violet. I told her the truth from the start. I'm not a big relationship guy."

"Is that why she had to go to your mother?" I snapped. "Who was awful to her?"

"No, she had to go to my mother because she couldn't reach me. I wish she'd figured out another way, but there really wasn't."

I sat back, confused. "Couldn't reach you? When?"

"When she decided she wanted to get in touch," Rain said. "She tracked me to Carla and moved here, hoping she'd find me. But I didn't make it easy for her, and neither did my mother."

Now I was really lost. I also noted how Rain called his mother by her first name. "What do you mean, she tracked you to Carla?" I asked. "I thought you two were dating."

Rain chuckled. "Is that what she told you? Hey, I never called it that. Seriously. We had a fling while I was passing through Chicago."

"Chicago?" I shook my head. "Maybe you better start at the beginning."

"I thought you said she told you this?" Rain shook his head, maybe remembering the watch. "Never mind. So we met when I was going through Chicago. Dated while I was there. I told her I had no plans on staying. She was cool with it." He shrugged. "I left, and didn't leave my number. She didn't give me hers either. But apparently years later, she decided she wanted me to know she'd gotten pregnant and thought I should meet my kid."

I gasped, my hand flying to my mouth. I'd had it all wrong. Syd wasn't pregnant now. "You're . . ."

"Presley's dad." He nodded. "I guess Sydney lost her dad recently and it made her think Presley deserved a father."

Holy moly. The last pieces clicked together in my head. Syd's appearance on the North Harbor scene two years ago. Reaching out to Carla, thinking she'd find a grandmother waiting with open arms. "But how did she track you to Carla?"

"This was before my Rain identity," he said, with that wry smile again. "I told her my real name and where I was from. It wasn't a huge stretch for her to look up Fernandez in the area. And I'd mentioned my mother's council position. So really, I made it easy for her."

"So she moved here to see if she could get to you through your mother," I said slowly. "But she's been here for almost two years."

Rain nodded. "As you know, my mother wasn't exactly the friendliest woman in town, especially if she thought you were beneath her. Syd's first faux pas, in my mother's eyes, was the tiny house parked on the street. She zeroed in on Syd even before Syd could think of how to make contact with her. She'd been out to get the house removed from day one. So Syd's been sitting on this, trying to figure out how to mend fences so she could broach the subject."

"So what did she do?" I asked, but I dreaded the answer.

"She went to her office with Presley. Told her this was her granddaughter. Expected my mother to embrace them both, call me, and never look back."

"And that didn't happen."

Rain shook his head slowly. "Quite the opposite, in fact. You may have noticed my mother wasn't known for her warmth," he said, so dryly it almost made me laugh. "She got very upset. Told her she was a liar and a gold digger and threw her out."

"Oh, man." No wonder Syd's hatred of Carla had seemed to get worse over the past couple of months. Her reasoning to me was about Carla upping the stakes and making life hard for Charlie, who didn't deserve it. And this explained her frozen reaction in the coffee shop Monday when Carla had come at us—at me—with figurative guns blazing. "But knowing Syd, she kept trying."

Rain nodded. "In subtle ways. But then she started getting angry. Like, really angry. She felt that Carla was making decisions for me without ever giving me a chance to weigh in. And she was right. But that's how Carla operated. God." He raked his hands through his hair. "I hear what I'm saying and I know how awful it sounds. To talk about her like this when she's gone, especially the way it happened. But it's true. All of it's true."

"So you just found out?"

He nodded. "Three weeks ago. My mother finally called me. But she had something to hold over my head." At my questioning look, he nodded. "My inheritance."

"Inheritance?"

He nodded. "My part of the family business. This was the birthday I was supposed to get it. The big thirty. It should've been twenty-five, or even twenty-one, but my mother convinced my grandfather to delay it even longer."

I was confused. "The realty business?"

Rain made a face. "God, no. That was her way of keeping herself amused. The family business, going all the way back to her great-great-grandfather. Mayfair Chemicals."

"Chemicals?"

Now he laughed out loud. "I'm glad the irony of that isn't lost on you. Now you see why I don't broadcast it?"

"Because of the circles you run in," I said.

"Bingo. I've worked really hard to get myself some standing in the environmentalist community. I'm writing papers, I'm out on the frontlines, and people are starting to know me. I didn't want to risk all that because of my mother."

"Well, you didn't need to take her money," I pointed out.

"I wish it was that easy. Have you tried living on a stipend from a university?" He grimaced. "I wouldn't recommend it to anyone who likes to eat."

"So she's been funding you this whole time?" I asked.

He nodded. "A monthly allowance. Until I got my inheritance. It's not exactly something I wanted to share with my friends. And when she found out about Syd, she thought she could use it as a threat. Tell me that if I didn't get rid of her, there was a clause in my inheritance that could make it so I didn't get it if this was really my kid and they would be entitled to anything. I'm not sure I understand it, or even if I believe her—I never saw the paperwork—but . . ." He spread his hands. "That's why I'm here."

CHAPTER 49

"So what were you going to do?" I asked. "Were you interested in seeing Syd and meeting Presley?"

He sighed. "Sure, I was interested. And don't get me wrong, she's a cute kid. But I'm not the daddy type. I don't stay put for long. I told her I'd help her out financially whenever I could, once I got this inheritance thing sorted out, and I'd visit when I was nearby. But I couldn't commit to more than that."

I thought about this. If Rain wasn't going to get the money because of Syd, had he found a way to get rid of his mother instead? Maybe he knew they were supposed to meet. Maybe he had shown up in her place. And maybe things had gone really wrong.

Would he kill his own mother?

"Are you sad she's dead?" I asked bluntly.

Rain's gaze slid away. His eyes turned cloudy with the question, as if the answer was so muddled in his brain it had taken on a physical appearance. "It's complicated. My mother and I disagreed about a lot of things. I haven't been home in ages. She was fine with it." He smiled wryly. "I think she wanted people to forget we're related."

"Why?"

"Because I was a troublemaker as a kid. Hung out with the bad kids, got arrested a couple of times. Something else I try to hide from my friends nowadays. It's only cool to get arrested if you're protesting global warming. And later, she was fine not being my mother because we don't align on anything. Because I'm protesting her pet project. Because I'm a scraggly, un-gainfully employed drifter who draws attention to himself and embarrasses her." That easy look was still on his face, but his tone had turned harsh. "And having to be responsible for my kid now? Well, that would've been more than she could stand."

"So do you get more money now that she's gone?" I asked.

He shook his head. "It doesn't work that way. It's a specific amount my grandfather designated for me, plus the interest. It's got nothing to do with my mother's portion."

"So who gets her portion?"

"Why, you need a loan?" He laughed at his own joke, then realized I wasn't laughing. Then it dawned on him. "You think I killed my mother?" His feet dropped to the floor, and he sat up straight. "Are you *kidding* me?"

"Why not? The police think *I* did," I shot back. "And I had way less of a reason to. You had an inheritance coming. And I'm hearing from you that you didn't like her much." My heart was pounding so hard I wondered if I'd hear his answer.

"Wait a second." Rain leaned forward earnestly. "You've got this all wrong, Violet. I needed my mother alive to get that inheritance. She had to sign it over to me at her discretion, once I hit this birthday. I was here to convince her she should."

I had no idea if I should believe this guy or not. "Okay, so she signs it. Now you're even angrier that you had to grovel for it. And now you don't need her anymore." I waited, holding my breath.

One side of Rain's mouth tipped up in a smile. "Good theory. Except for the fact that I didn't get it yet."

I sat back, confused. "What do you mean?"

He shook his head. "She didn't sign off before she died. I didn't get the inheritance."

Really? That seemed convenient. "Well, can you still get it?"

He shrugged. "Maybe. I need to talk to my grandfather. But he likes me even less than my mother did, so I'm not sure how that will go." His smile was wry, but I could feel sadness underneath his flip attitude. "Besides. I wasn't around Monday night. I had a meeting with some of the local chapter of my environmental group over in Monroe. I left here around four and didn't get back until nine. After Andrew called me."

Convincing, but it could all just be a good story he'd concocted to throw suspicion off himself.

"You do know Syd could be in trouble," I said. "Carla sent her a message telling her to meet her at 5:45 that day."

Rain frowned. "Did she go?"

"I don't know," I said. "She won't talk to me. But what I'm really struggling with is who else could've done it? I mean, I'm sure there were people who had issues with her, but I haven't found anyone who's a serious contender yet."

"I'm kind of at a disadvantage because I don't know who she deals with, really," he said slowly. "But I do know the business records are a mess, and the finances are a huge mess. I'm her executor," he added. "Since she and my dad are getting divorced, I was all she had for a safeguard. And I think that business partner of hers has been messing around."

"Andrew?" I was taken aback. "That can't be true. Is that why you went to see him the other day?"

"It is. Anyway, I don't know for sure, but I'm sitting down with the accountant to try and reconcile the books and see what's what. Which is upsetting her partner. I can't imagine why he'd be upset unless he had something to hide."

"Andrew's not like that," I insisted, but doubt was starting to creep in.

"Well, he's been pretty vocal about threatening me," Rain said. "Like he did at the protest."

"He *threatened* you?" I remembered seeing Andrew talking at Rain, waving his hands around.

"Told me to stay away from the office and the books or he'd have me arrested. That I was money hungry." Rain didn't seem too affected by it. "He can't do it anyway. And I don't feel the need to explain myself. Yeah, I want what's mine. After what I put up with from my family, I deserve it."

"Did you tell the cops this?" For Natalie's sake, I hoped not.

Slow head shake. "I want to be sure."

"Even if that's true, it doesn't mean he killed her," I said.

"Not unless she found out," he pointed out.

We both sat with that. Then I shook my head, suddenly remembering what Ginny had told me, and why it was important. "No. The waitress at the bar saw Andrew there during that window Monday night." While Natalie thought he was out posting flyers about our healing circle. Maybe he'd gotten cold and decided to take an hour to warm up.

"You know for sure it's the window?" he asked.

"Based on what the cops told me, yeah."

"Then I guess he's just a scammer. Or a bad record keeper." Rain shrugged. "There is one other thing that I found out this week when I was going through her bank stuff." He glanced at me.

"Okay," I said.

He was silent for so long I wondered if he was messing with me. Maybe he was going to bribe me to recoup some of that inheritance. "She was involved in a fledgling business deal with someone else. As an investor. And she pulled out recently. You probably know this, though, right?"

I was immediately on alert. "No. With whom?" I asked.

He grimaced. "I probably shouldn't be the one to tell you—well, anyway. Is what it is." He spread his hands wide. "With Todd."

"Todd who?"

"Todd Langston," he said, exasperated. "Isn't that your boyfriend?"

I wondered how he even knew that, but that was the least shocking thing about what he'd just said. I stared at him as the room started spinning around me. He was jerking me around. Had to be. Why would Todd be in a business deal with Carla? It was impossible. He didn't like her either.

"You have no idea what you're talking about," I said. I could hear the quiver in my own voice and felt my face reddening, and hated myself for all of it.

"I do," he said. "Sorry. She was going to be a silent investor in his pub franchise."

His pub franchise. Something he'd been talking about

doing forever. Something I didn't think he'd made any traction with.

Then I had another thought that left me cold—was Carla the off-site meeting he'd had on Monday? The day she died?

Rain watched me with those intense eyes. "She pulled out at the last minute. Said she didn't have as much investment capital as she'd initially thought after reconciling her books."

"What's the last minute?"

"It looked like just this past weekend."

Right before she died. The pit in my stomach was back, and pretty deep. "How do you know this?"

"I found some paperwork."

"Who have you told?"

"The detectives," he said. "I had to. They wanted copies of all her recent business records."

I let this sink in. My boyfriend had been doing a business deal with Carla Fernandez and hadn't told me. Heck, he hadn't even told me he was close with a deal on another location. He'd been vague about it lately, still talking about it as if it were in the future but not concrete yet.

And if Rain was telling the truth, she'd pulled out of the deal and been killed—what, one or two days later?

Had the cops been talking to Todd too? I felt sick.

"I'm sorry, Violet," Rain said. He sounded sincere.

"Yeah. Thanks. Anyway, I'm sorry to keep you. Thanks for shedding light."

He nodded and rose to go.

But I had one last question for Rain before he left. "Since you're not really Miguel Fernandez anymore, what last name do you use as Rain, since you don't want anyone to know who you are?"

He smiled. "I don't. I'm like the Beyoncé of the environmentalist world. So far, it's been working."

CHAPTER 50

After Rain left, I went down to Pete's for my coffee, since I hadn't made it there earlier. I walked down the street, feeling like I was in a trance. We'd gotten rid of one suspect—Andrew—but gained another one.

My boyfriend.

How could he not have told me any of this? Did that mean he was guilty of something? Or were we just that out of touch with each other that he didn't think it was important? Either way, this wasn't good. I remembered Fiona's assessment of him. *Subpar.*

By the time I got inside the café, I was feeling pretty low. Pete wasn't even behind the counter. I ordered my double-shot latte and picked it up at the other end of the counter. No Fiona today. I was sure she was waiting for me to come to her, after her dramatic proclamation and exit Wednesday. I hadn't seen her or Zoe since.

Just as well.

I walked out of the café, heading in the direction of my shop. Then I turned and went left instead. Before I knew it, my feet were in front of North Harbor Realty's building. I hoped Andrew was there. I didn't care if he was Nat's husband. I needed to know what was going on. Specifically, if he knew anything about the Todd-Carla business deal.

I went up to the fourth floor and walked right in, grateful to find the door unlocked.

Andrew was in the little kitchen. He turned when I blasted in. His eyes were red and puffy, and he looked worse than yesterday. When he realized it was me, his jaw set. "I told you, Violet—"

"Is Rain right? Are you messing with the books? Did Carla catch you?" I asked, cutting him right off.

His eyes widened. "How do you . . . no! I certainly am not messing with the books. I'm so sick of everyone thinking it was me who couldn't keep the business straight. Carla couldn't keep her finances straight if her life depended on it"—we both winced at his choice of words—"and now that she's gone everyone's blaming me. It wasn't my fault she fired the accountant. I had to hire a new one to dig us out."

I paused, uncertain. What if Rain was wrong?

"He just thinks there's more money than there is," Andrew said, as if reading my mind. "He's really a twit, that kid. His poor mother had her hands full with him, yet she still supported him."

His poor mother? Really? "So why are you acting so weird lately? And why were you in Todd's bar Monday when you were supposed to be out doing stuff for Natalie?"

Andrew sat down heavily in one of the waiting-area chairs, dropping his face into his hands. "I didn't want Nat to be disappointed in me. I promised I'd help her, and I . . . haven't been around much," he said. His voice was muffled, and I had to step forward to hear him. "But I was stressed because Carla wanted to dissolve our partnership." He looked up at me with bleary eyes. "Which meant I'd be out of a job."

I sat down next to him. "But why?"

"She wanted to expand the business. I knew we were stretched thin." He shrugged. "She didn't want to hear it. We've been arguing about it for weeks."

"Why were you stretched too thin?" I asked.

He shrugged. "A lot of expenses. This office," he waved his hand around, "is five thousand a month for the whole floor."

"But you guys sell million-dollar homes," I pointed out.

Andrew didn't have a good answer for that. I got the sense there were things he wasn't saying. I guess he didn't need to tell me anything, when it came down to it. But there was one thing I was going to push. "What do you know about other deals Carla had going on?"

"Other deals? Like what?"

"Like silent investor gigs."

Andrew shook his head. "I'm not following."

"Okay. I'll be clear. What do you know about Carla offering to fund Todd's next bar, then pulling out of the deal?"

"What?" He looked shocked enough that I not only believed him, but actually felt a little bad.

"That's what Rain said."

Andrew snorted and sat back, crossing his arms over his chest. "And you're going to believe him?"

"What reason would he have to lie about that?"

"Oh, I'm sure I could find a few," he said.

I shook my head, impatient. "I think he's telling me the truth. So how did you not know? Is that money from something else?"

Andrew sagged under the weight of what I was asking him. "I don't know," he said. "I don't know what she was doing or where the money was coming from. I was just trying to stay afloat and keep doing my job." I could feel the waves of despair rolling off him, and they were so great that I had to take pity on him and stop talking. There was more to this story—I could feel it—but he wasn't about to tell me, and I really didn't have any right to ask.

I left him sitting there, head still in his hands, and closed the door quietly behind me.

There was only one person who could tell me what I wanted to know, and that was Todd.

CHAPTER 51

I didn't bother to call or text Todd, figuring I'd just show up and hope he was there. And luck was finally with me when I arrived outside Luck o' the Irish a few minutes later. His delivery guy had just shown up. I followed him in through the open side door.

Todd looked surprised when he saw me coming. He gave me an uncertain smile. I'm sure after my lukewarm response yesterday, he didn't know what to expect. "Hey, Vi. I didn't know you were coming by."

"Yeah, I didn't either. Can we talk?"

He glanced at the delivery guy unloading the beer, and said, "Just leave the slip on the bar."

The guy nodded, and Todd led me out back to his office. "Want anything?" he asked.

I shook my head. He perched on the edge of his desk, motioning me toward the chair. I stayed standing.

"What's going on?" he asked finally. Todd hated silence. He always tried to fill it.

But I wanted him to sweat a bit. I took my time answering. "When were you going to tell me Carla Fernandez was going to invest in your next bar?" I asked.

He hadn't seen that coming. He opened his mouth, closed it again, then said, "Vi. I'm sorry I didn't tell you. I wanted to make sure it was really happening. And then, all of a sudden, it wasn't."

"It still seems like a big thing to leave out of conversations with your girlfriend, no?" I continued.

Todd shifted uncomfortably. "I'm sorry."

"You've been sorry a lot lately," I said. "Why wouldn't you tell me, Todd?"

He shoved off the desk and walked around the room in a little circle. "I don't know, Vi. Because I knew she wasn't your favorite person. And like I said, I didn't believe it was going to happen. By the time I did believe it, the rug got pulled out a couple days later." He shrugged. "Then I was back to square one anyway."

"Why did she pull out?"

"I don't know. She just said she didn't have as much liquid cash as she thought."

I thought of Andrew and Rain and botched financials. "And she told you last weekend?"

He nodded.

"And?" I asked. I hadn't seen him much over the weekend, come to think of it. He'd worked both nights. We'd spent some time together Sunday, lunch and a movie, and he'd been distracted. But I was used to it lately, so I hadn't thought twice about it.

"And I was upset. I've been waiting for this, Vi. You know that. But on Monday I got a call from a guy."

"A guy."

"Yeah. He said he was interested in backing me and did I want to meet. I asked him where he'd heard about me and he said, around town."

"And it was for real?" I asked skeptically.

"Yeah, it was for real. It's a guy named Chad Woodley. Turns out he and Carla had this rival investment thing going on. He'd gotten wind of our deal—and then our no-deal—and took advantage of it."

I studied him. He looked earnest, like he really wanted me to believe him. "You know this looks bad, right?" I said.

"What do you mean?"

I ticked off points on my fingers. "Carla was backing you. You've been wanting this for years and were finally going to get it. Then she bailed on you this weekend. On Monday evening—when you lied about the bar being busy and you being here—she winds up dead."

Todd looked like I'd just punched him in the stomach with a particularly violent fist. "Violet. Seriously, you can't—why would you even say that?"

"I'm telling you how it looks," I said, spreading my arms. "Especially from my perspective. You were absent Monday and you lied about it."

"I told you. I was at that meeting with the investor and I couldn't tell anyone. Not even you. He said if I did, there would be no deal." He came over and tried to put his arms around me, but I stepped away.

"So you left and no one knew where you went. And if the police asked you about this investor, you wouldn't tell them either? Because once the cops start digging into the financials, I'm sure they'll be all over this idea that she stiffed you. And you weren't accounted for when she died."

"Vi. Not gonna happen. I promise."

"It happened to me!"

"Believe me, they'll be more interested in Andrew," Todd said.

"If he hadn't been here when she got killed, with witnesses, maybe."

Todd shook his head slowly. "They'll just assume he had someone do it. Once they find out about recent circumstances."

I frowned. "What, you mean that she wanted him out of the business?"

"That, and that she'd broken up with him."

"Broken up . . ." I stared at Todd as it slowly dawned on me. "No. No way."

Todd nodded. "Yeah. They were having an affair."

Now I sank down onto the chair. "You're kidding."

"Wish I was. This was their rendezvous most days."

I remember Ginny saying Andrew and Carla had a lot of *business meetings* here. "You're *kidding*."

"I just told you I'm not. He was here Monday all mopey. She wasn't only breaking up with him, she wanted him out of the business. If he didn't go quietly, she was going to tell Natalie. And that fool? He was only concerned with her breaking up with him." Todd laughed, a sharp, quick sound. "He actually told me he loved her."

CHAPTER 52

My phone buzzed just as I was about to go to bed that night. Granted, it was only eight, but Todd's revelation about Andrew and Carla had been enough to sufficiently rattle me. I'd gone to my store and worked until four, then I'd slunk home and stayed there, snuggling with Monty, not sure what to do next. I hoped the police would get their act together and get this thing solved, but I was starting to wonder if I even wanted to know what the outcome was going to be.

I wondered if Natalie knew. Or suspected, even. She'd been preoccupied and not herself lately, for sure. I felt awful for her. And I was going to see her tomorrow at our healing circle, and I had no idea what to say. I'd chosen some crystals for her, trying to tune into her energy from here. I wasn't sure I'd done a great job. In addition to the stones I'd picked for grief and dealing with romantic troubles, howlite kept coming up, which was my go-to stone for dealing with rage and anger. Which was also understandable, if she knew.

This was all going through my head as I reached for my phone. Sydney.

"Hey," I said, hitting speaker.

"Hey." She sounded subdued and very un-Sydney-like. "Are you home? Can I come over?"

"Sure," I said.

"Good. I'm outside."

I forgot she couldn't get into the building anymore. Since she didn't live here and all. I closed my eyes and concentrated on the door downstairs unlocking. "Try the door," I said, once I'd heard that click in my mind.

"Huh. I swear it was locked when I tried it a minute ago. I'll be right up."

I smiled, a little, as I went to unlock my door. Maybe this stuff could come in handy.

Syd came through the door a moment later. She looked like she hadn't slept in days either. I locked the door behind her and motioned toward the kitchen. "Tea?"

She shook her head. "I can't stay long. Presley is with Charlie. I just . . . wanted to come see you. I have to tell you something." She clasped and unclasped her hands together. "I just left the police station."

I sank onto my barstool and waited for her to go on.

"They brought me in to talk about Monday because . . ." She closed her eyes, seemingly trying to drum up strength. "They thought I was meeting Carla."

"Were you?" I asked evenly.

Sydney shook her head. "I wasn't. I almost did, but in the end . . . I couldn't anyway. I had something else to do."

"What, Syd? Where were you, really?"

She shook her head. "That's not important. But I wanted you to know why." A deep breath. "Carla is Presley's grandmother."

I kept my gaze on her. "I know."

She gaped at me. "You *know*? How?"

"I talked to Rain," I said simply. "He told me the whole thing. Why didn't you tell me?"

Syd pulled out her own barstool and sat. "I don't know," she admitted. "I was embarrassed. Especially when it didn't go as planned. And then I was here and I didn't know what to do, and she kept getting meaner." She brushed away a tear. "I just wanted Presley to know her family."

I went to her and gave her a hug. I could feel the desperation, fear, and grief that had obviously been plaguing her for a long time now, and I wanted to weep. "I wish you'd told me. I could've helped," I said.

"No. You couldn't have. And I didn't want to put anyone else in her line of fire. Although you seemed to get there on your own," she said with a little laugh.

"So what happens now?" I asked. "With Rain?"

Syd's face fell again. "He's leaving. Once he gets the inheritance sorted out. He's not the dad type, I guess." She gave me a rueful smile. "He said he'd help with support. Which is good, because I'm struggling. It's one of the reasons I decided to look him up. I wanted her to know her dad, but I also wanted some help. I've been trying to find ways to make more money, but . . . it's not really working out."

I nodded. "So what happened with the police?"

"They found out she invited me to meet. Luckily, I could prove I didn't. Otherwise, man, that would've looked really bad, right?"

"For sure," I said, hoping she would never know I'd wondered the same thing. "But we still don't know who killed her."

"I know. It's kind of freaking me out."

"You said Presley is with Charlie," I said, suddenly catching up with that. I remembered Ginny telling me

Charlie hadn't been in the bar in a while. Yet Charlie told me that was where he was when Carla was killed.

"Yeah. So?"

I chewed on my lip, trying to think how to say this. "Are you sure . . . about him?"

She stared at me. "What on earth do you mean?"

I told her about his blown alibi. "So where was he? He couldn't stand her either. Especially if she was targeting him because of you."

"Oh, Vi." She looked sad. "Of course he lied about where he was. Guys like Charlie don't like to admit they need help. He was at his grief counselor. It's right around the anniversary of his best friend's suicide. He's embarrassed to let anyone know. I only know because he needed a ride once and he trusted me enough to ask me."

Now I really felt like a jerk. "Crap," I muttered, tugging at my hair. "I'm sorry."

"Don't tell him I told you," Syd warned. "He'll disown me. But I think the cops know he would never do this. No matter how much he disliked her."

I thought of Gabe. "Yeah. I'm sure you're right. So is this . . . your connection to Carla . . . why you didn't want me looking into her murder?" I asked.

She nodded, sheepish. "I panicked. I didn't want you thinking it was me, and I wasn't ready to tell anyone about . . . the other stuff." She reached for my hands. "Can you forgive me, Vi?"

I nodded. "Of course." I still felt there was something she wasn't telling me.

"Thank you. So much." She got up and reached into her jeans pocket. "And I've got my stones. I love them. I think you've changed my mind about all this stuff," she declared. "I want to come to your healing circle."

"You do?"

She nodded. "I do. Can I bring Presley? I think it would be good for her."

"Of course," I said, wondering what had happened to my friend. "Four o'clock tomorrow at the yoga studio."

"I'll be there."

CHAPTER 53

When I got to the yoga studio at three on Friday to set up, the door was still locked. Carissa Feather waited outside, wearing a turquoise outfit that made her look slightly like a peacock and shifting the weight of three giant bags, which I knew held her singing bowls. She looked annoyed.

"Hey," I said, walking up to her.

"Hello," she said, giving me a nod. Guess she was still mad at me about the medium thing. "I thought we were supposed to be here early?"

"We are." I peered inside. It was dark. I rapped on the door, then pulled out my phone and texted Nat.

We're outside.

I flashed Carissa a smile. "She'll be right out." I hoped. Actually, I hoped nothing had happened with Andrew. I thought of Todd's comment about hiring someone to kill Carla. Did Andrew Mann really know a hitman?

Natalie came to the door, jolting me out of my traitorous thoughts. She unlocked it and held it wide. "Sorry," she said. "I was on the phone out back and lost track of time." Her hair was wet like she'd just had a shower, hanging down her back. She wore her typical yoga pants and a heavy sweatshirt in which she looked lost.

Carissa brushed past her with her bags, barely muttering a hello. Natalie sent me a raised-eyebrow look as if to say, *What's with her?*

I shrugged and followed her into the studio.

"I'll be right back," Nat said, and vanished back into her office.

I wondered how any of us were going to heal the collective consciousness when we all seemed like we were in pretty bad moods. I went into the studio. "Everything okay, Carissa?"

She glanced up from where she was laying out the lovely tapestries the bowls sat on. "Not really. My medium lady is a fraud."

"What?" I sat down cross-legged on the floor next to her. "You're kidding."

Carissa shook her head. "And I hired her for another event. Already paid her when the story came out yesterday." She glanced at me. "You were in part one, but they retracted what they said about you."

It clicked, then. Mazzy. "Wait," I said. "How was there a story? Who wrote it?"

"I don't know. I have it here." Carissa reached into her bag and pulled out a paper, folded to the right page.

I glanced at the byline. Not Mazzy. Which made sense, since she was a pile of slime now. Maybe she'd been working with someone on it. I skimmed the article. Lilia Myers had been unveiled as a fraud when she was discovered using a staff of people to feed her information during her sessions. I sighed and abandoned the rest of the article. Next to it was a small paragraph declaring that any mention of The Full Moon and its proprietor, Violet

Mooney, had been made in error and there was no evidence her practice was fraudulent.

At least Mazzy had gotten that done before she was slimed.

I glanced up as Presley raced into the room, giggling as she threw herself at me. "Hey, sweetie!" I gave her a hug. I hadn't seen her in days and realized how much I missed her.

Syd followed her in. "Hope it's okay that I'm early," she said, then stopped dead, staring.

I looked around, confused, and realized she and Carissa were staring at each other.

"Ohmigod," Carissa squealed, jumping up in a rustle of satin. "It's you!"

That was unexpected. "Get out. You guys know each other? How?" I asked. Up until, well, this week, Syd would've rather walked on hot coals than associate herself with characters like Carissa.

But Sydney didn't look amused. In fact, she looked ill.

"Did you get in any trouble? I have to admit I'm disappointed," Carissa continued, disregarding Sydney's discomfort. "I thought she was the real deal. She seemed so good. I wonder if she'll do time?"

"Carissa," I interrupted. "What the heck are you talking about?"

"Sorry, Vi. Forgot you weren't in the know." She waved at Syd. "This here was one of Lilia's backups. She was working Monday night when Lilia got discovered."

CHAPTER 54

Sydney had gone from green to red. I was staring at her, openmouthed, not sure what to say. Natalie walked in and stopped, looking from one to the other of us.

"What's going on?" she asked.

Presley broke the silence with a loud *gong* on one of Carissa's singing bowls. Carissa whipped around. "No, honey, you can't do that," she admonished, sending Presley running to her mother.

Syd hugged her daughter against her legs. Her eyes met mine, pleading a little.

I dragged Syd into the reception area. "What's she talking about?"

Syd picked up Presley, hiding her face against her daughter. "I'm sorry, Vi. This was the part I left out. I told you I'd been trying to find extra income. Well, I picked up a gig. With this psychic." She sighed and walked to the far end of the room and then back. "It was supposed to be harmless. We were in the wings, doing research on the people who came in to try and find nuggets she could use. But then Monday night it went kind of bad. She was trying to get this really rich woman to buy a ring that she said would bring her love. But it was like a fifty-thousand-dollar ring. Or so she said." She grimaced a little. "I'm sure she got it out of a vending machine. Anyway, when I realized what she was doing and how much money was involved, I was out. But we didn't know it was a reporter posing as a client."

Ouch. "Monday. So that's where you were when you said you were at the paint party?"

She nodded.

"Are you going to be in trouble for this?"

"I got a fine." She grimaced. "That I really didn't need. But I guess that's what I get. At least it gave me an alibi for Carla's murder."

"Syd. Don't you know I'd never judge you? You can talk to me," I said, exasperated.

"Violet. I've spent the entire time I've known you telling you how I don't believe in any of this. And then I'm going to tell you I work with a medium? A fake one, to be exact?" She shot me a skeptical look. "I can't imagine even you being supportive of that."

"No, but I could've helped you in other ways," I said, then trailed off as the door opened. People were starting to arrive for the event. "We'll talk later," I said, and moved over to greet the newcomers.

I stayed out front while people trickled in, greeting and sending them to the studio. Nat had disappeared again. She was so distracted. I'd brought her crystals, and decided I'd stay after the circle and try to talk to her.

I was surprised to see Zoe come through the door. I briefly wondered how I'd explain her to Syd and Natalie, but then brushed that aside. If they were here to stay, I'd figure it out.

"Hey," I said. "What are you doing here?"

"I'm here for the circle," she said, as if it should be obvious, even though the last time I'd seen her had been over a puddle of slime. She held out a paper boat of fries. Looked like she'd been back at Potatoes from Heaven again. "Want some?"

"You're going to develop a habit," I teased, and reached for one, dipping it into the little container of orangey sauce nestled next to the fries. But on the way to my mouth, I stopped. Instead of the delightful smell that usually sent my stomach rumbling, I smelled something . . . rancid. Something I'd smelled before. On my scarf, when the police brought it to my door.

And the last pieces flew into place. Nat, saying she'd been meditating Monday and lost track of time. Sydney, in her usual judgmental way, mentioning that Nat had been at the french fry truck when she'd stopped there after closing up shop.

"What?" Zoe asked, staring at me.

I dropped the fry back into its container and walked out back to Natalie's office, pushing the door open without knocking. She sat at her desk, staring at the wall.

"Nat," I said.

She didn't look at me. "I can't hide it anymore, can I," she said.

I took a seat across from her and reached over. She moved her hand out of my reach.

"Did you know?" I asked. "About Andrew and Carla?"

She looked at me. Her eyes were dull and empty. "I knew about him. I didn't figure out who until . . . I bumped into her Monday. I was going to meditate, but I couldn't resist getting some fries. I'd skipped lunch," she added, as if she still felt the need to justify herself in that setting. "And she grabbed me when I was going in the back door. Said she was sorry to tell me this way, but she'd been seeing my husband." Tears bloomed in her eyes, but her voice remained steady. "And that she'd broken up with him, but she needed him to leave the office. I don't even remember the rest of it. Honestly," she added, imploring me to believe her. "I'd been so worried and sick and anxious for weeks now, and I just . . . I lost it. I had your scarf with me. You left it here. I was going to bring it by your store."

I swallowed. Until that moment, I'd been holding out hope that it wasn't true. That there was some good explanation for all of this. That my Zen friend who didn't even like to kill spiders could never hurt another person.

She still didn't look at me. "I guess I couldn't accept it. And she started walking away from me like I was nothing, like all of it was nothing, and I just . . . reacted."

I could feel my own tears welling up as I frantically worked out what to do here. Maybe she could claim insanity. Maybe they'd let her off since it was her first offense. "We can fix this," I said, grabbing her hand. "We just need to talk to Gabe. He'll know what to do."

But Natalie shook her head. "I already called the police. Told them I had information. They should be here any minute," she said. "I'm sorry about the healing circle, but you should go ahead." She smiled at me with wet eyes. "You're the real healer here."

CHAPTER 55

A Week Later

"Violet Mooney. Do you swear your allegiance to the Magickal Council, beginning today, the fifteenth of January 2020?"

"I do."

"Do you promise to help rule the witch realm with justice, fairness, and an eye to all that your ancestors before you have pledged?"

"I do."

"Do you promise to carry on the Moonstone tradition while you do so?"

"I do."

The tall, serious woman with the glasses halfway down her nose nodded at me, then turned to the rest of the solemn circle assembled around me. "Then I pronounce you our newest council member."

Cheers erupted all around me. I saw Pete in the crowd, clapping, along with some of my other friends from town.

I saw Fiona wiping away tears out of the corner of her eye. As everyone dispersed, she came over to me and grasped my arms. "I'm so proud of you, daughter."

I smiled, feeling on the verge of tears myself. I still wasn't sure what I was doing, or how this would all play out, but it felt right. Aside from feeling responsible for maintaining the power of female witches, I had a responsibility to my grandmother. If her death was suspicious, I needed to find out what had happened. Fiona had already committed to helping me.

And this was the only way we could do it.

"So now what?" I asked.

Fiona smiled. "You go back to North Harbor and live a double life, I guess."

I thought about that. North Harbor was where I belonged, no doubt, and it looked like there were plenty of people from my other community there. "What about you?"

She laughed. "We're right behind you. I'm going to give your other world another try. Something tells me it may be better this time. Besides, your sister is so smitten with that police officer." She grimaced. "I have to keep an eye on that."

Zoe and Gabe had started dating once Carla's case had closed. Nat's confession had stunned everyone, including her husband. Now her fate rested in the hands of a jury. She'd made the enormous amount of bail the judge had set, using their house as collateral, and had basically shut herself away awaiting trial. Things had started to get back to normal, now that the case was closed and the bridge protesters, including Rain, had packed up and left town. The bridge project had been defeated in the special referendum, so the problem of what to do with the old bridge had been tabled for the moment.

"But we're going to find another place," she said. "Apartment buildings just don't work for me. We need a little house in the country." She looked at me, waiting.

I took a breath. "Grandma Abby's house. I'm sure she'd be good with it." I hoped.

"I thought you'd never ask," she said with a wink. "I've already moved your friend back."

"Syd?" I clapped my hands together. "Thank you!" I would need to keep an eye on her, after everything she'd been through. Plus I'd convinced her to come work at my shop for some extra cash. It had taken some doing, but she'd accepted the job.

"We'll move in this weekend. I have a few things to deal with here. And we need to get ready for your first meeting," she said. "I have a lot of reading for you. You have some catching up to do."

I nodded. "I will." But first, I had other reading to do. And other things to deal with. Including what I was going to do about Todd. Which I still wasn't sure of, but the fact that he'd kept so many secrets from me wasn't sitting well. "I'm going to go home, okay?"

She nodded and kissed my cheek. "Welcome home, daughter," she said softly.

I kissed her back and tugged at my earring, pleased with my landing in my living room a second later. I'd even managed to bring some of my own glitter with me. I was learning.

I went to my bed and pulled the book I'd found at Grandma Abby's out of my nightstand drawer. This time, it opened easily. Monty settled on one side of me, the black cat—Xander, I'd decided—nestled on the other.

I opened the book, and began to read.

ACKNOWLEDGMENTS

I have been fascinated with witches and magic for most of my life. As a college student in Salem, Massachusetts, I was in my element being around all of that history and watching people pay tribute to witches daily. It was there that I learned about magic and crystals and tarot, and even had the opportunity to meet Laurie Cabot. Exciting times for sure. But even back then I didn't fully understand the implications of what was done to women throughout history and why—the patriarchal attempts to squash the incredible powers all women have. As I began learning more about that history, coincidentally the opportunity to write this book presented itself, and I knew that had to be a thread within the narrative. All the strong women I've met over the past two years have all had a hand in this—from my Saraswati's Yoga Joint community and the incredible healers I've met by extension, to the Kundalini boss babes I've been honored to encounter and learn from, to the amazing women in my "ordinary" life. You've all shown me how much I'm capable of when I put my mind to it.

Thank you to my editor, John Scognamiglio, for suggesting witches for this series—how did you know I've been dying to write something like this for years? And to the rest of the Kensington crew, from cover art to copyedits, thank you for all your hard work. My agent, John Talbot, for his continued support and willingness to listen to me negotiate deadlines—thank you.

Special thanks to Nicole at Sacred Mystery Arts for

my first-ever tarot lesson—and the awesome reading I got in the process.

I've visited many crystal shops throughout the years, and I'm currently fascinated with The Funky Hippie and its amazing proprietor, Nicole Simonelli, who is not only a wonderful teacher but has also become a good friend. both of which are local to me. Anytime I can spend hours looking at crystals and letting them speak to me is a good time, so thank you for sharing your wisdom and your treasures. Many thanks to Jessica Ellicott, who took time our of her own writing to plot with me.

And to my ultimate posse of strong women—my fellow Wicked Authors, Maddie Day, Jessica Ellicott, Sherry Harris, Julia Henry, and Barbara Ross—thank you for your always positive influence in my life, and your constant friendship and support. Love you all.

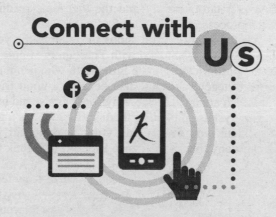